Forever Loved

Women of Prayer Series

Book Three

Darlene Shortridge

Darlene Shortridge

I Peter 5:10

Books by

Darlene Shortridge

The Women of Prayer Series:

Until Forever ✓
Forever Blessed ✓
Forever Loved ✓
The Letter
The Perfect Gift
&
40 Day Publishing

Forever Loved

This book is available in print at most online retailers.

Published by 40 Day Press

www.40daypublishing.com

Oklahoma City, Oklahoma

Cover design by Jonna Feavel

Author photo by Photography by Jonna

Published in the United States of America

To A True Life
Woman of Prayer

Valerie Stanley Burg

October 30, 1945 - May 21, 2012

Acknowledgements

So many hands help write a story of this nature. Many tears are shed, personal stories are shared, and old wounds are sometimes re-opened. What brings healing to some can ignite tender flames of hurt for others. Yet so many willingly gave of themselves so others could hear truth.

Everyone I mention here, in no particular order and for some particular reason which shall remain anonymous, has reason to be thanked: Stephanie Bloy, Barbara Kopitzke, Deb Knitter, Beverly McGinnis, Elaine Littau, Kim Painter, Amanda Stephan, and Mary Findley.

I would also like to thank all my readers. Every time I read one of your emails or Facebook messages, I am the one who gets blessed. I have the best readers ever.

Danny, thank you for being my partner in this crazy world we have chosen. It may be crazy, but it's ours and we wouldn't have it any other way. Thanks for everything you do! From layout to graphics to editing, you are irreplaceable. Jonna, I know you're many miles away. I still appreciate everything you do to make this dream possible. Jeremiah, you are awesome at promoting your mama wherever we go. Every time I hear you tell someone they need to read my books, I say to myself, *that's my boy*!

What a wonderful blessing to be able to do what I love. I sometimes feel guilty because this really doesn't feel like work. I believe that is what our calling is supposed to feel like. Thank you, Lord, for calling me to this. I love it…and I love You!

Foreward

Having shared friendship with Darlene Shortridge through pleasant times and tumult, plenty and lack, nearby and far in distance, I've seen her deep commitment to the Lord and His Truth. Her gift for writing is focused on more than producing a good read, it's a platform for speaking the Truth of God in a lost and confused world. People who deeply love God live the life of Christ on a daily basis, extending themselves as God's arm to fulfill His purposes and serve others. I've seen Darlene go from intently writing her next best-selling book to making a meal for the family down the road who's struggling with illness. She's the teacher at your Church or the Mom you chat with while you're watching your son's swim lessons. These real life experiences are woven into her writings, giving depth and believability to her characters. As 'Forever Loved' unfolds to the reader, Darlene reveals a solid Biblical stance in dealing with current 'hot button' issues such as homosexuality, adultery and suicide. What's more impressive in Forever Loved, however, is seeing God's grace extended in the face of gross sin and its devastating results. This is the over-riding theme of Forever Loved and it leaves the reader with a desire to the same. Be prepared to feel happy, frustrated, sad, concerned, thankful and pleased! In essence, you will be inside of each character, feeling what they feel and seeing what they see. Once you have finished 'Forever Loved' you will likely be contacting Darlene Shortridge to ask her the release date of her next book.

Barbara Faber Kopitzke
Hospice Chaplain, Pastor, Teacher and Accountant

Chapter One

Rachel spoke louder into the receiver, as if that would somehow get her point across. "I told you, this charge is erroneous. We have never been to this hotel."

She was silent a moment then her face started turning red. "No, my husband could not have come by himself or with someone else. He's a pastor for heaven's sake. He doesn't frequent hotels with other people." She tried to tame her temper. "Look, I don't want to argue with you. I just want this charge taken off my account. It is obviously a mistake. If you can't do it, then I will contact my credit card company and have them look into this matter."

She listened, nodding her head. "Good idea, why don't you talk with your manager? Maybe they have the power to do something." She didn't mean to sound sarcastic. At least that had not been her intention when she'd made the phone call.

She waited. She heard voices in the background.

Rachel rolled her eyes. This is why she usually had Ryan deal with these types of matters. She didn't have the patience that he had.

Again, she listened to the voice on the other end. "Ma'am, we're sorry, there must be some sort of mistake. When we looked up who registered the room, it was under the name of a Terri Schmidt. When we looked at the credit card bill, a Ryan Bradley signed for it. Ma'am, if I am not mistaken, that would be the same pastor Ryan Bradley that is your husband. Have you asked him about this charge?"

Rachel hung up the phone, sure she was correct. She would have to wait for Ryan to get home. He had a staff meeting at four then he was leaving. She would ask him about it then and he could call and take care of it.

Rachel pulled the meatloaf out of the oven at precisely six o'clock. She already set the table, the potatoes were mashed and the broccoli was steamed. She looked at her watch. Ryan should be home by now. She heard the garage door and smiled.

She called up the stairs, "Shelly, come wash up for supper."

Rachel listened for the familiar patter of her teenage daughter's feet on the hard wood floors above her. They had pulled all the carpet out years ago when they found out their eldest daughter had bad allergies.

She turned back to the kitchen and her husband, who had just walked through the door leading from the garage.

She leaned in to kiss him. "Good day?"

"Not bad, you?"

"Oh, it was pretty good. I got a lot done." She took the lid off of the potatoes, turned them into a bowl and added a dollop of butter to the top.

Shelly washed her hands at the kitchen sink. "Mom, what can I do to help?"

Rachel motioned to the microwave. "You can put the broccoli on the table."

The three of them joined hands to pray. Once upon a time it had been five of them huddled around their table, enjoying the family meal. Now, her two older daughters were off to college. Rachel snuck a peak at Shelly, their youngest, while her husband prayed. She was fifteen. It wouldn't be long before she would be out of the house as well. Then it would be the two of them. What would she do? Her whole life had been centered on taking care of her family.

She closed her eyes and finished out the prayer.

Later, when she and Ryan were alone in their room, Rachel brought up the hotel charges. "Can you take a look at this? I called them to tell them it was a mistake but they insist you signed for the room." She handed him the credit card bill then continued brushing her hair. She had no idea why she still counted the number of times she ran the brush through her thick black hair. Old habits sure are hard to break.

She heard her husband shuffling around behind her and turned. "Do you recognize the charge? I told them there had to be a mistake." She started brushing again when she remembered the name of the person checking in. "They said someone by the name of Terri checked in."

If she didn't know her husband as well as she did, she might not have seen him stiffen. It was slight, over as fast as it happened, but she caught it. Rachel rose and walked to him. "Do you know this Terri person?"

He smiled, "Yes, now I remember where I heard the name. The church rented a room for this guy for one night. He was in a tough place."

"Oh, I was thinking Terri with an I, as in a woman." Rachel cocked her head. "Why did you use our personal account?"

"I must have grabbed the wrong card by accident. You know how it goes. I was in a hurry. Probably trying to get home to you." He bent down to kiss her cheek. "I'll talk to the board about getting a reimbursement."

Rachel took off her pink robe and crawled between the sheets and turned to Ryan who was already closing his eyes. "Hey, remember me? Your wife?" She propped her head up on one elbow. "Not even a good night kiss?"

"Sheesh, I'm sorry. I'm just beat." Ryan reached over and pulled his wife close for a tender kiss. He brushed her black bangs off her pale forehead. "You are beautiful. I'm sorry I don't say that enough." He lay on his side facing her.

15

Rachel took her husband's hand. She loved this man. Her spirit was troubled, she knew something was wrong, but whatever it was would never change her love for him. Over the years, they had endured a lot and come through every trial with their marriage intact. Their faith had seen them through. Something was telling her the hardest was yet to come. She felt him squeeze her hand. They would make it. They had to. She loved him too much to let him go.

Three days later Rachel sat on the front pew, listening to the words her husband was preaching. After all these years, he still moved her to examine her heart. About halfway through the message, she heard the door open. The church was fairly small, a hundred or so attended on any given Sunday. It was hard to mask any noise. She turned and watched a man, relatively the same age as the two of them, sit down in the last row. She turned back to her husband who suddenly looked as if he was going to be ill. He stammered and fumbled with his notes before resuming the message.

Rachel turned again and looked at the gentleman sitting in the back row. He turned his eyes toward her and locked glances. She turned away, suddenly feeling uncomfortable.

Her husband was acting strangely out of character. He ended his message rather abruptly and excused himself to the back office. The gentleman in the back row didn't move. Several of the regular members greeted him with a smile and a handshake.

It was a few minutes before Ryan came out of his office and when he did, Rachel watched him act as if nothing had happened. She made her way to her husband's side as he shook hands with the parishioners. Finally, the gentleman was standing before them. She was surprised when her husband introduced her. "Rachel, this is Terry Schmidt. Terry, this is my wife, Rachel."

Rachel recognized the name but couldn't remember why. She extended her hand. "Hi Terry, I'm glad you came. It was good to have you."

"It was good to be here." He smiled, gave her husband a look she couldn't interpret then turned and left.

Later on, after the noon meal dishes were cleared away, she was thinking about the man at church, about the haunting look he offered her husband. She sat quietly on their back porch enjoying the summer breeze with a tall glass of fresh squeezed lemonade and a book that was just begging to be read when she remembered where she'd heard the name Terry. For some reason she had thought the Terri from the hotel was a woman. Instead, Terry really was a he, just as her husband had said. She should feel relieved. Somehow that wasn't the case.

Rachel absentmindedly rubbed her hand across Romeo, their golden Lab, as she looked out across her lawn. She put so much time into the yard, into her flowers. Had she been neglecting her husband? Had she set him on the back burner to tend to everything else? She prayed that hadn't been the case. She tried to remember the last time he reached for her in the quiet of the night and could not. What happened? They used to be close. They cherished that time together and dreamed about the day it would just be the two of them, living out the rest of their days enjoying one another's company.

She stepped off her back porch and walked among the roses, Romeo close on her heels. Rachel loved her roses. She spent a lot of time in her greenhouse, cross breeding flowers. She bent down to smell her latest creation. She named it Forever Loved. It was an unusual cross between two very different roses. It kind of reminded her of her own union with Ryan. They were so different, yet they fit together perfectly, like this flower. She bent and deeply inhaled the fragrant scent. She broke off a flower and carried it with her back to the porch.

She looked into the brilliant blue sky. *Lord, will you help me with my marriage? Will you bind us together with unbreakable chords, like this flower that was created from two and is now one?*

17

Her heart still hurt yet she clung to a peace that passes all understanding. *God, grant me the strength to make it through this trial. I need you now more than ever. I know this from the bottom of my heart. Give me wisdom. Show me mercy and grace as I accomplish your will in my life.*

Rachel waited quietly for a moment, for the settling of her soul. She knew it would come. He was with her. He would never leave nor forsake her. He would be her rock. She felt him stronger than ever. He was there. He would see her through this thing. She stood.

Okay Lord, I'm ready. She walked in her house and headed straight for her husband.

Chapter Two

Rachel leaned against the door jam of her husband's office. The door was open and he was sitting at his desk staring out the windows that allowed the sun to rise in full view from his workspace. Their back and side yard shared a border with the fairway of the ninth hole that made up the nucleus of their subdivision. Many of the girls' friends had attempted to jump in at the ninth hole and play through. Rachel had laid down the law regarding that unethical behavior. She was certain they found another hole to weasel their way onto and out of paying, but she supposed that is what kids do.

She looked hard, trying to see what he saw. She noticed nothing out of the ordinary. Golfers in their plaid shorts and polo shirts swung their golf clubs and gathered in small clusters. Nothing different from any other warm summer Sunday in their subdivision. Her husband was deep in thought.

She cleared her throat and he turned, looking for the world like he'd just been caught stealing a cookie from his mother's cookie jar. His natural charisma quickly kicked in and he smiled. She noticed the lines originating at the corners of his eyes and the slight gray at his temples. When did that happen?

"Can we talk?" She looked around the room. His domain. Cherry wood and leather spoke of the man sitting before her. "Can we move to the sunroom?" She walked toward the kitchen. "I'll get us some tea."

She found him sitting on the love seat, waiting for her to sit next to him. She handed him the cold glass of tea and sipped hers as she contemplated her options. Where to begin? She began as she always did. Abruptly and to the point. It was her way.

"What is going on with us?" She waited, searching him as he pondered her question. This man hated conflict. She knew he'd rather be anywhere than here, under her scrutiny.

He tried to escape in his usual manner, avoidance. "What do you mean?"

She shook her head. "That isn't going to work this time. I mean it. I want to know. What is going on with us?"

He tried his next tactic. He took her hand in his. "I'm sorry, Honey. It's my fault. I've been so busy with the church…"

She wouldn't let him continue. She pulled her hand from her husband. He would take the blame and promise to do better and they would never get to the bottom of what was going on. "No, Ryan. It's more than that. I know it. I know you. There is something going on and it's pulling us apart. I don't like it."

Ryan stood up and paced the length of the small sunroom. His tea was sweating and had a layered look from the melting ice settling near the top. Her's was half empty. Nervous habit. She had to be doing something with her hands. She lifted the glass to her lips as the seconds continued to tick.

Ryan ran his hand through his tousled blond hair then turned and faced his wife. He wasn't ready to deal with this. "Rachel, I need you to trust me. I have a couple of things I have to deal with but everything is going to be fine, I promise."

"Ryan, I've heard that before. Things are not getting better." She stood up and faced her husband. "I'm concerned. If I didn't trust God, I'd say I am worried. Ryan, we need to tackle this together. Whatever it is, it's too big for just one of us." She took his hand. "I need to know, do you trust me?"

"Yes, of course Rachel, but I just can't. I just can't." Ryan practically ran from the room and Rachel could do nothing but watch him.

Shelly came up from behind her. "Hey Mom, what's up with Dad? He took off and didn't even wave as he pulled out."

"Oh, Honey, I don't know. I wish I did." She rested her hand on her daughter's shoulder. So, tell me about your afternoon. Did you have fun?"

Shelly had spent the afternoon swimming with her best friend, Emily. "It was great. Tell me again why we can't have a pool?"

Both of them turned toward their backyard and started laughing. Rachel looked at her daughter. "So, you think you could fit a pool in there somewhere?"

"Alright, point taken, we couldn't fit a wading pool back there with all your flowers everywhere."

"In a few years it's going to be just me and your dad. Yes, you'd enjoy the pool for the short time you have left, but I will enjoy my flowers until I die. Which do you think is more important?"

"Okay, okay, I'm done asking. I won't ask again. I'm just glad Emily lives down the street and has a pool and likes me. That works." She started to leave the room to go change then turned back toward her mother. "You'd tell me if something was wrong between you and Dad, wouldn't you?"

Rachel didn't know what to say. Would she tell her youngest daughter her problems? Is that what parents were supposed to do? She smiled, hoping that would appease her daughter. "Go change. Let's go get a hamburger."

"Awesome. I'm starving." She took off at a run for her room calling for Romeo as she ran. The dog leapt up from his perch under the table and followed his playmate.

Rachel picked up her purse wondering where Ryan took off to in such a hurry. Did she upset him that much? Did he run to find consolation in someone else's arms? And if so, then who? She prayed it was the arms of God who was consoling him. Any one else was not an option she cared to think about. She remembered when it would be the five of them racing for the car in a hurry to put their seat belts on. The last one would be the rotten egg and would warrant ceaseless teasing from the non stinky riders. Even with her two oldest off to college, the three of them still played the game. Until recently. Ryan no longer had time for such frivolities. He didn't seem to have time for any of the family, let alone his wife.

She heard running in the hallway then headed for the car. Might as well get a jump-start on the seat belt. She didn't want to be the rotten egg today. Even if it was just her and Shelly.

Chapter Three

Shannon walked through the door. "Mom, we're home."

Rachel skipped down the stairs and embraced her two oldest daughters. They both had jobs on campus and chose to stay the summer so they could keep working. It was one of the ways they could afford a college education. With two college age kids to foot the bill for, they needed all the help they could get. In fact, Rachel had been considering a job that would make things a lot easier. Now that Shelly was fifteen, she was much less dependent upon her. "It's so good to see you both. I missed you."

Samantha, her eldest, stopped to primp in the hall mirror before taking her bag to her room.

Rachel could only smile. She always was the girly girl of the three. "You're beautiful, as usual. Now go up and put your things away. I have chicken ready for the grill. We're just waiting for your dad to get home."

Samantha made a face then took the stairs at a run.

Rachel hummed along with the radio as she finished cutting up the big chunks of red potatoes, sweet potatoes and mushrooms. She sprinkled them with olive oil and sea salt and set them aside for the grill basket. The girls would fall into their normal routine as soon as they came back downstairs. From the giggling emanating from an upstairs bedroom it would be a while before they graced her with their presence. Shannon and Samantha, Sam for short, were probably filling Shelly in on everything going on in their lives. She went ahead and set the table. Now that her two oldest were in college, Rachel granted them a little more leeway when it came to household routines.

They weren't home that often for her to get uptight about a few rules.

Finally, what sounded like a herd of cattle came running down the stairs. She savored the sounds of familiarity. *It's so good to have them home again.*

The chicken was sizzling by the time Ryan came home. He was late, again. It had become a habit that he refused to address. She was to the point she just didn't ask any more. There was an understanding between them, and even though she didn't agree, she abided by the unspoken rule and didn't question him. He would tell her when he was ready, not before.

Dinner was on the table and her family was together, if only for a short time. Life didn't get better than this. Rachel shut her eyes, so aware of her blessings that it was hard to maintain her composure. She opened her eyes to find her husband and three daughters staring at her. Her husband had the "don't do anything to rock the boat" look. Shelly had the "concerned child" look and Shannon and Sam just looked confused. She smiled at them. "I was just thanking God for my blessings. Having you all around this table means everything to me."

The girls shrugged their shoulders and started passing dishes. Besides grilled chicken and veggies, there was a nice salad and steamed asparagus.

Shannon, her middle child who was also their peacemaker, took a bite of her chicken and groaned. "Mom, you have no idea how much I have missed your cooking. This is delicious."

Sam mumbled in agreement, feeling a little guilty for being the last one to compliment her mother on dinner.

Rachel watched her three daughters interact with one another as well as with their father. She knew them so well. She knew their strengths, their weaknesses, their habits and what made each of them tick.

She watched her oldest daughter who had already finished eating. She didn't think Rachel noticed, but she hardly ate a bite. Sam's need for approval was something they had been dealing with since her later years at grammar school. She pushed her food around on her plate and passed tidbits to Romeo under the table, all in an effort to make it look like she ate more than she had. Rachel knew better. There wasn't that much meat on a chicken wing. She would need to have a heart to heart with her daughter before she headed back to school on Sunday. She worried about Sam. She was attending a liberal state college and Sam's faith had always been haphazard at best. Would she survive taking the liberal college classes? *Lord, please protect her.*

Shannon was her people pleaser. She would be the one to get married and have five or six children. Her joy came from being around people she loved and she wanted everyone to be happy. That was always a concern for Rachel. How far would Shannon go to make sure those around her were happy? She often let her sisters take advantage of her. Did she allow that from her college roommates as well? How about her employer? The boys she dated? Rachel shuddered. *Father, please protect her as well.*

Then there was Shelly. She and Shelly were the closest. Having her home for the summer and still unable to drive, gave Rachel many opportunities to spend time with her youngest daughter. Ryan was gone most of the time so the two of them spent many hours side by side riding bikes, gardening, cooking and just chatting about life. Of all three girls, Shelly had the strongest faith. She wasn't sure why that was; maybe because her own faith had deepened to such a degree she couldn't help but pass it on to her youngest.

The loudening table conversation brought her back to the present.

Sam was in a defensive position and Shelly was just as vocal about her position on the subject at hand. Shannon was looking between the two, wondering how to smooth out the ruffled feathers. "I obviously missed something. What are you two arguing about already?"

Sam gave her sister a pointed look before answering her mother. "I was simply telling everyone about my latest discussion in my summer Psychology class. We have been discussing alternative lifestyles."

Shelly jumped in. "Yeah, Sam seems to have forgotten what the Bible says about it."

Sam gave her younger sister a dirty look this time. "What do you know? You're only fifteen. There are many professional, knowledgeable intellectuals who disagree with the Biblical position on homosexuality."

Rachel cringed. This is exactly what she had feared. Sam was so impressionable. She looked to Ryan who once again looked like he was going to be sick. She waited for him to address his eldest daughter but strangely, he remained silent. *I guess it's up to me.*

"In this house, the Bible is our measuring stick for all things, be it morals, values, attitudes, sinful behavior and being Christ like." She looked to her oldest daughter. "Sam, I'm sure your professors know many things I do not. I won't argue with you on that." Sam looked smug. "But, they cannot begin to understand or comprehend the ways of our God. God says homosexuality is sin. It is not an acceptable lifestyle." Rachel set her fork down. "Isn't that correct, Ryan?"

"Yes, Sam. You were raised in the Word. You know what the Bible says." He set his napkin on his plate, obviously finished. "Can we please talk about something a little more pleasant?"

Rachel raised her eyebrows. *Really Ryan?* She shook her head and started clearing the table. *What is happening to my family, Lord?*

"I'll help, Mom."

Rachel smiled at her youngest daughter as she noticed the retreating backs of the rest of the family. "Thanks, hon. Whatever happened to cleaning up as a family?"

"Well, Sam has a date, of course. And Shannon is hanging out with Maddie from youth group. Since Shannon left for school, she hasn't got to see her much. I think she misses her."

"I suppose. They have been friends since grade school."

Shelly put the leftover chicken in a plastic container and glanced sideways at her mom. "And Dad closed himself up in his office." She started to open the refrigerator but instead

26

leaned back against the countertop and started crying. "Mom, something is wrong. I know it is. Sam and Shannon might not see it cause they're not here most of the time, but I do."

Rachel wrapped her youngest daughter in her arms and held her. "Honey, just keep praying for us, okay? I don't even know what is wrong yet. Just pray. We know the enemy would love to destroy our family. But I'm not going to let him. I know where my strength comes from and I won't stop fighting, okay?"

Rachel kissed the top of her daughter's head then released her. "Want to watch a movie?"

"Can I pick?"

"Sure, why not?"

They finished putting the food away and loaded the dishwasher then cuddled together on the sofa for Shelly's favorite movie, The Lake House. "Mom, do you think anybody will ever love me like Alex loves Kate?"

"Romeo does." The big lug of a dog climbed up on the couch and settled between them.

"Mom! I mean real love. Romeo loves anyone who feeds him."

Rachel smiled at her daughter who had returned her attention to the movie which had just begun. "Yes, I know so."

"How do you know?"

Rachel tucked her feet under her and looked her daughter in the eye. "Because Shelly, God has the perfect man already picked out for you. And we have prayed for him since you were little, right?"

"Yeah."

"Well, do you think God will give you a guy that mildly loves you?"

"You've got a point. I want to marry a pastor like Dad. I want to be in the ministry."

"Honey, it wouldn't surprise me one bit if that is the plan God has laid out for you." She took a drink of her tea. "Should we get back to the movie?"

Shelly took the movie off pause and settled in to watch her favorite love story. She used to pretend this movie was about her parents. She wouldn't be able to do that anymore. It was obvious their love wasn't timeless. She prayed her mother was right. If that were the case, then maybe they would overcome just like Alex and Kate. She smiled at that thought. *Please God, heal my parents.*

Chapter Four

On the Saturdays that the girls were home, they spent the day as a family. It was the rule. No dates. No sleepovers. No outings with friends. It was family for the entire day. Rachel had laid down the law three years before when Sam left home her freshman year and somehow she'd managed to enforce it.

A family friend was letting them use their boat. She already had her duffle bag stowed in the van and was tucking the thawed shrimp in the cooler by the time Ryan made his way downstairs.

Ryan headed straight for the coffee pot. "You going somewhere?"

Rachel tilted her head. "Uh, yeah. We asked weeks ago to use Mark and Jessi's boat today for our outing. Don't tell me you forgot?"

He closed his eyes and jutted his bottom jaw out. "Yeah, about that. I'm not going to be able to make it."

"Ryan, we only get a few Saturdays during the summer with the girls. You know that. What is so important today that it takes precedence over spending it with our girls?"

He sipped his coffee. "Look, I don't want to fight. I just have a lot on my plate right now and I can't go. You go. Take the girls and make a day of it."

Sam chose that exact moment to walk in. "Hey, if Dad isn't going, then I'm not going. I have to go shopping for some new jeans." She filled a coffee cup and took it with her back to her room.

No, this can't be happening. "See what you've done? I hope you're happy. I don't know what is going on with you, Ryan, but I want some answers before you tear this family completely apart. So you know, I'm not going to let you do that."

"Rachel, you've become such a nag I have to ask myself why I would even want to spend the day on a boat with you. I think we do much better these days as far apart as we can get."

She started unpacking the cooler. "And just whose fault is that, may I ask? You refuse to talk to me. You haven't touched me in months. You treat your family like we're the plague. I have no idea how you stand up at that pulpit and preach every Sunday. You're living a lie."

"Stop, both of you."

Rachel felt her heart drop and felt horrible. It wasn't often she lost her temper. She turned toward her daughter who had entered unnoticed. "Shelly, I'm sorry."

Ryan didn't say a word as he passed his daughter and left the room. His half empty coffee cup was sitting on the counter.

Shannon bounced into the room. "Sam says we're not doing the family thing today. I'm gonna go shopping with her, okay?"

Rachel admitted defeat. "Fine. Go."

Shannon took off without noticing the turmoil her mother and sister were going through.

Shelly wiped her tears away. "Is it all right if I go to Emily's? I just want to get out of here for a little while."

"Yeah, sure Honey. I don't blame you. I kinda want to get out of here for a little while myself."

"Thanks, Mom. I'll give her a call, see if it's okay."

"Try and have some fun, deal?"

Shelly nodded her head. "Yeah, sure." She gave her mom a hug then left to call her friend.

Rachel finished putting the food away then took her own cell phone out to the sunroom. She dialed and waited. "Jessi, it's Rachel. Hey, I guess we're not going to be borrowing your boat after all."

Rachel listened to her friend and colleague. "Are you available to get together for a cup of coffee? I could really use a friend at the moment."

Rachel pressed the end button on her phone and sighed. She had to talk with someone. She couldn't keep everything bottled up like she had been doing. That didn't work out so well, obviously.

Ryan was locked away in his office, again. Rachel slipped into a pair of khakis and her sandals and left without telling him what she was doing. She prayed she was doing the right thing. If she could trust anyone, it was Jessi. She and Mark had had their issues and she was the most compassionate person Rachel knew. She would have some good advice.

Rachel pulled into the parking lot right behind Jessi.

"Perfect timing!" Rachel, who looked forward to her words of wisdom, hugged her friend.

Jessi opened the door and let Rachel pass before her. "I'm not sure I can do the hot coffee thing in this heat. Some ice tea sounds good."

"You know us coffee drinkers. Nothing like a good cup of coffee, doesn't matter what the weather's like."

The shop was quaint and despite the weather, there were a few people lingering over steaming cups of the rich brew the shop was known for. The ladies found a quiet corner table and settled in.

Rachel sipped the dark aromatic liquid in front her. "I'm sorry about today, the boat and all. I know Mark went through a lot of trouble getting it ready for us."

"Don't worry about that. I'm just sorry you weren't able to enjoy it. Maybe some other time?"

Rachel nodded her head and turned away. The way things were going she wasn't really sure there would be another time. "Maybe."

Jessi set her tea down and studied her friend. She knew how lonely it could be in the ministry and how hard it could be to talk about tough times. People expected perfection when it came to their pastors. As a pastor it was hard to know whom you could trust. "Talk to me Rachel, tell me what's going on."

Rachel found it difficult to talk. She was trying to hold back the tears but it wasn't working. "I don't know if I can trust myself to talk about this." She wiped her eyes with her napkin.

"It might not be anything at all. Maybe it's just me being supersensitive. I don't know what to think anymore."

Jessi reached across the table and took Rachel's hand. "It's okay, you can talk to me."

Rachel began again. "It's me and Ryan. I think something is really wrong. We've had our share of problems but this goes beyond that. I don't know how to explain except to say he's been so distant. It's like I don't know him anymore. I don't know this man who lies next to me at night and wakes up beside me in the morning. He's become a stranger to me. And I miss my husband." Rachel looked around to see who might be listening in on their conversation. "I think he might be cheating on me."

Jessi leaned back in her chair not sure what to say but knowing she needed to say something. This was every woman's fear, at least every married woman's fear. "Have you talked to him about this?"

"I have tried, God knows I have. But he won't talk to me. He avoids me at every turn. This could destroy everything that we have worked so hard to build. Our church, our family, our marriage, literally everything could just fall apart. It's like he doesn't care anymore."

"How long has this been going on?"

"There have been times over the length of our marriage that he has become distant. But he has always found his way home. This time, he's not coming back. He's been acting this way for the past six months. I don't know how much more I can take without knowing what is going on. How do I get through to him?"

"Do you think he would talk to Mark?"

"He might open up if he had someone neutral to talk with."

Jessie took a sip of her tea. "Do you think it would help if Mark approached him? Maybe coming from one of his peers he would feel free to talk about what's going on."

"I'm willing to try anything. I don't want my marriage to end. I don't want my girls to lose their father. Jessi, we need help."

32

"Rachel, I don't know why this is happening. But I know that God is in control. I know that his hand is on everything and in everything that we will ever experience in this lifetime. I do know that whatever you are going through, whatever you and Ryan are experiencing, this will be used for good. I know it doesn't feel like it now, but there is a light at the end of the tunnel. I'm here for you any time you want to talk. You know I'll be praying for you. Don't give up. Don't let the enemy win. He wants to destroy families."

Rachel listened as her friend spoke. She knew she should be stronger, but sometimes it was hard to be the strong one. She was tired of worrying about what everyone else thought. She was tired of putting on a façade for the world to see what the proper pastor's wife should look like. She stared out the coffee shop window watching the dark clouds roll in. She could only pray that after the storm passed there would be a rainbow reminding her of all God's promises. She was in desperate need of a rainbow.

Chapter Five

Ryan watched his family getting ready for church. The girls were running from room to room borrowing clothes and helping one another with their hair. Rachel was quietly sitting in front of her vanity fixing her own hair. No one seemed to notice that he was scared.

"Rachel, I'm going to take the car separately from you and the girls. There are some things I need to get ready at church and I want to get there early."

"Okay, I'll see you at church."

Ryan drove slowly looking at the devastation from last night's storm. It came out of nowhere, unlike the devastation that was about to hit his family. This current storm was a long time in the making, but even so he could do nothing to stop it. *God help me.* Where did that come from? He stopped talking to God when he knew he wouldn't be running from his sin. It was easier that way.

He sat on the front pew as the worship team led them in songs of worship and adoration. He could no longer discern between right and wrong. Rachel was right; he couldn't continue to live a lie. He didn't join the rest of the congregation in lifting their hands to worship their Savior. He was a hypocrite. God didn't want his leftovers and he wasn't willing to give him his first, not anymore.

More than anything he wanted to turn in his seat and see who was in attendance. His wife was sitting on the pew next to him and his girls were sitting next to their friends. But it wasn't his family that he wanted to see.

Finally the song service came to an end. Ryan took his handkerchief and wiped the sweat from his forehead. He was nervous, he wondered if anyone else could tell.

He stood and made his way to the podium. The people in his congregation had no idea what was coming. They expected another long drawn out sermon, words of wisdom from their pastor. What a sham. They were in for the surprise of their lives.

Ryan stood at the podium silently waiting for everyone to take their seats and quiet down. He did not like confrontation but there was no other way. He glanced at his wife knowing she would be devastated. Knowing he was going to hurt her tore him in two. He had promised at the altar that he would cherish and protect her, but he didn't want to live a lie any longer. He could no longer deny what he'd always known. He wasn't being true to himself by continuing to live the life that he was living.

He found each one of his daughters seated with friends in different spots throughout the congregation. Their faces showed a mixture of confusion and embarrassment. In fact the whole congregation was staring at him. It was time to tell them the truth.

"Good morning. This Sunday morning service is going to be like no other that you've been to. I inherited the pulpit from Rachel's father twenty years ago, shortly after I got out of Bible College. During those twenty years we've seen many people come and go. Some people moved away while others just moved away from their faith. Some found new churches that met their needs while God brought in those who would best serve and be served within these four walls. It is with a heavy heart that I tell you that this will be my last Sunday with you. Effective immediately, I tender my resignation. I'm positive that God has someone that will serve you better than I have. Thank you for all the support you have given my family and me. God bless you all."

Ryan heard the gasps coming from the congregation as he turned and walked from the platform. He went straight to his office and shut the door. He grabbed the duffel bag that he had packed earlier, left through the side door and got in his car and drove home. He didn't want to speak with anyone. He didn't want to answer any questions. And he didn't want to look into his wife's eyes as she dealt with the aftermath of his decision. He would deal with her after she got home.

Rachel was numb. She didn't have the energy to stand, let alone talk with anyone. This was as much a shock to her as it was to everyone else. She heard voices, obviously directed toward her, but she couldn't make out the words. *Why would he do this? Why wouldn't he talk to her first? Was he that unhappy?* She felt hands on her, shaking her. Her youngest daughter's voice was breaking through the shock.

"Mom, Mom what's going on?"

Rachel turned to her daughter not quite sure what to say. No words would form. She stood up, grabbed her purse and started walking. She walked past the older ladies, the deacons, the board and the elders. She kept walking. Standing by the doors to the sanctuary was that guy, the one who Ryan provided the hotel room for. He seemed to be staring a hole right through her. She froze. This had something to do with him, she just knew it. She looked straight ahead and pushed through the doors and into the lobby. Voices were calling after her, questioning her. She had no answers. But she knew where to find them. She got in the driver's seat of her van and waited for her daughters. As soon as everyone was loaded she drove toward home. She ignored her daughters' questions and soon they figured out she didn't want to talk. It wasn't like she had any answers anyway. Soon they would all have the answers they sought after.

Ryan heard them before he saw them. One by one the four car doors closed. He remained in the Victorian chair by the fireplace as, one by one, they filtered through the front door. Funny that he should choose that chair. He remembered fighting with Rachel about it. She insisted on purchasing that old thing from the antique shop. And true to her word she refinished it as she said she would. Now it was his favorite chair in the formal living room.

Rachel saw him first. For a split second his resolve waned. He almost rushed to her when he saw the pain in her eyes. She didn't understand, she couldn't understand. She was too good, too pure. He didn't deserve her anyway, so in truth he was doing her a favor. She questioned him with her eyes.

The girls nearly ran into their mother as they came in behind her. Unlike their mother they rushed to him with questions.

Shelly reached him first. "Daddy, what is going on? What happened in there?" She knelt by his feet, her hands rested on the top of his leg, as she searched for meaning in what he had just done.

The two older girls knelt beside their sister. Shannon questioned her father trying to fix what he had done. "Dad, is there something I can do? I'm sure everyone would understand if you want to go back. We can fix this."

Rachel joined the conversation. "Girls, come sit down. Let's hear what your father has to say." Rachel sat down on the couch and motioned for her girls to sit down as well.

Ryan waited for them to get comfortable. When he looked up it was as if his jury, his accusers were waiting to cast judgment. And they had every right to do so. He was about to tear their world apart. "I'm sorry that I didn't talk with you four first. I guess I didn't know how. I thought it would be easier just to tell you all at the same time. I guess I was wrong."

Rachel's heart was breaking. "Ryan, why didn't you come to me? If you weren't happy, we would have found a way. Is this some sort of midlife crisis?"

Ryan shook his head no. "Rachel, I haven't been happy for a long time. But I want you to know that it's not your fault." He looked to each of the girls. "None of you are at fault. It's me. I've been living a lie."

For the first time Sam spoke. "Dad, what do you mean you've been living a lie?"

Ryan started sobbing. He wasn't sure he could do this, but he had no choice. "I'm not who you think I am. I'm a fake. I'm not the loving husband or the wonderful father that I've been pretending to be. I don't deserve a family like you."

Shannon, ever the peacemaker, rushed to his side. "Oh Daddy, yes you are. You have been a wonderful father. The best. How can you say such a thing?"

Rachel waited for it. She knew it was coming. She just wanted to know who the woman was. How could he do this to their marriage? To their family? She stood up. She wasn't falling for his tears. She wanted to know and she wanted to know now. "Who is she? You might as well just tell me. I've known for some time, I just couldn't prove it."

"It's not like that."

"Don't you dare lie to me. I know you Ryan Bradley. Have you forgotten how long we've been married?" Rachel approached her husband. "At least be a man and tell me the truth."

"That's what makes it so hard. I wish it were another woman, but it's not." He turned his head in shame. "The truth is I'm gay."

Rachel stared at her husband. *No, he couldn't have said what I thought he said.* "What did you say?"

Ryan turned to face her and the truth was written all over his face. She started to shake her head no. She felt her insides begin to tremble. She ran as fast as she could afraid she wouldn't make it in time. She threw herself in the bathroom and knelt at the toilet and emptied herself of her breakfast. She screamed over and over again. *No, it can't be. He couldn't of done this. I would have known.*

The retching slowed down but Rachel didn't think she'd ever stop crying. The betrayal was more than she could stand. She started the shower and climbed in, clothes and all. She turned on the water as hot as it would go and scrubbed her skin as hard as she could, peeling off layers of clothes as she went. Even though it had been
months since he touched her she still felt dirty.

Finally she settled down into the corner of the shower and just sobbed. She heard a knocking at the door but she ignored it. Her raw scrubbed skin was shivering from the cold water making contact. Her teeth began to chatter and still she just sat there. She didn't think God created enough water to ever make her feel clean again. Every time she thought of her husband being with a man and then coming home to her she felt sick all over again. But there was nothing left to throw up.

The water ran as she pressed her knees to her chest and sobbed and rocked. She was unaware of her youngest daughter leading her from the bathroom, putting pajamas on her and taking her to the guest room to sleep. She fell asleep from pure exhaustion.

All through the night she cried out in her sleep. She felt her youngest daughter's arms wrap around her each time and heard her prayers before she would settle back into a restless sleep.

The next morning Rachel pulled herself together. It was time to face reality and with God as her strength, as much as she wanted to crawl back into bed and never wake up, she knew she had to face this.

Rachel nursed her cup of coffee as she waited to face her family. She watched each of her daughters enter the kitchen, pour themselves something to drink and sit quietly at the table. It seemed as if no one had anything to say. Finally, Rachel asked the question. "Where is your father?"

Samantha answered, "He left after you closed yourself up in the bathroom. I don't know where he went. But he said he'd be back." She sipped her coffee and stared at her mother. "You could have tried to understand, Mom. It's not like he wanted to be this way. It's just how he is, he can't help it."

Shelly stood up, tightening her fist at her sides. "Don't you dare talk to our mother that way. Dad knows better and what he's doing is disgusting. How can you think of defending him?"

Rachel listened and watched the exchange between her daughters. If she didn't step in soon they were going to come to blows. If she could only find the energy she would, but at the moment mothering was the last thing on her mind.

Shannon, her peacekeeper, stepped out of her comfort zone and spoke up. "Come on Shelly, Sam, stop. This isn't helping. You're only making things worse." She looked to her sisters. "Please, don't fight. Mom and Dad need us to be strong and not make things harder."

Shelly glared at her older sister. "Yeah, sure. If Sam can keep her mouth closed then I can too."

Samantha grunted in disgust. "I've got to get back to school. We're already leaving later than we'd planned. Come on Shannon. Get your stuff."

Shannon raised her eyebrows in confusion. "We're leaving? Now? With everything that's happened, you plan on going back?"

"Well of course I'm going back. Why wouldn't I? Mom and Dad are grownups, they'll figure it out. I have class tomorrow and work tomorrow night. I have to get back."

Shannon looked to her mother for direction. "Mom, I really don't think I should go back. I should be here for you and Dad."

"Honey, Sam's right. You need to get back. Thank you for wanting to stay, but there's really nothing that you can do. Your dad and I need to figure this out. Just pray for us, okay? We need your prayers more than anything right now."

Shannon hesitated a moment too long for Samantha. "Come on Shannon, quit trying to fix everyone else's problems. We have our own to deal with and it's not getting done sitting here. I'm leaving in ten minutes." She stood up from the table. "With or without you. Your choice." Samantha headed upstairs to get her bags.

Shannon slowly stood up, not sure she wanted to go. She wrapped her arms around her mother. "Are you sure? I can stay. I don't have to go back now. I can always get another job. They'll understand."

"No, Honey. You go back to school. One way or another, everything will work out. God has a plan." Rachel stood up and returned her daughter's hug. "Go get your stuff. You know your sister will leave you."

Shannon hesitantly walked up the stairs, leaving Rachel and Shelly at the table by themselves. Rachel wondered how their lives could truly go on, but what could she do? This was her and Ryan's problem. The girls were all grown up and had their own lives to lead. She couldn't push her problems off on them. That wouldn't be fair. She had to deal with this. With God's help that was exactly what she was going to do.

Chapter Six

Val Sutton looked around at the women seated in the circle. How could they act as if nothing was wrong? She knew most of these women and even if they didn't go to the same church, they had to have heard by now that Pastor Ryan resigned. And no one knew why, or they weren't talking, one or the other. She was going to get to the bottom of this. She took her seat and waited for Merry to begin the prayer meeting. She crossed her arms and pinched her lips together making it obvious she had no intention of participating in small talk.

She endured prayer group and paced back and forth waiting for Merry to finish up talking with a new prayer group member. She needed her advice and she needed it quick. She had a bad feeling about her church and she wasn't going to stand by and let the enemy destroy her lifeline. He had another thing coming if he thought he was going to take her church down. No way was she going to let that happen.

Val looked down at her pantyhose gathered around her ankles. She studied them, wondering how she ended up with Elephant legs. *Lord, when did I get old? And how come they don't make panty hose for short old people? Humph!* She continued her pacing. *Merry must know that I have something important to talk with her about. Why can't she hurry it up?* Shaking her head, she answered her own question. *Probably cause she's from the south. Laid back about everything. Doesn't she know some things require speed?*

She heard the door shut behind her and quickly turned around. There Merry stood with her hands on her hips. "Val Sutton, what is wrong with you? You made that new woman so scared I doubt she'll ever come back."

"Oh, phooey on the new woman. Merry, I need your help. Maybe you heard and maybe you didn't and I don't want to be spreading gossip, but I have to talk with somebody. And that somebody is you. Pastor Ryan resigned on Sunday. He just up and quit. He didn't preach a message and by the look on Rachel's face, she didn't know a thing about it. She had to be helped from the sanctuary and she wouldn't talk to anybody. Not even me. I knew her mama when she found out she was pregnant with her. I've been going to that church for so many years, I've lost count. What are we going to do, Merry? Something bad has happened, I just know it. We have got to pray. I feel like my world is about to collapse and I don't know what else to do. I need someone to pray with me."

"Settle down, Val, don't go and get yourself all worked up. We'll pray. I hadn't heard anything but God knows all about it. He's got this. We can trust him." Merry turned and looked around the room. "I am feeling an urgency in my spirit too. We need to drop to our knees and get before our Lord. I feel some hard times are about to come upon us."

Val grabbed a pillow for her knees and went down hard. Merry followed suit and both women prayed as if the lives of those they love depended on them. Had the very windows of heaven opened up to them, they both would have realized just how much that was true. The heavenlies were filled with anticipation as both sides prepared for battle. Two humans joined the fight that day, a fight that was going to be hard won. Many would be sacrificed in the process and many would lose their lives. Not because the darts of the evil one were stronger than the side of truth, but because those lost were too nearsighted to see truth. They refused to accept truth as a way of life and instead chose the way of darkness. As with any war, the losses would be great. But rest assured, the war would be won and in fact, had already been won on the day of the resurrection. The enemy was a sore loser and wasn't going down without a fight, without taking as many human souls as possible with him to the pit. This was one more pitiful attempt at deceiving the elect. Thankfully, warnings had been issued and the elect were fully prepared and protected in the full armor provided for them. The armor of God.

Chapter Seven

Ryan slowly drove past the house trying to gauge whether Rachel was home. He needed to get a few things but he didn't want to face her, at least not yet. Still, he had to get some of his things. He pulled into the driveway hoping for the best. He highly doubted she'd changed any locks or tried to keep him out, at least not yet. If she were home the garage door would have alerted her to his presence immediately. He opted to try his key in the front door. That would be the safer bet.

Please, don't let her be home. He quietly shut the door behind him and tip toed to the steps. He would start his new job tomorrow and needed his dress clothes. He would be selling used cars across town. He was thankful for the job. He shook his head. All he'd been trained to do was preach the Word of God. How hard can it be? It's not that different from trying to get people to live right, is it? He lifted his hands, two sides of a balanced scale and weighed his new career. Buy a new car. Clean up your life. He grinned. In fact, it was probably going to be easier. Getting people to change was hard work. How difficult could selling cars be?

All was quiet. He opened his closet door and pulled out his suitcase and garment bag. He would have to face her eventually, he was just thankful it wouldn't be today. He filled his bag and slung it over his shoulder then he took up his garment bag and started for the door. He paused briefly, feeling a pang of guilt as he glanced at the family picture hanging over the fireplace. *Is this what you want to do, Ryan? Is this the life I have chosen for you?*

He ignored the voice in his head, the one questioning his actions. It wasn't his fault he'd turned out this way. He shouted to an empty room. "Where were you when I needed you? Where were you when I was scared? You weren't to be found. Now you expect me to listen? Now you want my attention?" He opened the door and headed to his car. "Well, it's a little too late now."

Ryan was shaking as he backed his car out of the driveway. By the time he reached the first intersection, he was sobbing. "How come you didn't love me then? How come you didn't protect me? It didn't have to be this way. You caused this. I wanted to be the good son. I wanted to be obedient and serve you." He wiped his tears with the back of his hand. "God, why didn't you help me?" The voice was gone. He hoped for good.

By the next morning Ryan had regained his composure and was standing in front of his new boss waiting for instructions. He looked around the show room as he waited.

"Like what you see?"

Ryan quickly turned back to his boss. "Yeah, what's not to like?"

"These are the new cars. You'll be concentrating your efforts on selling our used selection. That's in the next building over. Come on, I'll show you."

Ryan followed him from the well air-conditioned showroom into the heat of summer and into the building next door. There were no cars, just a lot of small offices and the smell of warm bodies. Ryan instinctively reached to loosen his tie.

"We don't wear monkey suits in here. Makes the customers uncomfortable. I'll get you a couple of polo shirts with our logo on them. That should do it."

Ryan was left standing on his own while his boss went off in search of two shirts.

"Hey, you must be the new guy."

"Yeah, I'm Ryan. I think I lost Mr. Morrison in the shuffle. He went to get me a couple of shirts."

The guy in front of him stuck out his hand. "Well I'm Caleb. It's good to have you. And by the way, around here we call Mr. Morrison, Jay. We're too busy to be so formal. He'll be back; a customer probably waylaid him. Either that or one of the sales team."

Ryan shook Caleb's hand glad for a friendly face in his new workplace. The guy seemed all right.

Caleb turned toward an office with a few desks crammed together. "Come on in. This is where we work. We deal with the internet sales and incoming calls. Jay's office is right next door and the guys who sell the used cars off the lot have their office across the hall. Gotta watch out for those guys. They'll eat your mama for breakfast if they think it'll get them a sale."

Ryan chuckled.

"You think I'm kidding? You'll see. One lost sale to a crooked salesman and you'll be a believer, trust me. Besides, where else do you think an ex-con can get a job? Yep, you got that right. A used car dealership. Even Jay's done time."

Ryan quickly closed his gaping mouth. "You're trying to pull one over on me."

"Nope, scouts honor. Not that I've ever been in the scouts, but hey, if it works for them, it works for me." Caleb pointed to the desk next to his own. "That's where you'll be planted. Feel free to take a load off while you're waiting for Jay. He could be a while."

Ryan listened as Caleb made a series of phone calls wondering what he got himself into. About that time, Jay walked into the office and threw a couple of shirts at him. "Here you go. I see you found your way. Come into my office, I have some paperwork you have to fill out."

Like an obedient pup, Ryan followed the large man into his office.

Jay pulled some paperwork from a file cabinet behind his desk. "Hey, what did you do before coming here anyway?"

"I was a pastor."

Jay turned to look at him, silent, considering what the guy before him just said. "A pastor, huh?" He grinned. "Well, you should fit right in then."

Ryan looked at him quizzically. "Why is that?"

"Well, as I see it, if you can tell people there is a God when there isn't, you should have no problem telling them there is a car when there isn't." He laughed out loud at his own joke.

"Of course there's a God."

Jay pierced him with his gaze. "Then what are you doing here?"

Ryan stammered.

"Yeah, that's what I thought." Jay handed Ryan the paperwork. "Fill this out. I'll be back in a few minutes."

Ryan knew he was in trouble. He remembered the day he wouldn't defend his faith at the kitchen table with his daughter. Now this. He hung his head. He tried his best, he did. He pored over the Bible. He'd highlighted every verse about temptation and finding his strength in God. Maybe Jay was right. The strength never came. He couldn't help who he was anymore than a woman could help she was born a woman. He'd tried to be something he was not for far too long. It was time to be who he was born to be. If that meant he had to give up his faith, then he'd do it. If God wanted him to be something different, he would have made it easier. As far as Ryan was concerned, God didn't care about him. And if he did? He had a funny way of showing it.

Chapter Eight

Jessi handed Rachel a tissue and put her hand on her shoulder. "I'm sorry you're going through this."

Rachel blew her nose. "That's it, Jessi. It's over. We're through."

"Wait a minute. What happened? I thought you were going to fight for your marriage?"

"No, it's over. There's nothing I can do."

"What do you mean there's nothing you could do? A week ago you were telling me you would fight for your marriage. What's changed?"

"Jessi, he's gay. I can't compete with that. And even if I could I'm not sure I'd want to. Every time I think about him touching me I get sick to my stomach. How many times has he been with a man and then come home to me? It makes my skin crawl."

"Let's see if I have this straight. When you thought he was having an affair with a woman you were willing to fight for him. But when you find out it's a man, you give up. Is that about right?"

"You're making me out to be the bad guy here. I'm not the one running around destroying my marriage. He's living with a man, Jessi. A man! My stomach is churning just thinking about it."

"Rachel, I'm sorry. I didn't mean to sound harsh. I just want you to hear what you're saying. If Ryan had been having an affair with a woman you were ready to fight for him. God was big enough to take care of that problem and get you through it. But now you're saying that because he's claiming he's gay you're giving up and therefore God is not big enough to take care of this problem in your marriage?" Jessi paused, letting her words settle in Rachel's spirit. "Does that make sense to you?"

Rachel felt the heat of her tears as they slid over her cheeks. "It's not that simple. You don't understand."

Jessi clasped Rachel's hands. "I never said your situation was simple. I would never underestimate your pain. But, I do know God's love is simple. It's for everyone. His grace is big enough for all of us. Every sinner that has ever lived can know his love. But, you already know that, don't you? The question is, do you believe it?"

Rachel looked around her kitchen, remembering the good times. "I do believe God can forgive him. I really do. I'm just not sure I can."

Jessi didn't want to push it. She understood Rachel's pain and knew it would take time if there were to be healing within their marriage.

Rachel walked around her kitchen stopping in front of the window overlooking the golf course. She ran her hand along the cool slate granite of her countertop. In one fell swoop every good memory with her husband was tainted. *How could he?* "You know I'll probably have to sell the house. I won't be able to keep up the maintenance let alone afford it." She turned from the window. "I haven't worked in twenty years. The mortgage has been affordable thanks to my inheritance. I doubt I'll be able to find a job that will pay the mortgage, the taxes and all the bills. And what about the girls' college education? How can I continue to help them? And Shelly's private school? We'll lose her scholarship since we are no longer pastoring a church." She returned to the table. "I'm sorry. I just can't think straight. I have so much running through my mind. I can't stop it. The thoughts just keep turning over, as if I have all the answers hidden away in some secret compartment of my brain. If it wasn't for the girls..." Rachel let the rest of her sentence drift away, unfinished. She wouldn't voice those thoughts. She'd go on, she had to. The girls already had one parent who'd bailed on them. They didn't need another jumping ship as well.

Jessi set her teacup in the sink as the side door opened. She hugged the pretty teen. "Hey there girl. How're you doing?"

Shelly shrugged. "Okay, I guess." She turned to face Rachel. "Mom, can I spend the night at Emily's?"

Rachel nodded. "Sure, go ahead." Shelly raced up the stairs. "She's been spending a lot of time away from home. I guess this place holds too many memories. Maybe it's a good thing I'll have to sell."

"Maybe you won't have to sell. You have your degree and there has to be something out there for you. I'm sure God has the perfect job with your name on it." Jessi hung her purse over her shoulder. "I've gotta get going. Aunt Merry is with the twins and I try not to leave the three of them together too long. They have a little bit more energy than she can handle."

The two women walked through the garage and to Jessi's van. "Rachel, have you talked with Ryan since he left?"

"No. At first I tried to call him, to just talk. But he wouldn't answer my calls so I stopped trying. He did come home though, once, just to get his clothes. He waited until I was gone. It's over Jessi. I just have to accept it." She pulled the lawn mower out of the garage. "I guess it's time to mow the lawn. By the looks of it, it's well past time."

Jessi noticed the well-maintained lawns of all the neighboring houses. "Do you want Mark to come and help you with that?"

"No, I should be able to figure it out. It looks like I'll have to figure out a lot of things. No sense in putting off the inevitable."

Jessi hugged her goodbye. "Call me if you need me. I'm here for you day or night, got it?"

Rachel nodded, pursing her lips, she waved goodbye as Jessi backed out of the driveway. *It's time to mow this forest.* She tilted her head, trying to figure out how to operate the machine in front of her. *It can't be that difficult, can it?*

She located the drawstring and pulled. The mower roared to life. *Maybe I can do this.* She started pushing her way through the overgrown grass, moving slowly. The smell of fresh cut grass only took a back seat to her roses and to the smell of her children when they were babies. She kicked off her shoes, allowing the cool fresh cut grass to slide over her toes to tickle her ankles. She had made a half of a swipe when the mower suddenly   stopped.

She pulled the cord once again and when the mower started, she pushed through the thick grass at an even slower pace. Once again, it quit after a short time. After the fourth time of starting and stopping, she began to get frustrated. *Okay, maybe I can't do this.*

Rachel bent over and started to pull the chord one more time when she heard a voice behind her. She quickly straightened and turned around.

"Hi, I see you're having some trouble with your lawn mower."

"Um, yeah. It's indecisive. Can't make up its mind whether or not it wants to work. Kind of reminds me of my kids."

The man in front of her reached for her hand. "I'm Dillon. My son and I moved in across the street about a month ago."

Rachel extended her own hand, embarrassed that she hadn't noticed the new neighbors. "I'm sorry, normally I would have come to welcome you to the neighborhood by now. I guess life interfered."

"No worries. I thought I might be able to lend a hand here." He knelt down and opened a compartment on the top of the mower. "My guess is the air filter. If it's dirty the machine will keep quitting on you." He lifted up a small sponge for her to see. "Yep, it's dirty." He brushed the debris from the sponge. "Do you have a sink in your garage?"

"Uh, no. Will the kitchen sink work?"

"Oh yeah, sure." He followed her into the kitchen and proceeded to wash out the filter, explaining as he went. "You never know, you might have to do this again." He finished squeezing out the filter then turned toward the garage. "This is going to need to dry. I'll come back in about an hour and see how it's doing. Then I'll get you all set up. I'm sure the mower will run great once this is taken care of."

52

"I sure appreciate your help. I had no idea what to do."

Dillon wondered about her situation but he wisely kept his questions to himself. "Anytime, I'll have it up and running in an hour or so."

Rachel was dredging through help wanted ads on Craigslist when she heard the roar of the lawnmower. She peeked out her front window and watched Dillon cut two complete rows of grass. She grabbed a couple bottles of water and she went out to finish the job she'd started.

"Hey there. I see it's working much better. Thank you so much." She handed him the cold water and set hers on the grill. "I can finish up here."

He handed off the mower and waved as he took his leave.

Rachel finished the front yard as well as the large backyard with no more problems with the lawn mower. By the time she finished raking the excess grass, her hands burned from the torn blisters on her palms. *I won't allow it to get this long again.* She was busy for most of the day doing mindless work. She found herself wondering about her new neighbor. He had said he and his son moved in, he mentioned nothing about his wife. *Probably divorced.*

She wiped her feet on the entry rug then headed for the shower. She needed to find a job. She had enough in savings to get her through the next six months but she wanted to reserve as much of that money as possible. Nor did she want to take any money she and Ryan had put aside for retirement. She was thankful that Shelly was fifteen. At least that much was a blessing. She wouldn't need childcare.

Once she was cleaned up, she sat down in front of the computer, sifting through the want ads. *There has to be something here.*

She was about to give up when she noticed a want ad for a groundskeeper for the local community college. *That has to pay better than minimum wage, right?*

She forwarded her resume, praying that this was the job God has reserved for her then turned off the computer.

Rachel let Romeo out before she settled on the wicker couch with her salad. She contemplated reading her Bible. She hadn't picked it up for days. God seemed so far away. Then again, it was probably so because she was the one who had walked away from Him. And she knew better. How many times had she counseled young families regarding the very same mistake? God will never leave us nor forsake us. Why then, at the first sign of trouble, do we alienate ourselves from his presence? She set her salad on the side table and picked up her Bible and turned to Psalm 139.

You have searched me, Lord, and you know me. You know when I sit and when I rise; you perceive my thoughts from afar. You discern my going out and my lying down; you are familiar with all my ways. Before a word is on my tongue you, Lord, know it completely. You hem me in behind and before, and you lay your hand upon me. Such knowledge is too wonderful for me, too lofty for me to attain.

Rachel felt the pressure in her chest, tears unshed, hurts left to smolder. She should have given all the pain over to her Lord weeks ago. Why had she been so stubborn and held on to them? Was forgiving so out of the question that she had to put her relationship with Christ on the back burner to keep from being reminded to love? She kept reading.

Where can I go from your Spirit? Where can I flee from your presence? If I go up to the heavens, you are there; if I make my bed in the depths, you are there. If I rise on the wings of the dawn, if I settle on the far side of the sea, even there your hand will guide me, your right hand will hold me fast. If I say, "Surely the darkness will hide me and the light become night around me," even the darkness will not be dark to you; the night will shine like the day, for darkness is as light to you.

Lord, why did I run from you? I should be running to you. Only you can give me peace. Your presence is my lifeline, my strong tower. Oh God, please forgive me.

Rachel dropped to her knees, seeking comfort from the only one who would always be there for her. As she released, the built up tears were replaced with an unexplained joy. She may have lost the man she thought she'd be able to count on through everything, the one she would grow old with, but she knew no matter what happened, God would be with her and she could handle it.

She stood up and stretched then looked at the wilted salad on the side table. After letting the dog in, she tossed her salad, climbed the stairs and settled between the cool sheets. The next morning, she couldn't even remember having closed her eyes. It had been months since she had slept that well. She glanced heavenward. *Thank you Lord. This is the day you have made and I will rejoice and be glad in it.*

The phone rang, reminding her that while she may be in the center of peace, there was still a hurricane surrounding her life.

Chapter Nine

Rachel picked up the receiver on the sixth ring and made a note to cancel her home phone service. No need to have that extra bill when she had a cell phone that would suffice.

"Mom. It's Sam."

Rachel heard the fear lacing Samantha's voice. "Sam, Honey, what's wrong?"

"Mom, it's Shannon. She's in the hospital. You need to come."

"What happened? An accident? Is she okay?"

"Mom, you just need to come. She's alive, but I, I mean, we need you here."

"Okay, I'm leaving. Let me call you back on my cell."

Rachel hung up the house phone and ran for her car. "God, please let Shannon be okay."

She hit the speed dial on her phone. "Okay Sam, I'm driving. Now tell me what happened."

"Mom, it looked like she took a whole lot of pills. I tried to wake her up and she wouldn't. I called 911, then I called you and Dad. I'm at the hospital now. I don't know anything. I don't know if she's gonna be okay. Mom you need to hurry up and get here."

Rachel pulled to the side of the street and rested her head on her steering wheel. She heard her daughter's tears at the other end of the line. "Sam, it's time to pray. Pray hard, harder than you've ever prayed before. I'm going to get there as fast as I can. You said you already called Dad?"

"Yeah, Mom, he's on his way too."

"Sam, you'd tell me if she didn't make it, right? I need to know."

"Mom, I promise you, she's alive. The doctors are working on her now."

Rachel put the van in gear and took off for Emily's. "I'm picking up your sister then we're on our way. I better give her a quick call to let her know I'll be there otherwise I'll be waiting on her. Call me if you hear anything, and Sam, remember to pray.

Rachel called her youngest daughter. "Shelly, it's me. Shannon's had some kind of a medical emergency. I'm about to pull in the driveway. We need to hurry."

"All right, Mom, I'll be right there."

True to her word Shelly came bounding out the front door and climbed in the van next to her mother. "Mom, what happened? What's wrong?"

"Honey, it looks like your sister tried to commit suicide."

Shelly faced her mother with a look of horror. "What? Why would she do that?"

"I'm afraid it's my fault. I knew she wanted to stay home and I insisted she return to school. She isn't as strong as you and Sam are. With everything going on, and having no way to make everything right, it was probably more than she could handle."

The two drove the remainder of the way in silence, Rachel beating herself up and Shelly blaming her father. Both were praying, pleading for Shannon's life. She didn't hear back from Sam while driving and she counted that a blessing.

An hour later they pulled up in front of the hospital emergency room. Rachel was surprised to see Ryan had already made it. His car was parked near hers. He must have been driving faster than she was. She made her way to the desk, Shelly on her heels, and asked where Shannon was.

Sam must have been watching for her. "Mom, she's in here."

Rachel pulled Sam to her, breathing in her scent then released her so she could go to Shannon. She tried to put on a brave face. She tried to be strong for her middle daughter.

She entered the small room with a pasted on smile. Probably not the best entry she could have made, but it was either smile or cry. And she figured anything was better than crying.

Shannon looked away as soon as she entered the room. Ryan slipped out right after she entered. Well, that made two family members ignoring her. She could understand Shannon. She was probably embarrassed. Ryan was a different story all together.

Rachel sat down near the head of Shannon's bed. "Hi, Honey." She had yet to talk to the doctor but assumed Shannon was out of the woods as she was conscious. "I'm sorry you're going through this and I'm sorry I wasn't here for you."

"Mom, I just want things to be like they were. I want you and Dad at home, together. I want us to be a family again."

"I know you do, Honey."

"But you can't make that happen, can you?"

"No, I can't. A lot is up to your dad and he isn't taking my calls. Maybe now he'll talk to me and we can schedule some counseling. Remember Shannon, God is bigger than all this. He can make a way where there is no way."

"You would go to counseling?"

"Yes, of course I would."

"Will Dad?"

"Honestly, I don't know. But, no matter what happens Shannon, we have the strength to go on, to keep on living because Christ is our foundation."

"I know, Mom." Shannon rested her fingertips on her forehead then moved them over her heart. "I know that here but I can't make myself get it here. I tried to psych myself up but it didn't work. I just wanted it all to go away."

"Honey, that's not how life works. There are going to be hard times. We are supposed to be here for each other." Rachel wasn't used to making her own decisions. For the past twenty plus years everything she had done had been in conjunction with her husband. "I want you to come home. You can finish up your degree later. I think you need time to heal and I want to be there for you. Would you like that?"

Shannon nodded. "I want to be home."

"You're going to need to see a counselor yourself, you know that right?"

"I think I'll be okay once I'm home."

"Yes, I think you'll be better too. But, you will still need to talk with someone. Don't you think it will help to talk to someone neutral? Someone who will look at everything that is happening objectively?"

"I guess so."

Rachel pursed her lips. "I know so. Besides, that is probably going to be one of the conditions if they let you out of here."

"What do you mean, if?"

"There is a psyche ward here for evaluation. Most of the time, someone who tries to commit suicide is held for counseling. They will probably transfer you to that floor tomorrow or the next day, as soon as they know you are okay."

"What? I don't want to stay here. I want to go home."

"I know you do. But first, we need to be sure you aren't going to hurt yourself again."

"Mom, I won't. I need to go home."

"Sweetheart, that is up to hospital policy. Even if they do keep you, it won't be long before you're home. Okay?" Rachel stood up. "Your sister wants to see you. I'll be in the waiting room." She bent over her daughter and kissed her forehead. "I love you, Shannon. You scared me to death. I don't know what I'd do without you." She let her daughter rest against her pillow and left the room. She'd always hated the smell of hospitals. She'd always associate that smell with the death of her parents and she hated that her daughter had almost joined them. She looked upwards. "Life isn't supposed to be like this."

Shelly was waiting and hurried toward the room Rachel had just vacated. That left her to face Ryan. She'd been trying to call him and she'd left several messages, not that he'd had the decency to return a single call. He wouldn't be able to get away from her today, that she was sure of.

Rachel heard the thunder. It had been threatening to let loose the entire day. She hugged Sam then sat down next to Ryan. "I guess we can thank you for this."

Ryan wasn't sure he heard her right. "Say what?"

"Maybe if you had called me back, God wouldn't have had to get your attention this way."

"Mom, that was low."

Rachel cast a dirty look in the direction of her daughter, telling her to stay out of it then continued in a forceful whisper. "I'll tell you what is low. A husband who abandons his family. That is the worst kind of low. Then he won't even answer a simple phone call. What kind of man does that?"

Ryan stood up. "Really Rachel? You want to argue now? I would have thought even you would be mature enough to see this isn't the time."

She shook her head. "And here I thought this might be your wake up call, shake some sense in to you. I guess I was wrong about that too, now wasn't I?"

"What do you want, Rachel? After twenty two years of marriage, I am finally seeing the real you. Even if I was straight I wouldn't come back to this. Who'd want a nagging, whiny wife like you?"

"And you think I'd let you back in my home? In my bed? God only knows what kind of diseases you have now. That's sick, Ryan. Any woman with half a mind wouldn't want a man who lusts after other men. You make my skin crawl."

Samantha stood up. "Enough. This isn't about you two. It's about Shannon. Get over yourselves, would you?" She took off for the door in tears.

Rachel straightened her shoulders. "Now look at what you've done."

"Me? This is on you, Rachel. You started this."

"No, Ryan. You did the day you walked out and traded us in for your lover boy."

"Tell Shannon I'll talk to her tomorrow. I'm leaving."

"Yeah, go ahead and do what you do best. Leave."

Rachel sat by herself, tears flowing down her cheeks. She knew better, she really did. Every sane thought flew out the window the minute she saw him sitting there, pretending he cared. She had let loose. Truly there was no hope now. She was on her own. She had to face it. "Oh God, what is wrong with me?"

She felt Shelly's hand on her shoulder. "Where are Sam and Dad?"

"They left."

Three days later Rachel picked her middle daughter up from the hospital and took her home.

Shannon was settled and looking happier than she had in weeks. Rachel was grateful that her daughter seemed to be bouncing back. That was a relief. On the flip side, Shannon was adamant that she follow through with her promise of counseling. What could she do? Their marriage was over, done for. But a promise was a promise. She set up a counseling appointment with Mark and Jessi, knowing they were the ones she could confide in. With them she wouldn't feel self conscious nor would she have to worry about gossip.

Rachel poured herself a green smoothie then turned to the girls who were seated at the table. "You want to go to church with me this morning?"

Shannon was quick to reply. "Ah no, I don't think I'm ready to face that."

Shelly was a little more apprehensive about turning her mother down. "Do you want me to go with you, Mom?"

Rachel smiled at these two lovely young women. "No, I guess I need to go the first time on my own. Is that okay with you?" She knew she'd given Shelly an easy out, even so, it was true. She wanted to face their congregation on her own. She finished her smoothie, gave each of them a kiss, then took the first tentative steps toward facing her future.

She wasn't sure what to expect as she walked through the church doors. Word had gotten out about Ryan and a few people had called. Some, like Val, really wanting to know how she was doing, others simply wishing to get some juicy gossip to pass on. Still, she was the pastor's wife and had a responsibility to the flock. They had been left floundering by her husband; she wouldn't let them down too. If they wanted her there that is. That was yet to be seen.

She had purposefully waited until church was almost ready to start. Val told her that Herbert had been covering services for the time being, until they found a new pastor.

Rachel held her head high as she walked and took a seat mid way up the aisle. She was surprised to see Val, Bible in hand, asking her to scoot over. She could just kiss that woman. Having a friend next to her strengthened her resolve so she took a chance and looked around the room. Some smiled at her in greeting; others were whispering and looking her way. Some things never change.

She felt a squeeze and turned to Val.

"Don't you worry about those old biddies. Some people have nothing better to do."

Rachel smiled, grateful for the support.

The piano began to softly play and she quickly forgot about the whispering. She missed being in the house of God. She closed her eyes and let the soothing words of worship soak her dry and thirsty body. *Youtube just doesn't cut it Lord.* She raised her hands, allowing herself to concentrate on someone other than herself. *I've missed you!*

She looked around the sanctuary. The small building may not have been much to a passerby, but to Rachel, these four walls represented everything she held dear. To her, this place would always be about her faith, her family, and her church family as her extended family. When she lost her parents in the accident, these people were there for her. Many of them, like the man standing before the podium and his wife Val, had been here when her own father stood at the podium preaching sermons and loving his congregation, gently leading them toward a life with Christ as their head. Val had changed her diaper in the nursery. How could she have doubted their love for her? She should have run to this place instead of from it.

She listened as Hebrews 4:16 was read. *"Let us then with confidence draw near to the throne of grace, that we may receive mercy and find grace to help in time of need."* Herbert went on to the parable of the lost sheep, the one where the shepherd left the ninety-nine to go and find the one lost lamb. Rachel found herself crying, knowing that she had been that lost one. Even though only for a few weeks, she had turned her back on her Lord. One day should have been too much. She'd accepted Christ as a child. In all that time she'd never doubted his love until these past weeks and she was ashamed. Even when her parents were killed, her relationship with Christ had been what held her together. Never once did she blame him or accuse him. Why now? Why did she turn her back on him now?

She wasn't sure she'd ever know the answer to that question. She only knew her pain was deeper than any she'd ever felt. She felt alone, hurt, abandoned, rejected and unloved, all at the same time.

The message came to an end and service was dismissed. She was glad she came. She understood why the girls didn't want to go with her. They couldn't stand the thought of people whispering behind their backs. And she had toyed with the idea of staying home with them. But, she was also an adult and now the head of her home. She had to face her fears if she was going to succeed in holding together what was left of her household. That meant coming here today.

Rachel blinked and glanced at Val, realizing she had missed most of what the older woman was saying. "and I have too much for just me and Herbert. What do you say?"

"I'm sorry, Val. I missed most of that. I guess I was a little lost, reminiscing."

"Oh, it's okay, Honey. You probably have a whole lot on your mind. I was just saying I have a big ole' pot roast in the oven at home with all the fixings. Lord told me to cook it, said he'd provide the family who needed it. Now that would be you Honey. He sure did provide. Why don't you go home and get those girls of yours while I get the biscuits on? Can't have a roast without biscuits."

Walking as fast as her legs would carry her, Val left without waiting for Rachel to accept her invitation. Rachel just shook her head knowing better than to argue with the woman who had been like a mother to her, at least not when the Lord gave her the instructions. She and the girls would be having pot roast for lunch.

She received a few hugs on her way out and a few curious glances. No one was outwardly rude, minus the whispers of course. Some even thought they were being courteous by keeping their voices so low. *Oh well, let them talk. Talk never killed a person.*

Rachel and the girls arrived to the smell of roast beef and Val's famous creamed corn.

Val met them at the door. "You girls get on in here." She hugged each one. "Oh my, the Lord sure knew what he was doing. You three aren't nothing but skin and bones. You haven't been eating, have you? Well, I'll fix that. Come on. Supper's about on the table."

Rachel paused, not remembering the last time she grocery shopped or when she had last prepared a meal. She remembered buying several bottles of green smoothies. And the girls must have picked up some minor groceries. It was as if life had just stopped, as if the earth quit spinning. She found herself hungry, really hungry. As if she'd been asleep for a long time, Rip Van Winkle style.

Her eyes roamed the contents of the table, taking in the feast. Val had covered all the bases. Roast, potatoes, gravy, carrots, onions, cream corn, brussel sprouts, biscuits and glasses of iced tea. She could hardly wait to dig in. Only her well honed manners kept her from eating everything in sight. After Herbert said grace, she purposefully ate as slowly as she could manage. Although by the looks on her daughters' faces, she must have been inhaling. She set her fork down, wondering where that came from.

The comparison between feeding her spiritual soul that morning and feeding her body that afternoon opened her eyes. She'd been starving herself. Neither the soul nor her physical body had been nourished. It was time for a change. She couldn't change others, but she could sure change herself. She could let this whole situation change her, destroy her, or she could grow stronger from the experience. It was up to her. Her choice.

She picked up her fork once more, this time savoring the delicious meal that was prepared for her.

She felt restored, refreshed, and full of purpose. She had no idea what God was going to do through this mess she called her life, but she knew what she was going to do. She was going to live. As long as her creator deemed her worthy to breathe and walk this earth, she would do her best; give her best. And that would begin today.

Chapter Ten

Ryan turned the page of his Bible, reading verses he'd highlighted over the years. *God, are you still there?* One by one, he read verses that had impacted his life, made him stronger and given his life purpose. Every verse he found on the subject of temptation, he underlined and highlighted, praying that the words would give him direction.

From the doorway Terry watched Ryan pore over his Bible then shook his head. Why did he keep going back to that fairy tale? "I wish you wouldn't read that. You're just confusing yourself. You made your choice, and it was the right one. We need to get on with our lives."

"I'm just trying to align my life with the Word of God. I still believe Terry. Even with the choices I've made, I still believe."

"I know you do. It just hurts me to see you in such pain. I can't help you if you keep opening doors to past hurts."

"I'm reading about temptations and what God says about them."

"Are you saying I'm a temptation?"

"That's the point, Terry. I don't know. I'm so confused. On one hand, everything I know tells me to run. On the other, my desire is to cling and close all the doors and windows and never look out again. I'm torn. Where do I turn?"

"Well, it would appear you've already made your choice. You're here with me, right?" Terry walked closer to the old recliner that Ryan was perched in. "I mean, it's not like you can have everything go back to the way it was. Not now anyway."

"You're probably right about that." Ryan closed the Bible and set it aside. "I just need some time to think. Although it seems like that is all I've been doing. That and working. Between the car dealership and the stress of my life being torn upside down and inside out, I'm a mess."

"Well, I'm here for you. I've always been here for you. You remember the first time you came to my house? You were eight years old. You were scared to death. I think it's the first time you realized you could hide from your father. I hid you in my room until your dad had left to go to work. I was there for you then, I'm here for you now." Terry placed his hand on Ryan's shoulder. "You remember that, don't you?"

"Yeah. I remember. How could I forget?"

"I think my mom figured it out, but she understood and kept our secret. When he would come pounding on the door, she'd insist she hadn't seen you. Even though she knew good and well you were tucked in the corner of my room." Terry knelt down by the chair. "Don't you see? You were supposed to be there with me. How can these supposed Christians tell you otherwise? Why would God put us together as children then tear us apart as adults. It doesn't make sense. If God really loves us then he'd want us to be happy. This was his doing. He made us this way. He made us to love each other, Ryan. You know it's true. You can't deny it."

Ryan stood up and began to pace the room. "I don't know anything any more. I just need some time to myself."

Terry abruptly stood up. "Fine, I'll leave. Do your thinking. And when you are finished I'll be here, like I've always been here. You'll see that I'm the only one who will still be here for you no matter what. Everyone else will turn their back on you. Except me. I'll always be here, always."

After Terry left, Ryan dialed a number that was as familiar to him as his wife's. He immediately recognized the voice on the other end. "Mark? Do you think we could get together and talk?"

"Ryan? You bet buddy. Name the time and place and I'll be there."

"Can you make it now? At your church?"

"I'll meet you there in fifteen. Does that work?"

"Yeah, that works. See you in a few."

Ryan paced back and forth in front of the church, waiting for Mark to show. He glanced at his watch noting that it had only been eleven minutes since he'd called. Still, he wanted, no needed, to talk to someone who might understand. Mark had been his closest friend in the ministry and he knew Mark had been through the ringer before he was a pastor. If anyone could understand his pain, Mark could.

The family suburban pulled up in front of the church. Ryan still couldn't believe what Mark and Jessi had been able to accomplish in this neighborhood. They now had one of the largest churches in the city, as well as a school and a day care. They had Bible studies and life groups every day of the week. They served meals to the homeless and needy, handed out groceries and clothing as well as school supplies for underprivileged kids. They had a street ministry and the most important part of their ministry was they lived it. They truly loved and cared about everyone they met.

Ryan extended his hand. "Thanks for comin' man."

Mark nodded then opened the door and led the way. His office was floor to ceiling books. He had tried to keep a neat tidy office but found it just didn't work. He wanted a comfortable, lived in feel that made people feel at home. Fancy office furniture just didn't cut it in his line of work. He wanted people to know he had been there, that he'd been through it. So, he had a small desk to work at and the rest of the room consisted of some overstuffed chairs, side tables with more books and a coffee pot, which he walked straight to and started. "Have a seat. Want some coffee?"

"Yeah, that'd be great."

Mark waited patiently. He'd been praying with his wife and knew what Ryan and Rachel were going through. They had spent a lot of time on their knees. He had tried calling Ryan a few times with no return phone call, until now.

"I guess you know why I'm here. I've made a mess of things."

"Yes, you have. But, the bigger the mess, the more we know it's God on the clean up."

"I'm not so sure he can clean this one up. Maybe damage control would be a better goal."

"See, what'd I tell you? Even you think it's impossible. What does Matthew 19:26 tell us?" Mark read from his Bible. *"With man this may be impossible, but with God, all things are possible.* You have quickly forgotten, my friend, just how powerful our God is."

"I think it's more I question why he'd want to get me out of this. I turned my back on him. Even now, I'm not sure what I want. I'm so confused. The voices in my head keep saying two different things and I'm being pulled in two very different directions."

Mark poured the coffee, praying for wisdom at the same time. He handed Ryan a cup and sat down opposite him. "Why don't we talk about what's going on with you. What happened to cause you to make such an about face?"

"An old friend showed up. One I thought was out of my life. He brought many memories with him, many emotions that I had long buried."

Mark nodded. "Yes, I understand how the past shakes things up. Tell me about your friend."

Ryan was uncomfortable. It had been his choice to come here, to talk with someone so he continued. "He lived next door to us when I was a kid. He was there for me during some pretty hard times."

Mark waited for Ryan to go on.

"I had it rough. My dad was, well, pretty abusive. Terry was a little older than me and I would hide out at his house until Dad would pass out. As the years went by, we became close." Ryan met Mark's glaze, looking for signs of condemnation. He saw none, so he found himself pouring out his entire story. "I was only eight when I started seeking refuge at Terry's house. It became a pattern. My dad drank, a lot. So did my mom. Mom escaped into her own little world, and Dad ventured into mine, more specifically my bedroom. I began to recognize the sound of his footsteps in the hall and knew he was coming for me. I tried hiding under the bed, in the closet, even in the dirty clothes pile. But he always found me. He would tape my mouth shut with duct tape so no one could hear me scream. Not that my mom would have done anything but he feared the neighbors might. It was easy enough for him to hold me down and violate me, but he had a hard time keeping me quiet.

"The duct tape did the trick and he began coming to my room more often, just about every night. I can't tell you how many rolls of duct tape he went through. I started to notice a pattern; he was drunk and predictable, enough so that an eight year old could see what was coming. When I started to see the signs, I quietly climbed out my window onto the fire escape and waited for him to quit looking for me. One day, the kid in the apartment below us saw me sitting out there. It was freezing and I was in my pajamas. I had seen him at school. He was a tough kid, or so I had thought. He invited me to wait it out in his apartment. It was only him and his mom and she worked a lot. He never asked me what happened, although I eventually told him. We became inseparable. He became my protector. The one person I could count on, who was always there for me.

"I finally had the big brother I had always wished for. And for a while, that is what it was, a brotherly relationship. Then the years started to pass by and things started to change. I was thirteen and the only physical relationship I had had was with my father. That was messed up. I think my father finally figured out where I was going, but he apparently found comfort in other places and left me alone.

"I also found comfort in other places, namely with the sixteen year old who had been my refuge over the years. We continued to have a physical relationship all the way through my high school years. I spent the next five years living as a homosexual teenager. Life was hell at school. I was called every name in the book. Queer, faggot, and homo became synonymous with Ryan. If I heard those names when I was in the vicinity, it was my clue to run. I became very good at hiding. I'd had lots of practice with my dad and even more in my puberty years. If I got caught, I was beat up. It didn't help that I was small for my age. I was an easy target.

"At the end of my senior year I was invited to attend a youth rally. Up until that point, I had avoided religion like the

70

plague. A god that would allow a small child to be sexually abused by his own father didn't deserve to be worshipped. I had no use for that kind of god. Then I met Phillip. He and his young wife moved into our building. He was a youth pastor and he was always kind to me. At first I thought he was interested, ya know? But he never touched me. He always talked about God like he was his best friend. And he didn't force me to understand or accept it. He didn't hide his faith either, which was pretty cool to me. I wished I had been that brave, to openly share with the world who I was. But there was a part of me, inside, that knew what I was doing was wrong. I was ashamed. Yet, here was Phillip, announcing to his gay teenage neighbor that he was a Christian and proud of it. I still didn't want any part of Christianity, but I had found a measure of respect for at least one Christian. That was a big step for me, well, a baby step, but at the time that baby step seemed like a giant leap.

"Like I said, I was invited to this youth rally and I went. I don't know why I went. It changed everything. Nobody called me names. I sat, mesmerized, as I listened to the speaker talk about the hard times he'd been through. His story was familiar. Different, but I felt his pain. And I felt like he knew mine. At the end of the night, I was at the altar, giving my heart to Jesus.

"When some people accept Christ, everything changes for them. They make radical changes in their lifestyle, give up sinful passions and set the world on fire with their enthusiasm. It was different for me. I was still the same insecure teen who found his worth in the guy who had been his rock. After studying the Bible with Phillip and the youth group, and understanding God's expectation that we turn from our sin, I ended my relationship with Terry. That didn't go over very well. He hated religion. He hated that I'd let them brainwash me. I tried to explain but I was brand new at the Bible and had no words. I only knew what was going on inside of me. And that was hard to explain.

"Our relationship turned into an on again, off again relationship. We had this bond, this connection that I couldn't let go of. I went to Bible College and for months at a time, I'd be strong. Then I'd backslide and undo all the progress that I'd made. I hid it well. I dated in college and was just one of the guys. Then Terry would show up out of the blue and I'd be right back with him. It was a horrible cycle.

"One day Phillip showed up at group with a black eye and a bloody lip. He refused to say what happened, but I knew. I knew it was Terry. I told him to back off, to move on. Even then I wasn't sure I could stay away forever. He was the one I trusted, that I believed in.

"The day I met Rachel, everything changed for me. I knew she was the one. I met her at a hamburger joint. She attended the state college and was a senior in the horticulture program. I was a senior at the seminary. We became inseparable. We married two years later and the rest, you know. For twenty years I was the faithful husband. Terry had finally taken the hint when I married Rachel and stayed away. Every now and again, I'd see a glimpse of who I thought might be him. If it was him, he stayed in the background.

"That is until a few months ago. He showed up out of the blue. Twenty years and he still has a hold over me. I don't get it."

Mark had listened to the details of Ryan's past with a grieving heart. How much pain had this man endured? *Oh God, how do I reach him?* "Does Rachel know about any of this?"

Ryan shook his head. "No. No, I couldn't tell her. She was so pure, so good. She would never understand the evil that I had been through. I couldn't take that chance."

"If she knew, it might help her understand where you're coming from."

"No, it's too late for that. I'm just gonna walk away. I can't have either of them. It's not right that I'm with Terry and Rachel will never take me back. I'm too messed up for her. I make her skin crawl. I know, she told me."

"She only said that cause she's hurt and she doesn't understand. You know as well as I do, it's a defense mechanism. We protect ourselves when we're most vulnerable."

"You should have seen her Mark. Did I tell you how we met? She was waiting tables at a hamburger joint. Some buddies and I were sitting at a corner booth discussing theology. We

72

were loud but it was all in good fun. A few disagreements about lineage if I remember correctly then this beautiful raven-haired waitress pops up out of nowhere to take our order. She took my breath away, literally. It was just like in the movies, I was speechless. I heard the others place their orders and I kept staring. One of the guys had to hit me upside the back of my head to get my attention so I would quit looking like a fool." Ryan wiped his eyes with the back of his hand. "I really loved her, Mark. I truly did. I thought it would work. We dated the rest of that year before I proposed. She brought me home and introduced me to her father. Told me I had to ask her father's blessing before she would accept. I was scared to death. He put his arms around me and hugged me, welcomed me into the family. He insisted we date another full year before he would give his blessing. Said he wanted plenty of time to get to know me, make sure I was the one that God had chosen for his one and only daughter."

Ryan rose and retrieved the box of tissue. "The day before the wedding he took me aside and spoke a blessing over me. He said that I was now his only son and just as Isaac blessed his sons, he would give me his blessing. That I would be eternally joined to Rachel, and thus to him by marriage. He said Rachel and I were meant for one another, that God showed him we'd grow old together. He said there would be valleys as well as mountaintop experiences throughout our marriage, but that we would prevail because our foundation was the Almighty Lord himself. I've ruined everything Mark. I don't deserve her."

Mark sighed. "You've have taken the first step to making things right. You've opened up about your past, about what you've gone through. We're going to need to get together regularly to pray and to talk this out. Are you willing to do that?"

"Yeah. It's not going to change what's happened. But, maybe I'll be able to make sense of the future."

"Don't write off your marriage yet. Remember, with God, all things are possible."

Both men walked away with broken hearts. One man remembering his own sin and how God had proved to be merciful and faithful. The other fully expecting God to turn his back on him, just as his own father had done so many years ago. The first went home to hug his wife and his children. The other drove past his family's home then returned to the dingy little furnished apartment he'd rented on the other side of town. He found the corner that faced the bedroom door and sunk down to sit on his heels as he waited to be judged and abused by his father. Once again he was the little boy who was trying to be invisible. Only this time he expected retribution to come from the Father he had committed to serve all his days.

Chapter Eleven

Rachel entered the college administrative building and gave her name to the receptionist. She was nervous, but anxious. She needed this job. The information she'd been given didn't specifically address the pay scale, but prayerfully it would be what she needed. She brought her gardening journals with her that detailed the advances she had made in cross-pollinating. At least they would see she was still actively involved in her field, even if it was from home.

She fidgeted as she sat in the waiting area. The mirror had told her that her blue suit still looked good on her, even though she'd lost a few too many pounds. That was about to change. She had made out a menu and was heading to the grocery store after this interview. It was time to start being a mom to the girls again. She was done sulking and ready to live.

She heard a door open and turned to see if they were ready for her. One gentleman was leaving the office and the other headed in her direction. "Mrs. Bradley? I'm Peter Fisher. We spoke on the phone." He shook her hand then led the way back to his office. "Have a seat." As she sat down he went around and sat behind his desk.

"Thank you for taking the time to see me. I appreciate your consideration."

"Looking at your resume you are probably over qualified for the position. You seem to specialize in cross-pollinating. The ad you responded to was for the position of a groundskeeper. I just hired the gentleman who left my office for that position."

Rachel started to rise. "I'm sure he'll will do a wonderful job."

Peter motioned for Rachel to sit back down. "I believe I have a position open that would be more suited to your knowledge and experience. We have an assistant position open in the horticulture department. You would be working alongside our horticulture professor. We have a small but growing department and I believe you would fit right in. Of course Prof. Holcombe would have the final say. Are you interested in meeting with him?"

"Why yes, I would like that. Is he available now or do you need me to come back at a different time?"

"He told me to give him a call after I met with you. I know you have your journals with you and record of the work you've been doing but I just really don't get my hands dirty if you know what I mean. I think it would be best if he looked your work over and he'll know if you're the perfect fit for his department. Let me call him real quick and see if he's available."

Rachel listened to the one-sided conversation praying that Professor Holcombe could meet today. This position had to pay more than a groundskeeper. She just prayed it was hers.

Peter hung up the phone. "He'll be here in a few minutes. Do you want a cup of coffee while we wait?"

"No, thank you. I'm good."

She didn't seem to have much in common with the man sitting in front of her but she tried to make small talk anyway. They discussed the weather, the college and the local economy. Finally the door opened. She stood up and turned and about dropped her jaw. "Dillon?"

"Rachel?"

Peter looked from one to the other. "I take it you two know each other?"

Both Rachel and Dillon started speaking at once.

Rachel turned several shades of red and turned to Dillon. "I'm sorry."

Dillon smiled. "We're neighbors. Rachel lives across the street from me. She had lawn mower problems one day and I helped her fix it."

Peter grinned. "Well, I guess groundskeeper might not have been the perfect job for you after all. Hopefully this

76

assistant position works out a little better for you. I've got to run down to human resources. I'll leave you two to discuss things."

"I've seen her landscaping, don't be fooled. She may not know the mechanics of a lawnmower, but the lady knows her plants." Dillon picked up the journals. "So, you've been cross-pollinating roses? I would love to see what you've done."

"Of course. Anytime."

"Well, I think we are going to really enjoy working together. Maybe we ought to get our families together. I'm sure my son would love to meet your girls. Then we can talk more about the position. Since we are neighbors and all."

Rachel paused, wondering if that would be the right thing to do then reminded herself that her husband left her. "Sure, why not? Do you have plans for dinner? I was thinking about grilling."

"That sounds perfect. What time should we be there?"

"Seven?"

"See you at seven. Oh, I better warn you. Jacob has had a rough couple of years. Well, we both have. I'm sure he'll be fine tonight but he still hasn't fully recovered from his mom passing away."

Rachel reached out and touched Dillon's sleeve. "I'm sorry to hear that."

"Thank you. We're getting there. Well, I best get back to work. It seems like I have more summer classes than I do during the rest of the regular school year. Practical application in Wisconsin begins in spring and ends in fall. The rest of the year we use the green houses. I think you're going to love working here. I know I'm going to love having you on the team. I'll see you tonight at seven."

Rachel left the office wondering if she had the job. *It sure sounded like I got the job. Then again, an offer wasn't extended. I'll ask him tonight.* She did a quick readjustment to the menu and headed for the grocery store wondering if the girls would be okay with Dillon and his son, Jacob, coming for dinner. *It is a neighborly co-worker kind of dinner. It's not like it's a date. They should be able to handle that.*

She ordered some steak and chicken kabobs at the meat counter then hurried through the grocery store to finish her shopping. She settled on fresh fruit, angel food cake and homemade whipped cream for dessert. Sounded like the perfect ending for a summer meal.

She had the girls help unload the groceries, wondering if she should tell them straight out. If she hesitated, they would think there was more to this than a friendly dinner, which of course there wasn't.

Shelly gave her a hug. "How did your interview go?"

"Well, to be honest, I'm not sure. I went to the interview and the position I applied for was already taken. But, they had another position open. Come to find out, the professor is our next-door neighbor, well, across the street from us. He asked if he could come and see my plant experiments and I invited him and his son for dinner. I hope that's okay with you two."

Shelly acted if it was no big deal. "Sure, why wouldn't it be? Besides, I've seen his son. He's cute."

Shannon asked the obvious. "What about his wife?"

"He's widowed. His wife passed away a few years ago. It's just the neighborly thing to do and if our lives hadn't of been turned upside down, we would have already had them over. Besides, I need this job." The tone she ended the sentence with said in no uncertain terms that the topic was not up for discussion. She was now the head of this house and had to do what was best for all of them.

She assigned housekeeping chores to both girls then went outside to water and see to her plants. They had to be in tiptop shape. She had no idea that Dillon was a professor of horticulture. Rachel had to admit that her front yard was impressive. She had planned the landscaping down to the very last detail. Then she did most of the heavy lifting herself. She wanted this home to be a sanctuary for her family, and to her that meant living in the midst of the most beautiful of God's creation. She wanted their entrance to be a welcoming site, both for her family and for their guests.

On the flip side, if her front yard was impressive, her backyard would be compared to the Garden of Eden. This was where she planted her best. These were her babies. She worked outside pulling weeds for the better part of the afternoon. After her shower, she made up a cheese and fruit tray as a simple appetizer so the kids could eat a little something before supper giving her and Dillon the opportunity to look around her back yard while it was still daylight.

She set the platter on the kitchen counter just as the doorbell rang. Shelly yelled. "I'll get it."

Rachel grinned. Of course she would. There was a cute boy involved. "Okay, just send them in here. I've got some refreshments ready."

She wiped her hands on the dishtowel then started filling glasses with ice as Dillon and Jacob, followed by Shelly, entered the kitchen. Rachel greeted Dillon's son as Dillon greeted Shelly. "I thought you had three daughters?"

"I do. Samantha takes summer classes and works so she lives by the campus year round. Shannon is upstairs and should be down any minute now." She motioned to Shelly, who was already entertaining Jacob. "And Shelly answered the door. They are as different as three girls can be, but I love them all the same. They amaze me."

He took a long swallow of his ice tea. "This is good, refreshing."

"Thanks. It's peach tea. My girls prefer it and we use frozen peaches in place of ice."

"Well, what I want to see is your backyard. I've been thinking about it all afternoon."

"Follow me." Rachel led him through the sunroom and through the French doors to the back yard. "Here it is in all of its glory."

The sun had started to lower and a soft glow filtered between the gaps in the flowers. The water, still resting on the open petals, glistened as the sun bounced off of them, truly creating a paradise.

Dillon stopped in the middle of the yard. "You designed all this?" He looked at her, amazed at her talent. "This is crazy good. Wow. I think I'll be learning from you." He found her rose bushes and studied each one, sipping from his glass while he slowly moved from plant to plant. "Rachel, I'm in awe of your work here. These are some of the most beautiful roses I've ever seen." He stopped in front of her favorite. "What do you call this? I've never seen it before."

"I named that one Forever Loved." She offered no explanation.

"Interesting name." He moved on to the green house. It was after eight and the mosquitoes were buzzing by the time they re-entered the house. Dillon offered to start the grill as Rachel put the finishing touches on the rice and salad.

She looked at the near empty platter. "I think the kids were hungry. There is a little left." She handed him a small plate and added a few grapes and a piece of cheese to her own.

"Thanks. I should have warned you. Jacob is at the age where he eats the same amount as three grown men. I should have offered to pick something up. I was so distracted thinking about my new assistant who lives across the street from me, it just didn't cross my mind."

"So, I got the job?"

"Yes, I'm so sorry. I thought I told you."

"Well, in a round about way you eluded to that fact, but you didn't come right out and say it. I just wanted to be sure."

"Yes, I'm officially offering you the job. Did Peter give you the specifics?"

"No, I didn't even know the position was open. I had applied for the groundskeeper position."

"Let me turn the kabobs then I'll tell you all about it."

As soon as he turned around, Rachel closed her eyes and let out a deep breath. *Thank you, Lord.*

"They're almost done. Should we wait until after we eat to finish talking about the job?"

"Great idea. Do you want to call the kids up? They're in the basement, sounds like they're playing pool." She looked toward the stairs. "I'll get Shannon."

Rachel called for Shannon then placed the salad and the rice on the table. Dillon called for Jacob and Shelly then went to get the kabobs.

80

Shelly and Jacob were talking non-stop when they sat down at the table. Much to Rachel's dismay, Shannon still hadn't come down. "I wonder what's keeping her?"

Shelly took the hint and took off at a gallop to fetch her sister. When they both arrived a minute later, it was obvious that Shannon had been crying. Everyone pretended they didn't see her red streaked face, but conversation was a bit strained because of it.

Shannon remained quiet for the duration of dinner, picking at her food then turning down dessert, she said she had a headache and wanted to return to her room.

Shelly and Jacob returned to their game of pool leaving Dillon and Rachel the last two at the table.

"I've got dish duty. It's the least I can do."

"Tell you what, you can help. It won't take us long to clear these dishes into the dishwasher."

The two talked amicably while they worked, side by side. The easy banter made Rachel long for days gone by when she and Ryan would do this. Somehow doing dishes together had become intimate. Here she was rinsing dishes with another man at her side. It felt weird. She loaded the last dish. "That should do it. Do you want some coffee with your dessert?"

"Yeah, if you have some made. I don't want you to go through any more trouble than you already have though."

"Oh, it's no trouble. Then we can discuss the job over dessert."

She poured two cups and carried them, along with sugar and cream, to the table. "How do you like yours?"

"Black with just a touch of cream."

He stirred his coffee and explained the basics of the job. She would be working Monday through Friday from eight till four. Her duties would be varied. Students always made for an interesting day. "You just never know what they will bring to the table."

Rachel didn't want to seem forward, but she needed to know how much she'd be making. That was why she needed the job in the first place. "Do you know where the job starts, income wise?"

81

"Oh yeah, we haven't discussed benefits. That isn't my department, but I believe the base salary is a little over fifty thousand to start. Along with full health insurance, dental, eye and a tuition program if your girls want to enroll here."

That is what she needed to hear. She didn't want to clue him in on how desperate her situation was so she maintained her composure. What she felt like doing was jumping up and down and crying. Instead, she said a quick thank you to her provider.

The evening ended with a promise from Dillon to have Human Resources contact Rachel with her start date and confirm her beginning salary. Everyone said their goodbyes and Rachel closed the door after her guests left for home. For the first time in weeks, Rachel felt like things were going to turn out all right.

Chapter Twelve

Val sat on the edge of the chair with her old guitar on her lap. *How long has it been?* She strummed a few chords then added her voice to the mix. She loved the intimacy of having worship in her own living room. Here it was just her and her God. No pretenses. No images to keep up. No concern about what others were thinking. Just raw honesty and adoration. Here she felt free to weep, to laugh, to dance. Here is where she was the most real with her Lord.

Today was a good day. Not all days were like that. Initially she was told she'd have one year. It had been two. God was good. He must have known she'd be needed, that her little girl would need her. Her heart broke when she allowed her mind to rest on Rachel. Lord knows that girl would need a mother. *So, that's why you gave me more time, huh Lord?*

Herbert was picking up the slack where the church was concerned. He still had his health and for that Val was thankful. The church needed all the help it could get. So much to keep a handle on. Whew. It was easier on young folks. Being old and this busy just wasn't good for old bones, especially sick old bones.

She looked at the grandfather clock. She still had a half hour before prayer started. She had joined the ladies prayer group at Mark and Jessi's church. *It's about time churches started joining together instead of fighting. Imagine what we could do, Lord? If it worked for the tower of Babel, it could work for us. Nothing we couldn't do in your name, Lord.*

She'd invited some of the other ladies from church to go, hoping they would show up. *Time will tell. Lord, we need unification. It's the only way we're going to defeat the enemy,*

Father. There's been fighting between the denominations for so long the enemy doesn't hardly bother with us anymore.

Val put her guitar in the battered case and closed the lid. She had to see about Herbert's breakfast before she could leave. Of course, oatmeal was hardly difficult. Why they were trying to eat healthier at their age she didn't know, but if you can't beat 'em join 'em. She drew the line at those nasty looking green smoothies that Rachel drank. If she could get past the color, maybe they would taste all right. Then again, she'd probably never know.

The clock on the kitchen wall made that little clicking sound as she set the oatmeal to boiling. Ten minutes later she bade Herbert goodbye and started for Bible study, knowing there'd be donuts and coffee for her own breakfast. She smiled to herself. What Herbert didn't know wouldn't hurt him. *Oh, I'm sure he has his share of treats when he is out and about. A donut isn't going to kill me.*

During the short drive she had time to think. She had meant to call on Rachel but time got away from her. Lately that seemed the norm. She was always tired and couldn't do nearly as much as she used to do. Some people understood that. Some didn't. It used to bother her that some thought she had quit serving the way she used to by choice. Not that there would have been anything wrong with that. But, it just wasn't the case. Cancer zaps a person. Especially an older person.

She sure hoped Rachel was doing well. She seemed awfully down at dinner on Sunday. Maybe Jessi would have an update.

Cars were already parked in front of the downtown church making it difficult for Val to find a spot close to the entrance. *I should have made Herbert make his own breakfast.*

By the time she made her way into the building the ladies were already eating pastries and sipping tea. The pastries were especially good. The shelter down the street provided them through their tea shop. Val was always glad when that happened. If she was going to eat something that bad for her, then she wanted to be sure it was really good. She picked up a crazy eight;

one side filled with cream cheese and the other with pecans, and took a nibble, *ah heaven,* then sipped her coffee.

Just as she'd hoped, Jessi was chatting with a group of women. Perhaps she could get her attention. Just as she sided up to Jessi, one of the women stepped aside and Rachel came into view. She was smiling and sipping a bottle of that green stuff. Val's heart soared. Rachel looked happy. What had happened in the last few days? Val questioned Jessi with her eyes. Jessi shrugged her shoulders.

Val studied Rachel for a couple of minutes before getting her attention. She looked different than she did on Sunday. Not only happier, but somehow she looked like she'd filled out a little bit. Like always she was well put together in her white capris and navy and white button down blouse. Her toes and nails were painted and her dark hair was clasped at her neck with an oversize white barrette. She had a touch of make up, but only a touch and a glimmer on her lips. If you didn't know what was going on in her life, you would think her life was perfect. The only thing she couldn't hide from Val was the sadness that lived in her eyes, a hollowness that belied her smile and her perfect look. Val knew. Rachel couldn't fool her.

About that time Rachel noticed Val and gave her a big hug. "How is my favorite lady?"

"I'm doing pretty good. You look like you're doing well yourself."

"I am. I can't believe how great I feel. Finally, it's like I'm waking up and seeing there is a whole world out there, beyond the four corners of my home and church. I'm loving it, Val. I really am. I think everything is going to turn out great. I don't remember the last time I felt this happy." She took another sip of her green smoothie. "I mean, I got this really great job making some pretty awesome money. I can keep the house. I am independent, making my own way. The girls are doing great, even Shannon is improving. My new boss is just wonderful. I really don't remember being this happy, at least not in a long time. And you know what Val? It feels good. Like this is how I'm supposed to feel."

Val tried to be encouraging but she had a troubled spirit regarding all this happiness Rachel was talking about. Like it was superficial or contrived. Maybe she did feel happier, but was it just a superficial feeling? Or was she truly filled with joy?

Val watched Rachel turn toward the ladies who she had been chatting with. Suddenly the pastry in her hand no longer held its appeal. She found a seat and started letting the prayers roll off her tongue. The heavens were wide-open and taking requests. Time to petition the Father on behalf of those she loved.

Chapter Thirteen

As soon as the prayer meeting was over, Rachel followed Jessi through the halls and into Mark's office. "You know, I really don't think this is necessary any more. So much has changed this last week. For the better, really."

Jessi leaned against the chair's arm. "What changed?"

"Well, for one, I got a job."

"Really? That is fantastic. Did you get the groundskeeper position at the college?"

"No, but I did get hired to be an Assistant Professor in the horticulture program. I can keep the house. I won't have to sell. I'm thrilled."

Jessi truly was happy for her and gave her a big hug. "I'm so thankful, Rachel. That is one answered prayer."

Mark walked in. "Hey, what's this I hear about an answered prayer?"

Rachel filled him in as they all got comfortable. Jessi handed everyone a bottle of water then sat down next to her husband on the love seat.

Mark started the conversation. "I'm glad you decided to come in to see us. It's important that you can talk with someone, it really helps."

"I was just telling Jessi that I don't think it's all that important anymore. Ryan decided how he wants to live and it certainly doesn't include me. God has provided a great job so I'm capable of providing for our family. Everything seems to be falling into place."

Mark studied the woman sitting across from him. "It may seem that everything is unfolding perfectly, but that is exactly what the enemy wants you to think. He doesn't want you fighting for your family. He wants you to be happy with second best but we all know that God only wants the absolute best for us. He never intended for any of us to settle for second best."

Rachel started getting a little agitated. "That choice was made for me now wasn't it?"

Mark tentatively but carefully got right to the point. "Rachel, I know this has been thrust upon you. But you still have a choice to make. You can do what you're doing and take it all lying down, or you can stand up and fight using every bit of power that God has given you. You can either pick up the tools God has given you to defeat the enemy or you can allow him to walk all over you, and your family."

Rachel was furious. "What about Ryan? Where is he in your plan? I can't make decisions for both of us. Isn't he supposed to be the head of our household? Providing for and sheltering his family? I tried to make it work. God knows I tried. Every day he walked farther and farther away from us. He became more distant. He wouldn't even talk to me. Then he just sprung it on me, like that explains everything. 'Oh Darlin', by the way, I'm gay.' Well, do you know what that does to a woman? A wife? A mother? I'll tell you. It about destroyed me. I'm not going to take responsibility for this, I'm just not."

Mark scooted to the edge of the love seat. "I'm not suggesting you take the responsibility for what Ryan has done. That is his and he needs to own it. I am asking you to take responsibility for your part in this, for your actions, for your reactions. I know that you didn't do this. But, do you really want to give everything up? Everything that you and Ryan worked so hard for? Do you want your girls to lose their family? What about all the people you've touched in ministry over the years? Do you want all that to go up in smoke?"

Mark knew he couldn't betray Ryan's trust, but he had to give Rachel some hope. "I'm sorry if it seems like I'm placing all this on you. I'm not. I can't tell you about our conversations, but I can tell you I have met with Ryan and we are talking. Not everything is as it appears to be. Please don't give up hope. Please keep praying and seeking God's will in your life. This won't be easy. I can guarantee that. But God has such awesome plans for you, for your ministry. The enemy would do a happy dance if you were to walk away with so little fight left in you. Please keep hanging on. God will give you the strength. I know he will."

Jessi squeezed Mark's hand. "Can we pray together, Rachel?"

Rachel nodded. To do otherwise would seem rude. Besides, she did want God's will for her life. She just felt it was vastly different than what Mark and Jessi seemed to think it would be. She took their outstretched hands and bowed her head.

She listened as Mark and Jessi prayed for her, for her family and for her husband. She felt let down, like they thought all this was her fault. She hung her head; full of shame she questioned herself once again. *Did I cause this? Is this my fault?* She felt the tears form and fought hard to keep them from falling. She was over tears. Past them. They showed her vulnerability and she never wanted to be hurt again. As soon as the prayer ended she angrily wiped the back of her hand across her eyes and turned for the door.

Jessi stopped her. "Hey, how about a hug?"

Rachel allowed herself to be enveloped in a bear hug then she quietly walked out the door. She wasn't going to go through this again and again. She couldn't handle the emotional turmoil. The pain involved in hoping for her marriage was too great to handle. It was easier to admit defeat than to keep clamoring for what used to be.

Rachel found herself driving out of town, through the country. She rolled down her windows and let the summer breeze blow through her hair. She thought back to the day she met Ryan. It was at the diner where she was waiting tables. His smile and the light in his eyes mesmerized her. She remembered his laughter as she strained to hear what they were arguing about. Waiting on them, she realized their arguing had been nothing more than schoolboys discussing theology and she was relieved because that meant he was a Christian. When he showed up the next day and the day after that and each day thereafter when she was working, she knew he was the one. How could she have been so wrong?

She pulled into the driveway to find Dillon coming off her front porch. "Hey. What brings you this way?"

He smiled. "I was wondering if you talked with human resources and everything was set for you to start work?"

"I sure did. Looks like I'll be starting a week from Monday."

"Sounds good. Have you eaten lunch?"

"No. Honestly, I haven't even thought about it."

"Well, would you like to accompany me? I'd like to discuss some things with you and get your perspective. I know you haven't officially started yet, but I really am looking forward to working with you and I value your input. Would you mind terribly grabbing some lunch with your boss?"

Rachel felt that little tug reminding her she was still married. Once again she pushed it back. She may still be tied to him on paper, but that was the extent of it. And besides she was pretty sure Dillon wasn't interested in her in any other way but as a colleague. "Yeah, let me run in and check on the girls first. I'll freshen up and meet you out here in ten?"

"Perfect. I'll be here to pick you up."

Neither Shelly nor Shannon were home so she had no explaining to do in that area. Her hair, on the other hand, was severely protesting a brush going through it. After that ride in the wind, she doubted anything but a shower would take care of it. She quickly undressed and jumped in knowing it would take her a bit longer than the said ten minutes. When she emerged from the bedroom fifteen minutes later she was freshened up in a summer floral skirt and matching tank top. Her hair was braided and pinned to the back of her head. She slipped her feet in her sandals and headed right back out.

Dillon was leaning against his car waiting for her.

"Sorry I'm late. My hair was not cooperating."

"No problem. You look lovely. It was worth the wait. Before we take off, I have one question to ask you. I don't want to pry, but at the same time, I feel I need to ask. I notice you are wearing a wedding ring. I'm not the type of guy who takes a married woman out to lunch. Are you and your husband still together?"

90

"No, he's out of the picture."

"Okay. You don't have to go into details unless you want to. Let's get some lunch. I'm famished."

Rachel enjoyed having the attention of a man. It had been a long time since she had felt appreciated by her husband. To have a good looking successful man show an interest in her, even if it was just for work, gave her self esteem a major boost. He opened the car door for her then rounded the car to get in the driver's seat.

"Do you have any time constraints?"

"Not a one. I have nothing else in my planner and I left a note for the girls telling them I'd be out until they saw me. So, we're good."

"Great. I know this wonderful little restaurant but it's kind of a drive. Since it's such a beautiful day and obviously the company is pleasant, I thought it would be okay.   She smiled at him. "The day is indeed beautiful. And of course I have to say the company is pleasant. Otherwise I might get fired before I start."

They both laughed and enjoyed a very comfortable ride to Lake Geneva where he pulled his little red sports car in a parking spot in front of the lake. "Feel like taking a little walk?"

"I'd love to."

Dillon opened her door and helped her out. The touch of his hand on hers revived feelings in her that she'd thought she lost. This man was intriguing. She enjoyed the gentle banter they had and the way he remained focused and attentive. He was always considering her and her comfort. Whether it was the air conditioning in the car or her taste in food, he catered to her desires. She had to admit she liked it, and more than a little. She didn't protest in the least when he raised her hand to his lips.

"Thank you my lady for the pleasure of your company. I fear I would have led a rather bland day had you not agreed to accompany me."

"I'm happy to oblige. I had no idea my job duties would consist of lovely drives and even lovelier lunches."

He stared at her for a moment, making her wonder about his thoughts. She stepped out of his car and allowed him to lead her down the path to a little restaurant on the lake. "It would seem the restaurant doesn't open for another forty five minutes. Would you mind walking with me for a bit?"

"I'd like that."

They found themselves sitting on a bench facing the lake. "I must say, I find you intriguing. You're so secretive about your life. You've shared nothing with me."

Rachel's emotions were too raw to enter into a conversation about her. "Well, it's really not all that interesting. How about you? I know nothing about you either, save the fact that you are widowed."

"You got me there. What do you want to know? I'll tell you anything you want to know."

"Well, where did you live before you moved here?"

"That's an honest question. We lived in Colorado. My wife and I were both professors. After she passed away, the place just held too many memories for us. Even after two years the wounds were fresh and memories were everywhere. We decided to make a fresh start here. I searched for colleges looking for horticulture professors and tada, here I am."

"What was your wife's name?"

"Sofia. You would have liked her. She was a great mother, just like you. And she loved to garden. I think the first thing I thought when I saw your house was how much Sofia would have loved it. You have an amazing talent."

"Thank you. How did she pass away? Or do you not want to talk about that?"

"I told you to ask anything, and I meant it. She was killed in a car accident. It was raining and she was in a hurry. Her death was instant, or so they told me. She felt no pain. I was certain that was true because I was sure I had every bit of it. My whole body hurt. I mourned her. She had been my life for so long, I wasn't sure I would be able to go on without her. But, I had Jacob to think of. Being a parent stinks sometimes. To think we must be good parents and always think of our children first really puts a kink in a guy's death wish, you know what I mean?"

"I can relate."

"Anything you want to talk about?"

"Um, no. Not right now."

"Well, when you feel up to it, I'm here. I've been told I'm a good listener."

"I'll keep that in mind."

Dillon stood. "I believe what was our late lunch and what has now become our early dinner is waiting for us."

Rachel walked the path, forgetting for a moment that she was with Dillon and tucked her hand in the crook of his elbow. As soon as she'd done it, she quickly withdrew and let her hand hang at her side.

His voice told her that he'd noticed. "It's okay you know. I didn't mind."

The day was beautiful so they chose patio dining where they had a full view of the lake. "What is your pleasure?"

Rachel's face turned a crimson red. "Excuse me?"

"What are you in the mood for, for lunch?"

"Oh, yes." She quickly looked down at her menu but felt him staring at her.

"Are you okay?"

"Yes, I'm fine." She sipped her water. "Everything looks good."

The waiter approached their table. Dillon ordered a bottle of white wine and oysters on the half shell. "We'll need to have a few more minutes with the menus."

"No problem sir, take your time."

A few minutes later the waiter poured them both a glass of wine then left the table. Rachel wasn't one to drink; being a pastor's wife she always felt it would be a bad example. She wasn't a pastor's wife any longer. She lifted the glass to her lips and took a sip.

Dillon watched Rachel. She was a mystery to him. He virtually knew nothing about her. Her tentative sips at her wine indicated she wasn't a drinker. When he offered her an oyster, she was apprehensive. Who was this woman and why was she frightened?

Rachel watched Dillon lift the oyster shell to his lips then tilt his head back. He chewed a couple of times then swallowed. "I thought you were supposed to swallow oysters whole?"

"No, to get the full taste you need to lightly chew it, just a couple of times. It releases the full flavor of the oyster. They are really good. Perfect oysters for the beginner, they're from the west coast. Why don't you give one a try?"

"All right, why not?" She hadn't tasted seafood yet that she didn't like so she'd take a chance. She followed Dillon's example. She felt the smooth texture slide over her tongue. She clamped down a couple of times, relishing the flavor and swallowed. "Not bad."

"You did great. Have another."

The waiter brought each course, leaving plenty of time between for conversation and the cleansing of the palate. When Rachel finished her last bite of Key Lime Pie, she was beyond stuffed and suddenly remembered they did not discuss any business. "I've had such a great time tonight but I feel terrible. We didn't discuss work."

Dillon waved her off. "We can do that tomorrow or Saturday over coffee at my house. I'm not nearly as good a cook as you, but Jacob and I want to repay your kindness by having you and your girls over. I must say though, we do make a mean spaghetti sauce. We'll have Italian."

"We'd love it. Shelly will be excited. She thinks Jacob is so cute."

"Well, Shelly and I have something in common then, don't we?"

"You think Jacob is cute too?"

Dillon laughed. "Yeah, that's it."

It was after dark by the time Dillon escorted Rachel to her door. She said a cordial goodbye and sent him home. She was humming to herself as she kicked off her shoes and padded into the kitchen to put on tea water. Shannon was sitting at the table waiting for her. "Where were you?"

"I was out. Having dinner if you must know."

"With who?"

"With Dillon. Why do you ask?"

"Can't you see, Mom? He's after you. Doesn't he know you're still married?"

"Shannon, first off, he's my boss. He's not after me. Second, how is this your business?"

Shannon acted as if she hadn't heard her mother's question. "You're throwing everything away. You shouldn't be going out with him."

"I'm throwing everything away? Me? Your father threw everything away when he moved in with that man."

"What if Dad had come back home and seen you with another man? What if you weren't here?"

"I don't care who your father sees me with. I stopped being his business when he walked out the door. And where I go and with whom is none of your business either. I'm not going to sit here and hope and pray your father comes home. He made his choices and by doing so, he made mine. I'm living my life and I'm only answering to myself. Do you understand?"

Shannon busted out crying and ran up the stairs. The tea kettle whistled the same moment the door slammed.

Rachel turned off the tea kettle. She should have known Shannon wouldn't take this well. She would have to make Shannon understand she wasn't dating Dillon. She simply needed someone in her life to make her feel like she was a woman, like she was appreciated. She wasn't dating him for heaven's sakes. They had just met. She poured her cup of tea and sat at the table. A perfect evening once again tarnished. She wouldn't feel guilty. She did nothing wrong.

Rachel peeled her clothes off and climbed into bed. She raised her hand to her cheek then rubbed it against her lips. She fell asleep dreaming about the gentle neighbor from across the street and slept better than she had in weeks.

Chapter Fourteen

Shannon was seething. How dare her mother flaunt herself like a floozy? She was married. She knew better. She heard her come up the stairs and go into her room, not even bothering to see if her own daughter was okay. When had she become so selfish? *Has she always been this way and I've just not seen it?*

Shannon watched her mother come and go, doing whatever she pleased with no thought whatsoever for those she was supposed to love. She was even happy. Who could be happy? In fact, both her parents turned into selfish little brats. What happened to her family? Didn't they want to be together? Didn't they want to get back what they had?

She pictured her older sister, running with her friends, drinking herself silly. Her parents had no idea. Wouldn't good parents do something about that instead of being so focused on their own happiness?

Shannon thought back to her conversation with her mother. Her mother flat out admitted she didn't care. She paced, replaying the conversation in her mind. With each step she became angrier and angrier. With each line of the script her rational thought disappeared.

She picked up a bottle of perfume and threw it against the wall. The heady spice scent filled the room. She took a small piece of glass and studied it, intent on the light filtering through. Shannon held the glass between her fingers and made a small cut on her arm. She watched the blood drip, not caring that it spotted the cream carpet. She felt warm and peaceful. She felt her anger slip away like the pellets of blood on her arm. She stared long and hard, watching the small pool of blood around the cut start to gel and then dry. Suddenly tired, she curled up on her bed and closed her eyes.

When Shannon opened her eyes she lay still watching the sunlight dance across her room as the tree outside her bedroom window swayed with the wind. Still content with the world she took a shower, taking care to wash the dried blood from her arm.

Laying out her clothes, Shannon didn't give the cut on her arm another thought. She dressed in shorts and a tank top then went to the kitchen for some orange juice. Her mom was taking blueberry muffins out of the oven and Shelly was eagerly waiting at the table, butter knife ready. She joined her sister. "Smells good in here."

Rachel brought the muffins to the table, along with a fruit salad she'd already prepared. "Thought I'd make us a light breakfast." She sat down at the breakfast table then reached for a muffin at the same time as her middle daughter. "Shannon, what happened to your arm?"

Shannon instantly looked to the place she had cut the night before. "I broke a perfume bottle and cut my arm. It's no big deal. Just a scratch."

"I'll get some iodine after we eat and put a band aid on it. You need to be more careful. You could have really hurt yourself."

Shannon nibbled at her muffin. *I didn't exactly lie. So what if I didn't tell her I did it on purpose? She doesn't need to know. Like she'd care anyway.*

Rachel buttered her muffin. "I called your counselor, Shannon. I want you to go in and talk with her. I made you an appointment for later this morning."

"Mom, I'm fine. I don't need to go again. I just went a couple of days ago."

"I know. But after last night, I think you need to address some of these feelings you are having."

Shannon pushed her chair back and stood up. "Thanks, Mom. That's all I need."

"Shannon, sit down." Rachel waited her to follow instructions. "I've had enough of these temper tantrums. You're a grown woman. It's time you realized that not everything is about you. Your counselor will help you deal with these issues you are having. Now eat your breakfast."

"If I'm a grown woman why are you telling me what to do?"

"Because at this moment you are deciding to act like a child instead of the grown up that you are. When you start acting your age I'll start treating you as such." Rachel shook her head. She didn't need this. She had enough to deal with.

Shannon fingered the cut on her arm. Just touching it made her remember cutting and made her feel better. She breathed deep and ate the fruit she'd taken. "Fine. What time is my appointment?"

"Ten Thirty. I thought maybe the three of us would do some shopping afterward. If you feel like it, that is."

Shelly who had remained quiet up until this point chimed in. "Yeah, I need some new tennis shoes. Volleyball practice starts next week. Exercise shorts wouldn't hurt either. Mine are getting too short."

"You have gotten taller, haven't you? Well, we'll go to the mall after Shannon's appointment."

Shelly popped the last of her muffin in her mouth and took off to get ready leaving Rachel and Shannon at the table.

"Shannon, I know this has been hard on you. But sometimes life is hard. We don't ask for it, but it hits us upside the head anyway. I want you to know I had my first counseling appointment yesterday. Apparently your dad is also going. I just wanted you to know that. I'm keeping my word to you."

Shannon studied her mom. "Are you going to go together?"

"I truly don't know, hon. I just don't know. We'll see."

The day sped by and everything seemed to be going well. It wasn't until they were on their way home that Rachel let them know about their dinner plans. "We've been invited to Dillon's and Jacob's for dinner. They want to repay us for inviting them last weekend."

Shelly let out a yell. "Yeah! Jacob's a blast."

Shannon was sitting in the front seat. "I'm not going."

"Shannon, why? What is wrong with our neighbors?"

"You know what. We've already talked about it and I won't go."

"Fine. Suit yourself. But Shelly and I are going."

Shannon watched out her bedroom window as her mother and sister entered the house across the street. She felt the anger rising up in her again. Having cleaned up all the glass, she searched through her parent's medicine cabinet until she found some of her father's razor blades. She took one back to her room and made two cuts on either side of the one from last night. Again, she was mesmerized by the blood flow. She pulled her knees up to her chest and sat there, staring into the emptiness. She felt numb. Numb was good. She liked numb. It was better than anger and disappointment. Numb was better than the hurt that threatened to destroy her. She could handle numb. Later that night she heard her mother and sister come in and go to their rooms. The next morning Shannon wore a long sleeved shirt. No one seemed to notice.

Chapter Fifteen

Ryan walked out of his manager's office. Man he hated this job. *If they ask me to lie one more time I swear I'm quitting.* It wasn't as if they paid him like they were supposed to. Half the time his commission was drastically lower than he expected. And they always had some lame excuse for it. Today he found his thousand-dollar bonus was denied because one of his deals was split with the manager's pet. Yesterday he'd received a frantic phone call from one of his customers saying his bank accounts were frozen. Apparently the dealership hadn't paid off his trade in, from a month ago. He muttered as he headed back to the phone cave. *How do these guys stay in business? Is every used car dealership this crooked?*

Now he had to deal with Terry. He had met with Mark earlier to talk some more and Mark asked him a question that had plagued him since going into work earlier that afternoon. He had asked why after all these years had Terry shown back up in his life. He didn't have an answer for him. But he would. Just as soon as he got home.

Ryan pulled in the dim parking lot behind his apartment building and parked his car in his allotted spot. Terry pulled up right behind him. He closed his eyes. He hated confrontation and this felt suspiciously just like that.

He unlocked his door and held the door open. "Come on in. Can I get you something?"

"No, I'm good. What's up? You sounded awfully serious on the phone."

"I need to know why? Why after all these years did you come back? I mean, you knew I was happily married and I was honoring my vows to my wife. Why did you do it?"

Terry walked to the dirty window and peered out into the night sky. "The day you got married was the worst day of my life. I knew you'd turned your life around, that you'd gone straight. And as much as I hated it, I honored your decision. I started bouncing from relationship to relationship, but no one held my heart like you did. I was in and out of relationships for years. For a while, my only relationships were a series of one-night stands. I didn't want to risk being hurt again and I knew no one would ever measure up to what I had with you. I could always count on you being there. We knew one another, better than anyone else on earth and it's rare that you find that twice."

Terry turned around to face Ryan. "A couple of years after you married, I moved to San Francisco. Finally I'd found a place I fit in. It was there I became seriously involved with someone. It was there I buried him. He died of AIDS. I knew I had it too. The drugs weren't like they are today. Today you can almost live a life of normalcy after being diagnosed. By the time the new drugs were on the market, it was too late for me. I was already progressing from HIV to full blown AIDS. Yes, my symptoms have slowed, but it's only a matter of time before I'm gone."

He helped himself to a bottle of water. "I know it was wrong of me to want to see you before I'm gone. If you wondered why I have kept my distance, I would never put you in danger, or your family. I just wanted to spend time with you. I've been staying in a shelter that caters to AIDS patients. They see me at my worst. I've only allowed you to see me at my best. On my good days I get around okay. It won't be too long before I can't get around at all. I guess I wanted to be near someone who cared for me, who might have some answers."

Ryan was speechless. He could barely breathe. He held his head in his hands, waiting for the dizziness to pass. He met Terry's gaze. "How long?"

Terry shook his head. "There is no way to know exactly. There weren't many options when I was first diagnosed. Taking a handful of pills every four hours, day and night, got to be old fast. Especially when I wasn't experiencing any symptoms. It's hard to believe you're sick when you're young and when you don't feel it. So, I wasn't as diligent about taking the pills as I should have been. I'd already been diagnosed with HIV for ten years when things got easier, medically speaking. But for me it was too late. For whatever reason, my body has reacted well to the medication I'm on now, so my rate of deterioration had slowed, but now it's progressing. If I had to guess, I'd say less than six months."

"I don't know what to say."

"There isn't much to say. It's my fault. No one else's. I didn't come here to cast blame. I just wanted to see you, to spend some time with you before I pass. I'm sorry I caused such a mess for you. That wasn't my intention."

"Your showing up made me question myself. I was no longer sure of who I was or what I wanted out of life. I walked away from my children, my wife and my faith so you could have your hand held when you die? Just how selfish are you?"

Terry started shaking. He couldn't stop the sobs that emanated from his thin frame. "I'm sorry. I wanted to know before I die that someone loved me, that someone would sacrifice everything for me. I wanted that person to be you. You're the only person who has ever truly loved me."

Terry's words penetrated Ryan's mind, shocking him. He was dumbfounded. There was only one person who loved enough, who sacrificed everything, and it wasn't him. His mind immediately went to the cross. Jesus looked straight at him, not accusing, but imploring. "Oh my God, what have I done?" He fell to his knees crying out to his Father. "I'm so sorry. Oh God, please forgive me."

Terry watched Ryan, trying to grasp what was happening. Nothing made sense. What did he do? Finally, after what seemed like forever, Ryan picked himself off the floor. "What is going on, Ryan?"

"Don't you see the irony of it, Terry? You wanted to know that someone loved you, that someone would sacrifice everything for you. You don't need me for that. Jesus already did it. Because he loves you more than I ever could love you."

"Oh please. Don't start with the fairy tales. I don't need any feel good stories to make everything better."

"It's not just a story, Terry. He's more real than you and I ever could be."

"You know, when you found Jesus I swore I would never have anything to do with him. He took you away from me."

"No, Terry. He didn't. He gave us a wonderful relationship, a wonderful friendship. It was a gift really. We're the ones who twisted it into something it wasn't supposed to be. We were never supposed to be together like that. God's plan from the beginning was one man and one woman. The Bible tells us that Satan seeks to destroy everything good that God created. Satan is a master at making good things sinful, of turning the beauty of God's plan into a tool to be misused by our fleshly desires."

"No, I don't believe that. We were supposed to be together. You know that."

"No, Terry. We weren't. Not in that way."

"I won't stand here and listen to this. You go ahead and read your fables from the queen James bible. I've accepted who I am. You're still fighting it. You're the kind of gay that would keep us in the dark ages. This is who I am. This is how I was born. And you were too. Just accept it."

"No, Terry. I'm not. I've been set free. You can be too. Jesus loves you, Terry. He's the source of the love you've been seeking. I will fail you, I know I will. But he will never fail you. He'll never leave you, nor forsake you. But you must accept him and repent of your sin."

"Who are you to talk about sin? Look at you. You left your wife and your kids. You walked away from your church. Now you have some epiphany experience and you feel you can preach to me?"

"You're right. I'm sorry. I don't mean to preach. I just want you to know a love that is greater than any physical love you'll ever know. I've messed up, bad. I don't know if I'll ever get back what I had. Don't you see? Even though I may lose everything on this earth, I can't lose the love of Jesus. I've let my family so far down I don't know if I'll come up from that. My wife may not take me back and to be honest, I wouldn't blame her. My kids are messed up because of me. My little girl tried to commit suicide because of me." Ryan was openly crying. "And even with all of that, Jesus still loves me. He still wants me. Don't you want that kind of love? Don't you want someone who loves you no matter what? He's speaking to your heart Terry, you know he is. Won't you listen to him? Nothing will ever be the same, I can promise you that."

"Not on your life. I remember your promises. They don't mean a thing." Terry opened the door. "I'm done here. I thought I could count on you. Obviously I was wrong."

Ryan watched Terry stalk off into the night then he picked up the phone and called Mark. "Hey man, can we talk?"

Ryan gave Mark directions then waited. He paced, he cried, he knelt and he doubted. But through all the negative emotions and doubts regarding what his future might be, he held onto the peace that God had filled him with. No matter what happened in his marriage, in his girls' lives and in his job situation, he knew God was in control. And for that he was thankful.

The knock at the door brought him to his feet. "Mark, come on in."

Mark entered the tiny apartment, not sure what to expect. While it was dingy, it wasn't dirty. The furniture was clearly second hand, make that third hand and not exactly sturdy. He carefully sat down at the kitchen table and took the cup of coffee Ryan offered. "What's up? You sounded pretty serious on the phone."

"I asked him. Just like you told me to." Ryan started pacing. "You were right. He had a reason, a really terrible reason for coming back after all this time." Ryan explained the entire situation, or at least everything he knew to Mark. "What do I do?"

"I think you already know the answer to that."

"You mean talk to Rachel, explain everything and tell her about my past."

"Yes, you owe her that much."

"But, what if she doesn't want me back? What then?"

"Well, that's the chance you have to take. Every relationship should have honesty as its basis for survival.

Without honesty you lose trust. Without trust you lose respect. And when mutual respect is gone, your relationship is no stronger than those you had in the world. You have to tell her the truth."

Ryan blew out a deep breath. "I suppose you're right. My gut tells me it's too late, that I've gone too far."

"You won't know until you try. Besides, is it your gut? Or the enemy keeping you from trying?"

"Good point. I guess I've lost more than perspective."

"You'll get it back."

Ryan nodded his head. "What about Terry? If I don't see him through this, he's going to die alone."

"I think the first thing you need to do is get right with God. You need to be able to hear his voice again. Between the Holy Spirit, the enemy and your flesh, your head has to be spinning. Can you take a few days and just seek God's will? Don't make any moves without Him telling you what to do. I can go see Terry if you'd like me to, let him know that he has people praying for him."

"Would you? He left here pretty mad. Hurt too. I wouldn't expect a great reception."

"Well, I'll give it a few days and let God have some time to use the words you spoke. He'll try and push them out of his mind, but it won't work. God's word never returns void. Maybe he'll talk to me, since I'm a neutral party."

"He won't see you that way. He thinks religion took me away from him."

"Then we need to help him understand that the enemy did that, not God. God intended for you to have a great friendship your entire lives. The enemy twisted it into something it was never intended. That wasn't God's doing."

"Yeah, I tried to tell him that. He wasn't buying it."

"God has a way of revealing truth. He uses the words we speak and the actions we portray to start a garden in people's lives. At first they may look at the truth as weeds, but in time, they see the beauty of God's handiwork and realize all God has done for them. The truth always comes forth. You can count on that."

Mark walked through the door, emotionally exhausted and sat down next to his wife. "There's one answered prayer."

Jessi looked up from her book. "Oh?"
"That was Ryan."
The book closed and Jessi gave Mark her undivided attention.

"He questioned Terry, about why he came back. Let's just say he's done a one eighty." Mark shared everything that Ryan told him. "Do you think there's hope for Rachel? She's really been hurt."

Jessi inched closer to her husband and took his hand. "You of all people should know there is always hope."

"Yes, this is true. And I have you right here beside me to remind me of that."

"You know that's true. And I won't stop." Jessi closed her eyes, seeking God on Rachel's behalf. Mark, feeling the prompting joined his wife.

Chapter Sixteen

Jacob chewed slowly, wondering what to say. He knew his dad had feelings for the lady next door, Rachel. But, did he know her story? He doubted it. "You really like her, don't you?"

Dillon put his fork down. Was he that obvious? "Well, I guess I do. Are you okay with that?"

Jacob nodded.

"I miss your mom too, buddy."

"It's not about Mom. I don't blame you for wanting a girlfriend."

Dillon watched his son. He seemed nervous, out of sorts. He wasn't sure why his son would be acting this way. They had been so close since Sofia had died. "Jacob, what's up? Is something wrong?"

"Dad, you do know she's still married, right?"

"I know. She told me he was out of the picture though."

"Shelly told me what happened." He nervously glanced at his dad.

"Jacob, I think it's best that Rachel tell me when she's ready. I don't want her thinking I was checking up on her behind her back."

"Dad, you should know. Shelly thinks they could get back together."

"Rachel told me her relationship with her husband was over. I believe her."

Jacob averted his eyes.

"Hey, I'll be okay. I promise. I think I love her, Jacob. I'm willing to take a chance on that."

Jacob rose to get the door when he heard the bell chime. He led Rachel into the kitchen then excused himself.

Dillon stood up and Rachel put her hand out. "Please, finish your supper. I didn't come by to interrupt. I made some peach cobbler and wanted to bring some over. We'll never eat it all."

Dillon closed his eyes, breathing in the defining scent of fresh baked cobbler. "My favorite. Did you already have some? I have vanilla ice cream that would top this off perfectly."

"I thought you'd never ask."

He cleared the table while she took out the ice cream. *It's like she belongs here.*

Rachel dished out spoonfuls of soft peaches surrounded by delicate crust and topped them with scoops of the cold treat. "It's still steaming. Better eat it up before the ice cream melts."

They took their dishes to the back patio overlooking the pool. "Are you sick of my youngest living in your pool?"

"Nah, Jacob enjoys the company. She's welcome any time."

Rachel walked to the edge and dipped her toes into the water. "Feels good."

"You want to go for a swim?"

She remained silent. She used to love to swim. Then life got hectic. "I think I would. I'm gonna go change. I'll be back in a few minutes."

Dillon reached for her dessert, which was turning into peaches and cream and finished it off. He didn't think she would notice and if she did she wouldn't mind. They had been casually seeing one another for the past couple of weeks. Lunches and dinners, long drives and quiet picnics. They talked about everything. Everything except her ex-husband. He'd managed to keep their relationship strictly platonic, so far. He knew he wouldn't be able to keep that up much longer.

He took the steps two by two, hurrying to get changed. He beat her back to the pool and dove in, swimming from one end to the other. When he came up for air, she was standing before him. He immediately saw she had removed her wedding ring. He chided himself. *Maybe she always takes it off when she swims.* "Come on in. The water is great."

Rachel began to wonder if she'd made the wrong decision. Dillon staring at her wasn't helping matters. What if she repulsed him? What if he knew her own husband hadn't found her attractive and was more interested in men? Would he think it was her fault? Her constant questioning of herself made life extremely confusing. Would she ever live a normal life, with someone she could love?

She removed her cover up and dove into the water. The cool water felt refreshing. She swam a few laps, more to avoid Dillon than for exercise. Gasping for breath, she stopped. "I'd forgotten how much energy swimming requires."

Dillon swam toward her. "Every day during the summer I swim laps here. During the winter, I swim at the school gym. I enjoy it. It's one of the reasons I bought this house."

"Shelly has been bugging us for a pool for as long as I can remember. I don't have the heart to tear up my gardens. I reminded her she'll be leaving in a few years and going out on her own."

Dillon noticed she still used the word "us." He took her hand. "Us?"

"Old habits die hard. I'm sorry. I guess it's going to take me a while to get used to there no longer being an "us.""

"Don't worry about it. I just thought something might have changed."

"No, nothing's changed. I'm certain I wouldn't be here if it had."

He lifted her chin and felt her tremble. Not sure if it was the cool water or the idea of him kissing her that caused the tremor, so he let go. He pulled himself out of the pool. "You want something to drink?"

"Water sounds good."

"Coming right up."

Rachel leaned back in the water and closed her eyes. Her body buoyed, gently swaying with the motion of the water. She loved how the water muffled all the sounds of life. She was at peace, so she didn't hear Dillon re-enter the pool. By the time he dunked her it was too late. They both laughed in the late afternoon sunshine. Rachel couldn't remember the last time she'd had this much fun. "You are good for me, you know that? Thank you for being such a good friend."

Dillon kept his face expressionless. He wanted to be so much more than that but knew she needed time. Time to heal from the deep hurt she carried with her. He wished she would confide in him.

She climbed out of the pool and sat on the cement edge while she dangled her feet and dried her face. Dillon lifted himself out and sat near her, on the edge. "I take it you've had enough?"

"Yeah, I better get home before the girls send out the cavalry."

"Let me get my towel and I'll walk you."

"Not necessary. I know my way back."

"Yes, but a gentleman always makes sure the lady arrives safely to her door."

"Well then, lead on my valiant protector."

In spite of the light hearted fun they'd had that afternoon, Rachel found herself quiet on the short walk home. Once she reached the garage she turned to say goodbye and found she was face to face with Dillon. He was a single breath away. She stood still, surprised by his closeness. She was staring into his dark brown eyes when she felt his lips lightly brush hers. It was a gentle kiss, a tentative kiss, one with boundaries. She felt his restraint. Then she remembered her guilt and pulled away. A quick goodbye and she was behind the closed kitchen door, leaning against it while fresh tears permanently burned the memory of this kiss into her mind. *What am I doing?*

Rachel touched her fingers to her lips. No one besides Ryan had ever kissed her. She remembered the first time he kissed her. He had made it a habit of showing up at the diner and walking her home. He didn't like her walking home by herself at night. After a couple of months, he finally took her hand. It took a couple more months before he kissed her. It was that night she fell in love with him. He was supposed to be her first kiss and her last. She stood at the altar and pledged her love until death separated them. No one else had ever touched her. Until tonight. She felt dirty. Why had she let him kiss her? She wasn't fooling anyone, least of all herself. She wanted him to kiss her. She wanted to feel wanted. She needed to know she was still desirable, still beautiful as a woman. It had been too long and now she would never be able to take that kiss back.

Who was she kidding? Ryan didn't want her anymore. What difference did it make? Her marriage was over.

She fell into bed, wet hair and all, pulled Ryan's shirt close. She cried herself to sleep as she breathed in her husband's scent.

Dillon walked across the street in a daze. Why did he do that? He could have messed up everything, scared her off. He swallowed hard. What would he do if she pulled away? He shook his head, knowing if he had to do it all over again, he would. If he could he would hold her and protect her forever. He looked over his shoulder toward her bedroom window and wondered what she was doing. Was she thinking of him? Was she angry with him? Time would tell.

Ryan slammed his hand against the steering wheel. He was too late. He'd messed up and he had himself to blame. He'd followed Mark's advice and taken a couple of days to pray and get his head on straight. He knew now, more than ever, that he had to explain to Rachel, to show her that he really did love her and honor their marriage vows.

He saw the whole thing. He watched him walk her home. It was obvious they had been spending time together. Then he watched another man kiss his wife. He wanted to jump out of the car and beat the guy. Then he remembered why his wife was with another guy to begin with. Because he let her go. Because he told her he was done. Because he gave up everything they both considered precious.

This was his doing. He was entirely at fault. He swallowed the lump that had formed in his throat as he slowly drove away.

Chapter Seventeen

Herbert pressed the cool cloth to Val's forehead. After her last round of chemo she had been sicker than normal. The good news was the growth had slowed to the point of near stopping. The bad news was this last round still made her sicker than a dog. Which irritated her because she had things to do. Rachel needed her. She knew prayer anywhere was effective, but somehow she felt the release of God's power when she was praying with fellow believers. It made her mad that the enemy had a foothold in her life. This morning was prayer and she had missed it.

Herbert noticed her bad mood. "Hemming and hawing isn't going to change anything. Why don't you lie down and be a good patient?"

"Good patient my behind. If I had a nickel for every time I nursed you over the past fifty years I'd be a rich woman. And you were the absolute worst patient ever. You get a splinter and you think you're dying."

"Always bringing up the past, now aren't you woman?" Feisty was good. He'd take her feisty any day.

"I hate being sick. I just hate it."

"I know you do. You'll be better before you know it."

"I can't make you dinner, ya know that, right?"

"I'll manage. I think we still have some ham spread in the fridge. I'll eat that up."

Val knew she was having a pity party and quite frankly, she didn't care. "Everyone is wondering why I'm not helping more. I just hate that. They think I don't care"

Herbert shook his head. "Woman, there isn't a person alive who thinks that. Certainly not anyone who knows you. If you're not throwing up and in bed, you're giving everything you've got. I'm not sure I know a more selfless person than you. You have a heart of gold."

"It just bothers me that I can't help out more at church. The ladies are scrambling for Sunday school teachers and helpers in the kitchen. Why, I don't know if anyone realizes it's second Sunday potluck coming up this week. Who is organizing everything? Are sign up sheets posted? Oh Herbert, I just hate being down."

"They're going to get along without you. We'll make do."

At that news Val busted out crying. "I'm not needed. Oh God, why don't you just take me now?"

The doorbell kept Herbert from giving his wife a good talking to. It wasn't often she fell into one of these slumps, and he could understand her doing so, but he just couldn't take anymore stress on top of everything else. She needed to be thankful she was alive and quit putting one foot in the grave. "Wonder who that could be?"

Herbert opened the door to four ladies standing on the porch. "Well, what do we have here?" Merry was leading the way with a homemade pot of chicken noodle soup. Three women were on her heels. One with a loaf of homemade bread, another with a pie of some sort and the third had her Bible, and it was a big one. "Come on in ladies. Val will be glad to see you. She was just complaining about not being able to go to prayer. Now here you are bringing the prayer to her. She'll be mighty happy." He took the pot from Merry and walked toward the kitchen. "Mmm, this smells good. Beats ham spread any day."

Val quickly wiped away her tears before her friends saw her pouting. "Well, how did you know I was down and out today?"

"You weren't at prayer were you?"

"Well no, you know that."

"Then it doesn't take a rocket scientist to know you needed some friends today. And here we are. We've got lunch, our Bibles and our hearts ready for prayer. You feel like some praying company?"

Val started crying again. This time instead of feeling sorry for herself, she praised God. He should have been chastising her for her attitude and here he was blessing her. "Isn't that just like God? He knew I needed you today."

Herbert brought in a small cup of soup. Later, after her stomach had settled, she could try to eat some of the noodles. "Here drink a little of this broth. It just might stay down and it'll give you energy to pray with these ladies."

Merry took the cup from him. "You go on in the kitchen and eat your lunch. We'll take care of her."

Herbert didn't have to be told twice. Warm bread and homemade soup were calling his name.

Val looked at her friends. "I'm feeling better already. Just having you here, knowing you've been thinking of me and praying for me does me such good."

"Oh Val. You're always thought about. We love you. You do so much for others, it's about time you slowed down and let the rest of us care for you. We all need that from time to time."

Val sipped her broth but stayed where she was. The rest of the ladies found a comfortable chair and one by one began to read from the Word. Val watched her friends, so thankful for them. After reading the entire book of 1 John, the group started praying. First, they gathered around and prayed for Val, for healing, for strength, for courage and for peace. Knowing her heart, they joined together in storming the throne on behalf of Ryan and Rachel.

It wasn't every day that a house sees powerful prayer, especially when one of the prayer warriors is down.

One by one the ladies took their leave. Val was thankful for each of them, for their friendship and their support.

Her husband opened the door and peered cautiously before entering the room. "Are they all gone?"

"Mmmhmm, they just left."

"Then I guess it's safe to come back in here. Those women sure know how to pray."

"That they do."

Herbert sat down next to her and took her hand. "Are you feeling better?"

"Yes. He sure knows what we need when we need it, doesn't he?"

He kissed her hand. Soon they would be celebrating their fifty-year anniversary, if she made it that long. He prayed she would. They married young. She was only nineteen. She was more beautiful to him today than she was fifty years ago. He looked at his wife and saw the nervous, scared nineteen year old he'd married. She reminded him of that girl from so long ago. "Are you afraid?"

"I was. Most days I'm not. But today was one of those days. I needed a reminder of God's goodness and mercy and he gave me a good dose of it. I don't know why I get scared sometimes. Eternity is as real to me as this earth. I know I'm going home soon. But I feel like my job here isn't complete; like there is something I need to do before I'm released. Maybe that was why I was so anxious today. Rachel has been so heavy on my heart. The prayer time did me good."

"I'm glad they came. As much as I love you, there are times we need our friends to circle around us. Kind of like Job. Although his friends didn't always do right by him. They came around though."

"Yeah, God gave me some good friends." She squeezed his hand. "And an even better husband. Did you talk to the kids today?"

"Everyone sends their love and all of them are planning on coming for our fiftieth. We'll be seeing them soon."

"I pray I make it that long."

"You'll make it. You heard what the doctor said. You're surprising even the most stubborn of your physicians. They are all amazed you are doing as well as you are. God is going to give us this anniversary. And you will be well enough to enjoy it."

"You know what, I believe you. I have a peace about the whole thing." She took the blanket off her legs. "I'm even kind of hungry. Did you eat all the soup?"

"No woman, I didn't eat the entire pot. You sit down and I'll warm you up a bowl. Want a piece of bread too?"

"Sounds heavenly."

Chapter Eighteen

Dillon watched the clock. *She should be here any minute.* He shuffled some papers around his desk, trying to take his mind off her. *She'll get here when she gets here.* He paused. The problem was, he didn't want to stop thinking about her. And at the same time he berated himself for constantly thinking about her. He told himself he wasn't ready, that there wasn't a woman on earth he could love as much as he loved his wife. Then Rachel walks into his life and shatters that belief into a million pieces.

She had made herself scarce since the kiss. As much as he wanted to go over and check on her, he felt he should give her space. This would be the defining moment. He would know instantly if he still had a chance with her.

He held still, listening for her in the hallway. Nothing. He poured himself another cup of coffee which he needed like he needed a hole in the head. Anything to keep him busy. And to think he would be working with her from here on out. How was he going to get anything done? He sat back down and waited.

Rachel walked through the halls in the agriculture building looking for Dillon's office. If she didn't find it soon, she would call him. If she had had the guts to go over after he'd kissed her, she wouldn't be in this predicament. But she hid away like a child and was now lost in a maze of hallways, classrooms and lecture halls. She had no idea the college was this big. *Ah, there it is.* She read the name plate on the door. Dr.

Dillon Holcombe, Professor of Horticulture. *Tucked into a little corner, isn't it?* She found him sitting at his desk, staring into space. "A penny for your thoughts?"

Dillon felt his face redden. "Hey, there you are."

"I got lost. This place is bigger than I realized."

"Sorry I didn't give you better directions."

"I have to say, we could hide out here for weeks and no one would find us. This is really off the beaten path."

"Right you are. When they added the program, they had to find room for us." He motioned to the small quarters. "And this is what they found. We'll be sharing an office; I hope that is okay with you."

"I'm good with whatever. I'm just happy to have a job."

Dillon tilted his head, wondering how he could feel what he was feeling so fast. "About Friday evening…"

Rachel put up her hand, stopping his speech. "Not necessary. There is nothing to explain. I'm sorry I didn't call you or come by. I just needed a little time to process."

"So, we're okay then?"

"Yeah, we're great."

He watched her eyes for any sign that would indicate her feeling otherwise, he saw nothing but tenderness. She was stunning. Not just her looks, although he had no complaints, but also her heart. Rachel intrigued him, she compelled him to search deep inside of himself and find the good. He wasn't sure what it was about her, but he was drawn to her. He needed to know her better. And more than anything, he wanted to kiss her again. He managed to curb that temptation. "Great. Let's get you settled. I have a couple of weeks to get you up to speed, and then we'll be inundated with students. Summer classes just ended so we'll need to focus on the upcoming semester. Think we have enough time?"

"Absolutely."

"Good. How about a tour of the facility then I can go over class schedules with you."

"Does this tour include the greenhouses?"

"Sure does."

She walked toward the door. "Then what are we waiting for?"

Rachel had chosen wisely in wearing loose fitting culottes, low slung sandals and a breezy short-sleeved blouse. She lifted the stray hair that was sticking to the back of her neck and tried to tuck it into her gently clasped up do. "It sure is hot out today."

"Supposed to be even hotter tomorrow." Dillon stopped. "If we get some of the basics done here today, we can go over the class syllabus tomorrow at my house. We only have a couple weeks of summer left and the pool has hardly been used this summer. What do you say? Want to come over and take a working swim?"

Rachel tilted her head. She no longer felt guilty over spending time in another man's company. She spent a good portion of the weekend dealing with her self-imposed condemnation.

Dillon noticed her hesitation. "If you'd rather not, I completely understand. I will even refrain from kissing you again, unless you want me to." He questioned her with his eyes.

She exhaled through her mouth and upward to cool her obviously red face. "The kiss was nice. I just want to take things slowly. It's only been three months since Ryan left. I'm not sure I'm ready to jump right into another relationship."

"We'll go as slow as you need to go. I promise I'll behave."

She nodded. "All right, fine. Can we go see the green houses now?"

"Your wish is my command. Right this way."

Dillon felt as if he were walking on air. She didn't hate him, in fact, she was willing to spend more time with him.

The rest of the afternoon was spent with their heads bent over class schedules and giving Rachel a list of her duties. Since her true talent lie with actually planting and cross pollination, Dillon was more than willing to let her take control of that department and he would handle the class room instruction. Of course he would be overseeing the projects, but Rachel would be working one on one with the students in the greenhouses. She was thrilled.

"Dillon, this is like a dream job. I can't believe I'm doing this. Am I really even qualified?"

"You wouldn't be here if you weren't qualified. Trust me, this job needs you as much as you need it. I need a good partner. My wife handled the hands on back in Colorado. It's not my forte. I'm gifted in the classroom. Not with my hands in the dirt."

"I seem to remember you doing a pretty good job with my lawn mower."

"Yeah, but uh, I also had some pretty good motivation. A pretty lady in distress never hurt any."

Rachel playfully smacked his arm. "Here I thought you were a farm implement salesman or something."

Dillon smirked. "Funny." His stomach rumbled then he looked at his watch. "Whoa. I had no idea it was so late. I'm famished. Want to grab a bite before we head home?"

"Sure." Knowing his penchant for lovely cafes out of town she felt she better set some limits. "If it's local."

"Alright, fine. We'll do simple. There's a great new diner that opened up on Milton Avenue. They serve a mean Reuben."

"I think I'll leave the Reuben to you, thank you very much. And yes, I've been there. See, you're not the only one up on the new restaurants in town. The girls and I stopped there one day after shopping. It was pretty good. Service was a little slow though."

"You   want   to   go   somewhere   else?"

"Nah, at this time of day it should be okay."

Rachel followed Dillon to the café. Surprisingly there were still quite a few patrons. They were seated toward the front of the restaurant and looking at their menus when Rachel heard her name. She looked up and found her husband and oldest daughter standing in front of her. Rachel stood up and gave Sam a hug. "Hey Sweetie. I didn't know you were in town."

"I came to visit with Dad."

Rachel felt her eyes tear up and blinked. "Oh, well, that was nice of you." She turned toward Dillon. "Dillon this is my daughter, Samantha, but we all call her Sam. And this is Ryan. This is Dillon. My boss and neighbor."

Ryan extended his hand and leaned forward. "Her husband. Pleasure to meet you."

Rachel rolled her eyes and sat back down. "We were about to order."

Sam looked from her mom to her dad. "Well, we just came in for a late bite and there doesn't seem to be any tables open. Do you mind if we sit with you, Mom?" Sam sat down at one of the empty chairs without waiting for the okay. "So, what's good here?"

Dillon piped up, determined to make the best of this situation. "The Reuben. It's great."

Sam read the description out loud. "Rye bread, sour kraut, corned beef, horseradish…who eats this stuff? Yuck."

Rachel took the menu from her daughter. "Like you're going to order anything besides a side salad." She silently pleaded with Dillon to end this debacle.

Ryan took the menu from Rachel. "Well, I'm starved and I'll have something besides a salad."

Rachel stood up; she couldn't do this. "I'm really not all that hungry. I'm gonna get going." She kissed her daughter's cheek. "Sam, next time you come to town, I'd appreciate a call." She left the restaurant in tears and hurried to her car.

Dillon reached her before she had a chance to get in. "Come here." He pulled her close and let her cry on his shoulder. "We're going somewhere to talk. We'll come back for my car." He took her keys and opened her door for her. He got behind the wheel and pulled out of the parking lot.

Rachel wiped her eyes and nose. "I'm so sorry. I can't believe they did that. It was Sam's doing. I know my kids. They keep hoping we'll get back together." She blew again. "Trust me, Ryan does not want to be in my presence. I revolt him."

Dillon drove to a small out of the way park and shut off the engine. "Come on. Let's sit outside. There's a nice breeze."

He opened the door for her and led her to a picnic table.

Rachel looked around and noticed they were completely alone. She sat down and poured out the whole story, everything from beginning to end. "So you see, he wouldn't want anything to do with me. Our whole marriage was a lie. He was trying to be something he wasn't. Every time I think of our marriage, of the way I must have repulsed him, I just start crying. I've never felt so rejected, so humiliated in all my life." She started crying all over again and tried to stutter through it. "How can anyone ever love me? My own husband didn't find me attractive. He'd rather be with a man."

Dillon pulled his handkerchief out of his pocket and handed it to her. What could he say? How could he comfort her? "If it helps any, I find you much more attractive than any man I've ever seen."

She started crying even harder.

"Rachel, listen to me. What your husband did was stupid, foolish. You are the most beautiful woman, the most attractive woman I have had the honor of spending time with. Every minute we're together just makes me want to see you more. I was married for a long time and I loved my wife with all that I am. But when I look at you my relationship with her seems like it was so very long ago. I sometimes feel guilty because of how I feel about you. The voices inside my head argue. They tell me it's too soon and I'm betraying her. But then I just look at you and all the negative thoughts flee. I love you, Rachel. I don't expect you to say anything. I know it's too soon for you. But I'm here for you. You are not repulsive or revolting. You are very much a beautiful, desirable woman."

Dillon just held her and let her cry. He didn't expect any sudden proclamations of love or adoration. He just wanted to hold this woman and comfort her. She had no idea how much she had come to mean to him. Even if she heard the words he spoke she still didn't fully understand. She breathed new life into him. She gave him hope. He wasn't going to let go easily. He had never been a praying man but he sent a silent plea to anyone who might be listening. *Please don't make me give her up.*

Chapter Nineteen

Shannon and Sam conspired at the breakfast table while waiting for their mother to get home. Sam had explained everything that happened at the restaurant. Mom had a lot of explaining to do. Especially since she had said there was nothing between her and her boss. It was bad enough they worked together. Going out on dates, swimming in his pool, making him desserts, all of it was too much for Shannon to handle. Mom was throwing her marriage away. Maybe she didn't see it but Shannon sure did. According to Sam, Mom was all smiles sitting next to Dillon. And Dad walked in on them. It had been obvious Dad was hurt. How could she?

Shannon heard the garage door go up and braced herself. Her mother wasn't going to get away with this.

Rachel walked in the door and set the bag of groceries on the counter. *Oh, so it's going to be like that is it?* She raised her eyebrows at her daughters. "Yes?" She started putting the food away.

"I think you already know."

Rachel turned at the sound of scorn in her daughter's voice. "So, Sam, you can't call your mother when you're in town but you can rush right over to cause trouble, huh? So, what, am I a child again that I am tattled on then taken to task?"

"Mom, you were out to eat with another man. Another man you said meant nothing, who was just your boss. And to make matters worse, Dad saw you. Doesn't that bother you?"

"You know what bothers me? The fact that my daughters are still blaming me for something their father has done. He left. When are you going to get it? I didn't ask him to, he just came home one day and decided for all of us. We didn't get a choice. I didn't get a choice. That is what bothers me."

Shannon stood up and crossed her arms. "Don't you want to get back together with Dad? Don't you believe it could happen? Seems to me I haven't heard much talk about God lately. Maybe you stopped believing God can do anything. So, all that preaching to us kids was nothing but a nice lie, huh? When things get tough, you don't even believe it."

Rachel closed her eyes and tightened her lips. *God give me strength.* "Shannon, God released me from this marriage when your father walked out that door and into the hands of his lover. I don't have to explain myself to you or to anyone else. Maybe someday you'll understand that this is not all about you. The hurt your father caused me doesn't just disappear with a nod and a smile. It will be a long time before I'm ready for a relationship. But I tell you what. It's nice having someone who will actually listen to me, who isn't judging me because they aren't getting their own selfish way."

Shannon felt her anger start to rise and started fingering the cuts that lay under her long sleeve shirt.

Sam interrupted her sister with an apologetic glance before addressing her mother. "Mom, you make it sound like Dad had a choice, like he chose to abandon you and us girls. He didn't choose his life. Do you think anyone would choose to be gay? I mean, come on. He didn't mean to hurt you. But, he couldn't go on the way things were either. He wasn't being true to himself."

"So, is this how he explained himself to you? Is this how you two talk behind my back?"

"No, Mom, he hasn't said anything to me about your relationship. I just came down to spend some time with him, to let him know I still love him and support him. He doesn't have to say anything. I have lots of gay friends at school. Believe me I hear it all from them. Dad doesn't have to explain a thing. I know how it works."

"Yes, being in college, surrounded with liberal college kids makes you an expert in all things gay. You seem to think your liberal professors are demi gods. Have you forgotten everything you were ever taught? What about the Bible? Do you want your father to go to hell?"

Sam rolled her eyes. "Mom, that's where you're wrong. The Bible isn't against being a homosexual. As a matter of fact, some of my Christian friends are gay. They're not going to hell. They love Jesus as much as we do. If you're worried about Dad's soul, you can stop. He's going to be just great." Sam took a ponytail holder out of her purse and pulled her hair into a side ponytail. "If you want to hear more about how Jesus really felt about homosexuality, you should come with me to church some time. I found this really cool church. Mom, it's all about loving people. We've missed the boat. Dad deserves our love and our support. If you really loved him you'd be happy for him." Sam looked sheepish. "In fact, did you know that there are several homosexual relationships in the Bible? Most likely David and Jonathon were lovers. Ruth and Naomi too."

Rachel was so shocked by what her daughter said she found it hard to form words. "What? Sam, what happened to you?" *Oh God, where have I gone wrong?*

Shelly, who came through the door in the middle of Sam's rant went off on her sister. "You have lost it. That is wrong on so many accounts I don't even know where to begin. First off, I didn't hear one scripture to back up your theories. Because that is all they are, messed up theories trying to justify sin. This feel good stuff is going to send a whole bunch of people to hell. Dad included if he doesn't get right with God. I've been doing some studying, too. Except I went straight to the source and didn't depend on people who want their own way to convince me of what is right."

"What do you know? You're only fifteen. Wait until you're older, then you'll understand."

"Don't pretend that you understand me and how mature I am. What I want to know is, what are you hiding? What sin are you trying to cover up and make yourself feel better about?"

"I'm not hiding anything because I have nothing to hide. I'm an open book. What I've learned is, Jesus never meant for us to feel guilt. I'm just so much happier. I've learned so much since I started going to this church. They have such a different perspective on the Bible and on Jesus' teachings. If you would only listen, you could be happier too." Sam turned to Shannon, grabbed her arm and pulled up her sleeve. "Shannon, wouldn't you love to be happy and free from doing this?"

Shannon jerked her arm away and quickly pulled her sleeve down. "Just leave me alone."

Rachel covered her mouth with her hand. "Oh dear, Lord." She took her daughter's hand and gently pulled up her sleeve. She did the same to her other arm. "Shannon, why? Why would you hurt yourself like this? What is wrong with you?"

Shannon lost control. She pulled her sleeves back down. "You are what's wrong. All of you. Just leave me alone." She ran up the stairs and slammed her door shut.

Rachel closed her eyes. Her family was completely falling apart. Sam was lost, trying to find acceptance in a Godless world. Shannon was inflicting physical pain upon herself to try and cover the real problem and Shelly was spending more and more time away from home. She'd had her head in the sand and had not realized just how much her daughters were hurting.

"Sam, how did you know, about Shannon?"

"Mom, she's wearing long sleeves in August. That would be the first clue."

"I didn't ask for attitude."

"Sorry. Girls cut at college. Long sleeves are a way they cover up what they do, even in hot weather."

"I had no idea. None whatsoever. I saw the long sleeves, of course. But when I would question her she either claimed she was chilled or shrugged me off. I didn't want to push it."

"Mom, with Shannon, sometimes you just need to push things." Sam picked up her purse and gave her mom a hug. "Hey, I gotta get back. It's already late and I have to work in the morning. I'll talk to you later. And let me know if you want to go to church with me sometime, okay?"

Rachel watched Sam leave and turned on the tea water. "I'm going to check on Shannon. Would you watch this for me?"

"Sure. Want jasmine?"

"You know me too well. I'll be back in a few."

Rachel knocked on her daughter's door. "Shannon, it's me, Mom. Can we talk?"

"Go away."

"Listen honey, I know you're upset, but we need to talk about this. Please open the door." Rachel heard the lock turn. She opened the door to Shannon's retreating back. "Hey. I'm sorry I got so upset downstairs. Things are crazy and sometimes I just don't know what to do."

Shannon sat on her bed, not saying a word.

Rachel walked closer to where her daughter was sitting, glancing in the wastebasket as she went. Her stomach turned at seeing bloody tissues. "Can we talk about what you've been doing?"

"There's nothing to talk about."

"Shannon, of course there's something to talk about. You're hurting yourself. That is just not acceptable. At the very least I want you to talk to your counselor about this."

"I already have."

"She didn't say a word to me."

"I asked her not to."

"Shannon, why? I'm your mother. You didn't think I'd want to know or be concerned?"

"Look, Mom, I'm tired. We can discuss this tomorrow at my counseling appointment, okay?"

Rachel leaned over and kissed her daughter's forehead. She felt her flinch and pulled back to see a slight look of disgust on her face. "I love you, Shannon."

"Goodnight, Mom."

Rachel quietly shut the door to the bedroom and walked downstairs. Her tea was steeping in her favorite mug with a little note next to it.

Tired. Went to bed. Enjoy your tea. Love you, S.

She turned off the lights, picked up her mug and headed upstairs. Rachel stood in front of the window looking at Dillon's house. He raised a hand from his lit bedroom and she followed suit then turned from the window.

128

After setting her tea on the nightstand, she went to the back of her closet and pulled a box down from the overhead shelf then took it to her bed. One by one, she began removing the items from the box. The last in came out first.

The memories made her smile. Shelly had refused to crawl. Not even for her favorite toys. Then one day she received this little piece of pie on wheels in a child's meal from a fast food restaurant and that changed everything. Rachel could set that on the floor and Shelly would army crawl to get that thing. Anything else, forget it. But there was something about that pie.

Rachel lifted what was left of the worn baby blanket to her cheek, remembering Shannon refusing to let her wash it. Shannon had been her most attached baby. Besides her security blanket she'd had her nook. Rachel had received some grief about allowing Shannon to carry the blanket and suck on her nook well into her second year, but she wouldn't listen to the naysayers. She fully believed that Shannon would give them up when the time was right. Rachel had been correct. Shannon ended up with the flu and puked all over her two favorite things. After that, she wouldn't take them. They had become "yucky." She was thankful she'd never made the child endure the trauma of going without them.

She traced the faint outline of a turtle on the blanket. Shannon was their little surprise. According to the ultrasound, she was supposed to be a boy. Rachel had decorated in shades of blue and green in preparation for their little boy. Little animal print sleepers and soft gowns filled the small dresser she'd put in the nursery. The crib was outfitted in smiling turtles. Eventually, everything had been replaced, everything except that one blanket with turtles. Shannon was attached to it and nothing else would calm her down when she was upset. Rachel felt the knot begin to form in her throat. How could she have not known how much pain her little girl was in? How could a mother no longer understand her own children?

Next, she picked up the frilly pink dress that was carefully folded. Samantha was her girly girl. Rachel started it, of course. Being her first and being a girl, Rachel dressed her little girl in dresses and ruffles every time they went anywhere.

Most people thought Samantha would rebel and become a tomboy. But no, Sam remained true to her diva ways. Rachel tried to remember how many tubes of lipstick Sam had ruined. Or how many stains in the original carpet had been caused by stolen bottles of fingernail polish, but she lost count. She held these tangible memories close, breathing in the faint scent of her babies.

All the memories were as close as her last breath. How could she feel so distant from these same children who nursed at her breast, whom she would gladly give her life for? When did everything change? Why did they all of a sudden doubt her love? After everything she had willingly given up for them? Her career, her own dreams and ambitions, everything she had wanted in life was put on hold. Did her sacrifice not mean anything? Didn't they realize that she loved them more today than she did the day they were born? Just because it was time for them to go out into the world and live according to their purpose didn't mean she stopped being their mother, it just meant she was finally able to see to some of her own dreams come to pass. Even if her original plan had included Ryan, he had made it painfully clear he wanted nothing to do with her now.

She looked into the box once again. Her veil and the poems Ryan wrote for her, including the one he read to her on their wedding day were among the remaining items. She didn't have the strength to pull them out. A different day maybe. Once the hurt had subsided, she'd revisit those memories. Her heart couldn't take it right now.

She sipped the last of her tepid tea and turned off the lamp. Rachel cuddled into bed with her memories as her daughters' laughter filled her dreams while she slept soundly. When morning arrived, she wanted nothing more than to escape to that place of joyful laughter. Then she remembered her daughters were almost grown and needed her just as much today as they did in days past. She set aside the summer quilt and reached for her robe, ready to face whatever this day brought.

Chapter Twenty

Mark looked at the grey house sitting on the corner. The size alone made the house a foreboding structure. He wondered why he'd never noticed it before. There was a ramp leading to the front porch as well as a set of stairs. He climbed the stairs and knocked on the front door. As he waited, he contemplated the house. The porch seemed endless. *Jessi would love this place.* The frosted glass on the front door was surrounded by a burgundy trim with a darker shade of grey painted wood. The outside of the house was in beautiful shape.

The door swung open and a beautiful woman, who was by Mark's guess, in her sixties, greeted him. Mark reached for her hand. "Hi, I'm Mark Jenson. I'm here to see Terry Schmidt."

She tilted her head, questioningly. "Are you the Mark Jenson of the Community Church, downtown?"

He nodded. "One and the same." He wasn't sure by her expression if she approved or disapproved. It was hard to tell.

"I'm Maria. It's nice to meet you. Is Terry expecting you?"

"Uh, no. I was asked by a friend to come and talk with him. It's pretty important."

"He's had a few hard days. I'll see if he is up to visitors."

Mark waited while the older lady chatted with someone else. He wasn't sure if she was an employee or a resident. It didn't take long before the second woman was climbing the stairs and Maria was walking toward him.

"Why don't we go into my office for a chat while we wait, shall we?"

Since it was more of a command and less of a request, Mark followed Maria into a well-appointed office with a large sitting area. "Would you like a cup of tea, or maybe a cup of coffee?"

"Coffee would be nice."

Maria motioned toward the sitting area while she texted from her phone. "Refreshments will be in shortly."

Mark watched the woman handle her smart phone as adeptly as his teenage daughter.

Maria laughed. "I find technology as challenging as it is useful. I have a motto though, the day I stop learning is the day I might as well give up and give in. And I just don't see that happening."

"I'm impressed."

"No offense, but impressing you is not my goal. I could care less about impressing anyone. Efficiency on the other hand is extremely important to me." Maria rose to greet the same young woman she had talked to earlier. They spoke in hushed tones so Mark concentrated on the artwork that was hung throughout the office. Maria returned with a tea tray in her hands.

She handed him his mug of coffee and poured her own cup of tea from a stylish infuser. She nodded toward the contraption. "As you see, I was serious about embracing the future. Besides, this little contraption makes the best tea I've ever tasted."

He added a little cream to his mug then sat back and waited for her to initiate the conversation. He was at a loss as to why she wished to speak with him. Nothing he could do but be patient so he leaned back and enjoyed the quiet.

Maria studied the man in front of her. She would have had to be living in a hole in the ground to have not heard of him. His work in the downtown area was impressive. She didn't know him personally; therefore she was hesitant to start the conversation. Yet, the reason he was here still needed to be addressed. She had been praying for help, for someone to come along and lend a hand. The need was great. People assumed the advances in AIDS treatment absolved the need for houses such as this. They were wrong. "I bet you're wondering why I asked you into my office."

Mark had to refrain from contradicting her choice of words. "The question has crossed my mind."

Maria stood up and walked around the room. "Mr. Jensen, this place is home. The people between these four walls are family. Granted, they are family with problems but who doesn't have problems, yes?" She turned to gauge his reaction without giving him a chance to respond. "I often find do-gooder's motives for coming here a bit skewed. Everyone in this house already knows about Jesus. We'd be doing them a great disservice if we failed to offer them an eternity with our Savior. We know all about the great commission. But what happens after the truth is presented? Yes, many here come to know Christ in a real and meaningful way before they pass on. Others absolutely refuse and will spend eternity in a worse pain than they had here on earth. At least here there is hope, is there not?"

Mark nodded, fascinated by this woman.

Maria continued. "What we offer here is a peaceful place to live for the remaining weeks or months of one's life. We offer the dying some dignity and respect. God loves all, the sinners and the saints. He loved us all so much he sent his son to redeem us." She raised her eyebrows. "All of us."

She returned to her seat. "We do not distinguish between the saved and unsaved in this place. All are dying. All have a choice to make. We love them and care for them regardless of their decision. It is our hope that by our love, even the most stubborn will relent and see Christ in us, and how much he loves them. To the last breath there is still hope." She sipped her tea. "Just as in blood families, we rejoice when one who has made a decision for Christ goes to spend eternity with him. And when one chooses not to spend eternity in heaven we mourn. Our hearts break. Yet, we go on. There are many who need to be loved while they are here. As David did when his infant son died, he removed the ashes and sackcloth and ate a meal. What is done is done. Our hope lies in presenting the love and truth of Jesus Christ to each person here. The choice is theirs."

Mark wasn't sure if he was to respond. He remained quiet, listening to the wisdom in her words.

"I certainly didn't want to categorize you before I learned of your intentions with Terry. But, I thought in fairness, I should make you aware of what we do here. Terry is one of our tougher cases. He adamantly refuses anything to do with Christianity. His hurts run deep, as do the hurts of most of our residents. Terry's seem particularly rooted though. Perhaps in my younger days I would have burned Terry's file and deemed him hopeless. But, knowing my God like I do, and seeing the miracles he has performed, I know that there is hope even when circumstances seem hopeless. I'm holding on to that hope for Terry. I will stand in the gap and fight for him. I'll be his prayer warrior. I won't lay down my sword until the fight is finished."

"I understand and I won't undo the good you have done. Upsetting balances and bringing division is a concept I am familiar with. I also understand what it means to be forgiven when unworthy. I've been there. I want to talk to Terry about his relationship with a good friend of mine. This is a difficult and delicate situation. I know that. But resolution and healing needs to take place in many lives and I must be able to speak with Terry."

"I thought you might say that. But not today. I want you to go home and pray about this situation. Come back tomorrow and I'll make sure you have an opportunity to talk with Terry." She rose making it obvious this meeting was over. "If those terms seem agreeable to you, then I will see you tomorrow right after lunch. If not, then we'll count this as goodbye." She shook his hand in hers, walked him to her office door and shut herself in the room without another word.

Mark stood staring at the door, wondering, what just happened. Stunned, he drove home and tried to explain the situation to his wife. "I feel like I've just been given a homework assignment by my teacher." He shrugged. "I guess I'll be in my office praying."

Chapter Twenty-One

Ryan opened the letter and read the contents. How could she do this? In front of all the guys at work, the customers, his boss, everyone had seen him being served. She filed for divorce and now the world knew. He felt a hand slap him on the shoulder. "Hey man. Welcome to the club!"

Ryan turned to his co-worker. "The club?"

"Yeah, the club of freedom. No more chains. No more nagging. No more to do lists. No more spending all our money. Most of us guys are already members. Some of us have joined the club more than once if you know what I mean." There was laughter all around the small office. Ryan didn't see the humor. He closed his eyes and uttered a quick prayer. He felt the oppression every time he stepped into the car dealership intensify. He knew for certain this wasn't in God's will, yet there was nothing he could do. She'd made her decision. He wondered how much her filing had to do with her new boss. He should have punched him out while he'd had the chance.

He counted down the minutes until he finished out his day. He prayed he didn't get any latecomers who wanted to purchase a car through him. He wanted out on time so he could meet with Mark. He needed to talk with someone. The someone he used to talk to was now talking with another man. *Ryan, you only have yourself to blame. You did this. Don't be down on her.*

He tossed his briefcase in the passenger front seat and rolled the windows down. Although the polyester shirts the dealership provided were hot, he was thankful he didn't have to wear a tie. That would have been much worse. He flipped the air conditioner on the off chance it decided to work. Nope. *Guess I'll keep the windows open.* His stomach rumbled. Too upset to eat, he had missed lunch. The coffee he had been downing all day started to turn in his stomach. He knew from experience he'd better add some food to the mix.

He arrived at the diner first and ordered the soup and sandwich special. He doubted Mark would be eating with him. His aunt cooked home made meals almost every day. He missed Rachel's cooking. In fact, he missed almost everything about her. He shook his head. He didn't want to be any part of "the club." They could have it. Whether or not he wanted to be a part seemed to be irrelevant. For him, membership wasn't optional.

Mark approached the table and motioned for the waitress. After he ordered some coffee, he turned his attention to Ryan. "What happened?"

Mark took the envelope and read the letter. "I take it this came as a surprise?"

"You could say that. I had no idea."

"What are you going to do about it?"

"What do you mean? I'm not going to do anything. She's been seeing another guy. She filed for divorce. I don't think there is anything for me to do."

Mark shook his head. He truly wondered if men would ever get it. "Ryan, have you ever stopped to think your wife might want you to fight for her?"

"Trust me, she was pretty clear. You didn't hear her. It wasn't just her words, but how she said them. Remember what I told you? The thought of me touching her makes her skin crawl. It's over." He held up the certified letter. "This is just the exclamation point."

"Did you ever go talk with her?"

"I tried. I pulled up in front of the house just in time to see the guy across the street kiss her. At first I was so angry I could've punched the guy. Then, I admitted defeat and left."

Mark pulled out his Bible. "I want to read you something." He turned to Ephesians. "I'm sure you've heard this passage many times. I'm also certain you've preached on it. The other thing I'm certain of is a portion of scripture never comes completely alive to us until we are right smack dab in the middle of it. When every word completely fits in with what we are living, that is when that particular scripture speaks the loudest." He began reading from chapter five.

"Wives, submit to your own husbands, as to the Lord. For the husband is the head of the wife, as also Christ is the head of the church; and He is the Savior of the body. Therefore, just as the church is subject to Christ, so let the wives be to their own husbands in everything. Husbands, love your wives, just as Christ also loved the church and gave Himself for her, that He might sanctify and cleanse her with the washing of water by the Word, that He might present her to Himself a glorious church, not having spot or wrinkle or any such thing, but that she should be holy and without blemish. So husbands ought to love their own wives as their own bodies; he who loves his wife loves himself. For no one ever hated his own flesh, but nourishes and cherishes it, just as the Lord does the church. For we are members of His body, of His flesh and of His bones. For this reason a man shall leave his father and mother and be joined to his wife, and the two shall become one flesh. This is a great mystery, but I speak concerning Christ and the church. Nevertheless let each one of you in particular so love his own wife as himself, and let the wife see that she respects her husband."

Mark closed his Bible. "If husbands loved their wives like Christ loved the church, there would be no divorce. Can you imagine if Christ had said, ah, forget it, I came here because I love my church but all she is going to do is crucify me? I'm giving up. I'm not gonna go through with it. Obviously she doesn't love me. She isn't going to accept me. She doesn't respect me. Why should I give up everything for her?" He paused. "Thank God he didn't, right? Instead he said, this isn't about what she does. This is on me. He knew that he had to love her through it. He had to show her that she was everything to him. Not just when she was returning his love, but when she was rebellious and unsure, when she turned her back on him and cursed him and when she pushed the sword through his side and the nails through his hands. And instead of cursing her and giving up, he asked for her to be forgiven. That, my friend, is how a man should love his wife."

Once again Ryan saw Jesus on the cross. This time he pictured himself, being willing to sacrifice everything including his own life, for Rachel. Yes, he loved her that much. Giving up was a cop out. It was easy to walk away. The idea of fighting for her scared him though. What if she rejected him? He had never been a fighter. What if he said or did the wrong things? "What if I fail?"

"You won't. If you give everything, just like Christ did, then it's up to her to accept you, just like the church must do with Christ. When he gave everything, he put the ball back in our court. By doing so he didn't fail, he made the way. You need to pave the way for Rachel to come to you. You need to show her she's welcome, wanted and most of all loved. When she sees how much you cherish her, she will find her way back. Don't give up." Mark stood up. "Speaking of wives, mine is going to kill me if I don't get back in time for the twins' baseball game. We're praying for you and Rachel both. God is going to use all this. He'll give you the strength you need to get through. Give me a call later if you need to."

"Thanks, man. I appreciate you taking the time. I know you have responsibilities and your own church to take care of."

Mark shook Ryan's hand. "Hey, we are the church. We have to be there for each other." He downed the rest of his coffee and nodded goodbye.

Ryan watched his friend leave and imagined himself leaving work to head home. He used to take the simple things for granted, like dinner on the table when he returned home. He knew he had taken advantage the last few months they were still together. Dinner was often cold by the time he got home. He didn't even bother to call to let her know he'd be late. He accused her of nagging when in truth, all she wanted was communication. He had to talk to her.

Ryan turned on the windshield wipers as fast as they would go. He grinned as he imagined Mark's boys' baseball game getting rained out. Unfortunately, the rain meant the windows had to stay up as well. *Sure is warm out this fall.* His tires sprayed water as he traveled across town. Surely she would be home in this mess. A bolt of lightning and the sound of thunder made him jump. Rachel always loved a good storm. He pulled up in front of the house. No lights were on. It looked deserted. He ran from his car to the front porch and rang the doorbell anyway. He was soaked all the way through. No answer. He rang it again, still no answer. *Why didn't I call first?*

Rachel loved thunderstorms. She closed herself off on the back screened in porch and listened to the sounds of rain pelting the metal shed roof. She deeply inhaled the sweet heady scent of roses mingling with the rain and earth. This is where she felt the closest to God. No distractions. No golfers on the course. No neighbor kids running and playing. No music blaring or barbeques taking place. Nothing but her and creation.

The leaves were already starting to turn. Soon it would be time to get her garden prepared for the long winter ahead. Not yet. She had this moment to enjoy first. She closed her eyes. A loud bolt of thunder startled her. She cocked her head, listening for another sound that was playing with her ears. Nope. Nothing.

No one understood what she had done. Well, no one except Dillon. He supported her. She had tried to explain to Jessi. It was for the best really, filing for divorce. After her talk with Shannon's counselor, she had felt she needed to make a decision. Shannon needed to be able to deal with her circumstances and take action to adjust. Of course the counselor didn't tell her to file, but it was easy to see how living in limbo was hurting Shannon as well as the rest of the family. She needed permanence if she was going to avoid being hospitalized for mutilating herself. The cutting had to stop.

Jessi had some misguided idea that Ryan would come to his senses, that he would rethink his leaving her. As much as Rachel missed having a family to take care of, she knew that once a guy decided he was gay he'd pretty much announced a woman just wouldn't do it for him. She didn't think her fragile ego could take another rejection from the same man. Besides, it didn't matter, Jessi was wrong. Rachel informed her that she wouldn't need her counseling services anymore. She was done. As much as she was thankful for her friend, it was time to move on. Time to put some things to rest.

The wind was picking up and Rachel wiped the rain that blew into her face. Sudden flashes of light revealed the trees and bushes as they flexed and swayed. Another out of place sound caught her attention. *The doorbell. Who would be out in this mess?* It's probably for one of the girls. Shelly was gone but Shannon was home. At first she ignored it, but then thought better. She opened the front door to retreating taillights. The car reminded her of Ryan's but why would he be in her neighborhood? Unless he'd already received the divorce papers. If so, that was quick. She wasn't ready to talk to him anyway. He would probably insist she sell the house so he could have his half of her inheritance.

Rachel turned on the teapot then pulled her favorite teacup from the cupboard. It had been a gift from her mother and she mainly used it when she was missing her mother's presence. Rachel would give almost anything to have her mother sitting across from her. She could use someone who loved her unconditionally. These were the times she really felt the void in her life. She breathed deeply of the rising steam. Jasmine. Her favorite.

She turned off the lights and returned to the back porch. The lightning lit up the sky as she turned to face a man staring through the back screen door. Her hands flew up sending the scalding liquid into the air and the cup to the tiled floor below. Her scream interrupted a familiar voice. "Rachel, it's me, Ryan."

She tried to still her shaking hands. "Oh heavens! You scared me to death. What are you doing back here?" She looked at broken pieces of china littering the checkerboard tile. "And Mom's cup. Ryan, look what you've done." She turned to Romeo who was lying on the floor by the door. "And you. Why didn't you warn me someone was outside our door?"

"I'm sorry. I tried the front door but no one answered. On my way home I remembered how much you love to sit back here during storms. I turned around and came back. I'm sorry, I really am. I didn't mean to frighten you." He bent down to pet Romeo's head. "Don't yell at him. He knew it was me. If it had been someone who was intending to harm you, he would have let you know."

"Well, you scared me nearly to death. I need to get this mess cleaned up before I get cut."

"Just stay where you are. As usual you're barefooted. Let me get the broom and clean it up. You'll never make it through unscathed."

She reached over and let him in. What he said made sense, even if it unnerved her to be in close proximity with the man who left her for another man.

Rachel stood completely still and waited for Ryan to return with the broom. Her emotions started coming loose at the thought of her mother's teacup being swept into the dustpan. Ryan flipped on the light and immediately Rachel noticed how much weight he had lost. Was he not eating? He'd always been fit, but he looked more like a hanger than a living breathing man. What happened?

Ryan swept the last of the remaining glass into the dustpan.

Rachel watched him as he headed for the kitchen then curled up on the love seat. She felt a prick and removed a small piece of china that had landed on the couch. She studied the china. Her mom loved this cup. It wasn't valuable, it wasn't an heirloom, but the memories attached to it were priceless. Her mother had prepared tea and allowed Rachel to use her special cup more than once. The memories were still there. She set the piece of china on the side table, nostalgia enticing her to keep a small part of the past.

Ryan quietly entered the sunroom. He watched Rachel, wondering what her thoughts were. "A penny for your thoughts."

She looked up and half smiled. "Just remembering."

The answer satisfied him. It didn't matter what part, only that she was missing the past. "Yeah, I seem to do a lot of that myself."

He sat down opposite her, in the matching wicker chair. "I got the letter today."

"I didn't think you'd get it so soon."

He nodded his head. Not really knowing what to say. "I'm sorry, Rachel. I'm sorry for everything."

This time she nodded. So much had happened, so many ugly words said. The fight had gone out of her when she filed the paperwork. There was nothing left to fight for. "Me too."

Ryan held the letter in his hand. "We don't have to do this, ya know."

Rachel lifted her eyes to meet her husbands. They were dull, lifeless, hopeless. Not the eyes he fell in love with. "Ryan, I'm not sure I have the energy to fight anymore. Our entire marriage was a lie. What purpose would we serve in going on?"

He leaned toward her. "It wasn't all a lie, in fact, the only thing I lied to you about was my past. I should have trusted you enough to tell you the truth about my life before you were a part of it, but I was afraid. I was afraid you'd never love me like I loved you. That you wouldn't give me a chance because of what I once was."

"You say that like it was over when we met. But, you sat in our living room and told me, told us, you are gay. That's not the past, Ryan. That is now."

"I know. I'm sorry. I was so confused. When Terry showed up, it threw me. He had been an intricate part of my growing up years. Terry protected me from all kinds of bullying. We had developed a bond that got me through a lot of painful experiences. When he came to me, I couldn't just turn my back. It made me question everything I had done, everything I had become. When I found out he only came because he didn't want to die alone, I felt betrayed, taken advantage of. He thought I would drop everything, you, the girls, the ministry and most importantly my faith because he needed me to hold his hand." He looked toward the floor. "And I did exactly what he asked of me." Ryan looked back up at his wife. This was the hardest thing he had ever done. He was good at running. He was good at sweeping things under the rug, but facing the issue was never easy for him. "I was wrong."

Rachel was trying to grasp the words flowing from Ryan's mouth. She stopped listening at one sentence. Terry was dying. "What do you mean, Terry is dying?"

Ryan tilted his head. "He has AIDS. He doesn't have much time left."

Rachel placed her hand over her mouth. "And this was your partner before we were married?"

"Yes, but Rachel,"

Rachel cut him off. "Do you have AIDS? Do I? What about our girls? This just keeps getting worse and worse."

"Rachel, listen to me. He got AIDS after we were together. I don't have AIDS."

"How do you know? Have you been tested? Are you sure he didn't have it before you? How much do you know about his life before you?"

Ryan let the questions sink in. She was right. He had no idea, he was a child. HIV can sit dormant in a person for years before they realize they're sick. Even then, most don't attribute their sickness to HIV. He ran his hand through his hair. He may have put his whole family at risk. "I'll go in. I'll make an appointment tomorrow and go in. I'll make sure."

"Ryan, our girls." Rachel started sobbing.

Ryan moved closer and wrapped his arms around her. Holding her felt good, it felt right. He should never have let her go. For the first time in months he felt hope. Maybe God would allow him to hold her again, this time for forever.

Rachel felt Ryan's arms go around her. How long had she longed for this? She allowed herself to be sucked into his embrace for nearly a minute before she realized what she was doing and pushed away. "Wait, no. This isn't right. You're the reason we're like this. You need to go." Anger began to surge within her and she quickly opened the door he entered through. "It's time for you to leave. Call me when you get the results."

"Rachel, I'm not giving up. I'm not going quietly on this." He clenched the paper in his fist. "I've let you down, I know that. But, for the moment I'm still your husband and I still believe in miracles. There is always hope."

Ryan walked back to his car. He did not care about the drenching he received. In fact, he felt he deserved it.

Ryan left the doctor's office, paper in hand. They would notify him when the results were in. Shouldn't be more than a couple of days. Until then, he was pretty sure he was going to have a tough time sleeping.

He pulled out his cell and called Rachel to let her know it would be a couple of days before he had any news. The chill in her voice reminded him of their pending divorce. How he thought a few minutes of intimacy could change things, he'd never know.

Could he really have been sick all these years and not know about it? He didn't think so. He wasn't ready to head to work so he started walking. He concentrated on his body and how he was feeling. He had lost weight, had lacked energy and ambition, but all that he attributed to his separation from his wife. He knew major life changes could bring about health problems too. Was he misdiagnosing himself? The thought made him shudder. He hadn't felt normal in months. How can a person tell if there is something wrong with them? Had he been walking around with a life threatening illness and not known it? *God, I know I don't deserve it, but would you please take care of this?*

Ryan sat down on a park bench and watched the leaves blow in the early fall breeze. For a while he just sat there. Then he prayed. Not the desperate prayers of a dying man, not that he hadn't prayed those in the past, but the prayer of a man getting to know his best friend once again. He looked upward. *It's been too long since our last visit. I'm sorry.*

Chapter Twenty Two

Val marched into the sanctuary. Today was the ladies meeting at her church and she'd had about enough of the gossip. These were supposed to be Godly women, women who cared about one another. Instead, they stabbed a gal in the back as soon as something bad happened. What happened to sisterly love? What happened to lifting one another up and being there for each other when times got tough? These women were worse than a bunch of cackling chickens.

She set her bag down on her chair. Yes, she was tired. And yes, she was on all kinds of medications. But enough was enough and if she held her tongue any longer, she would probably bite it off. Just because she was down for a while didn't mean she still didn't hear what was going on. And boy was she embarrassed. As long as she was still breathing she wouldn't put up with the kind of talk that had been going around.

She watched while everyone got into their little groups, chatting in small voices. She may have cancer but there wasn't a thing wrong with her ears. And the first news everyone was intent on catching up on was Rachel and Ryan. It made her even madder. "Don't you ninnies have enough to worry about without dragging a poor girl and her husband through the mud?" Every woman's face registered shock. Dorothy was the first to break her silence, although not her eye contact, and lean in to whisper to Betty.

Val called her on it. "Dorothy maybe we should be talking about when your husband had an affair with his secretary?"

Dorothy's face turned ten shades of red. She pursed her lips together.

"Not so much fun when the gossip is about you, huh?" Val started to circle the room deciding which carcass to land on next and stopped in front of Betty. "Still taking a little nip from the bottle every now and again?" She could hear the gasps from around the room and turned her head. "Still self righteous? Well, let's see what we can do about that." She startled circling once again. She was gonna have to repent later, she just knew it. "Edith, do you realize you can spray that smelly ole aerosol can till the cows come home and it isn't gonna cover up that cigarette smoke? So, next time I come over, don't bother."

"Why, I never."

"You never what? Thought anyone would have the audacity to call you out on that?"

Edith clamped her mouth shut.

"I'm just getting started. Anyone else want to spread gossip about Rachel and Ryan? Cause I have more where that came from, don't I Rose? How about you Judith? Eleanor? Anyone want me to go on?"

Eleanor's eyes grew wide silently pleading with Val to not go there. "I think we get the message, don't we ladies?"

Val allowed herself to feel compassion now that she'd made her point. "I'm not sure you do. I'm not saying we don't deal with sin. I'm not saying what is happening is right or that we should turn a blind eye to it. But, our hearts should be breaking for Rachel and Ryan. We should be on our knees praying for restoration. We shouldn't be the ones pounding the hammer. We should be here for them, supporting them. We should be reaching out just to let them know how much we love them. Do you really think Rachel will want to come back to this church? Her daddy and mama built this church from nothing. This church is as much a part of her as living and breathing. The way you have been carrying on, I'd be surprised if she ever stepped foot in here again. Is that what you want this church to be known for? For kicking our sisters and brothers when they're down?"

Val let her words sink in. "We are supposed to be a family. Not like worldly families that hurt one another and stab each other in the back, but the way God said a family should be.

Ladies, one of our own is hurting too bad for words. What are we going to do about it?"

Val watched as one by one, each lady went down in prayer. This is what the church should be doing. Not spreading gossip like the flu bug. She found her own quiet place and joined them. Her first order of business was repenting; the second was Rachel and Ryan.

The ladies spent the next hour and a half rotating between prayer and discussing the current needs of the church. As with each ladies meeting, the competition began after the praying when lunch was served. Each lady tried to out do the other with the dish she brought. Even though Val was beginning to feel zapped, she knew the offerings would be better than anything a restaurant could serve up. She had just finished filling her plate when she heard a pounding on the church's front door.

"Ugh. Probably a salesman." She unbolted the door and a microphone greeted her mouth.

"Hi, I'm Julie Prescott with Channel Five news. Is it true that your pastor was fired because he is gay?"

Val sputtered. Completely taken off guard she backed up, shut the door, and locked it. "Oh dear, Lord, help us all."

Chapter Twenty Three

He was clean. No AIDS. No HIV. He hadn't been infected. Praise God. He had thought Rachel would have been more excited to hear from him than she'd been. Yes, he heard relief on the other end of the phone but she'd cut the conversation short, making some excuse to hang up. Now what? He rested his head in his hand. "Lord, what do I do now?"

Ryan lifted his head and smiled. He would court her. When they were first dating he had wished he could do more. Well, he may not be the richest guy in the world, but he had some resources put aside. She may not have noticed it yet, but he had still been making payments on the house. She had probably been doing the same thing. It was time to let his right hand see what his left was doing. He wanted his wife back. In fact, he wanted his life back.

After making a few phone calls from his favorite park bench, Ryan left for work. "Hmm, that is strange. Wonder what News Five is doing here. No one told me about any promotions going on. I bet it's going to be busy."

He parked and headed toward the side door entrance and was accosted before he could get in.

"Mr. Bradley? I'm Julie Prescott with News Five. Is it true that you were fired from your position as the pastor of Hope Center because you came out and announced you are gay?"

"I really don't think that is any of your business." He looked toward his office and saw all his co-workers watching through the glass with grins on their faces. He probably wouldn't have a job when this was through. "I need to get to work. Please, I have no other comments."

Ryan pushed the microphone out of his face and started for the door. Ms. Prescott wasn't far behind. "Mr. Ryan, I have it on good authority that is indeed the case. I plan on running this story live. I can do it your way and run with what I have, or you can be a gentleman and let me interview you. At least your voice will be heard. What do you say?"

He turned toward her once more and considered what she was saying. Maybe she would let him say anything he wanted. Maybe, just maybe he could get Rachel's attention this way. "Tell you what. I get done with work late tonight but I'm off tomorrow. Can we meet tomorrow, say ten? I'll give you your story as long as you promise to keep it real and not distort or twist what I tell you."

Julie extended her hand. "You've got a deal, Mr. Bradley."

He could hear the chuckles as he walked into his office area. He thought he'd heard every gay joke known to man. He was certain he was going to hear some more. They wouldn't listen to anything he had to say. But, he would have a captive audience when his interview was aired. Maybe then people would listen to him.

Rachel was exhausted. Between her students, her daughters, Dillon, and the weight of Ryan's blood test results, she just wanted to draw a bath and soak then pass out for the night. Her clothes were hanging on her again and after seeing what Ryan looked like, she didn't fancy being compared to a human hanger. She flipped on the news while she made herself a sandwich. She had to eat something. Dillon had tempted her with dinner, but she was just too tired. She took a rain check.

A familiar sounding voice coming from the television caught her attention. "There you have it folks. How this has been kept under wraps for as long as it has, we'll never know. But Julie will have the full story of that pastor who was fired from his church for being gay later this week. We've already started receiving calls from all over the state, frankly from all over the country, from individuals as well as gay rights groups wanting more information on this firing. Our little town is about to attract some major national attention.

Rachel dropped the mustard knife, stunned by what she was hearing. The door bell ringing in the distance didn't register. At least until Shelly pulled on her arm, demanding her attention. "Mom, there's someone at the door for you. I think you're gonna want to get this."

"What? Oh, yeah, right. I'll be right there."

"Should I let them in?"

Rachel couldn't pry her eyes or ears from the television set. "Sure. I'll be right there."

Shelly rolled her eyes and went to open the front door. "Come on in. Mom will be right with you."

Julie glanced at her camera man, surprise etching her well made up features, then followed the young teen to the kitchen where, to her amazement, Mrs. Bradley stood watching her news channel. "Is this where you want us to set up?"

Rachel turned, confused. "Excuse me? Oh, it's you. Get out. Get out of my house."

"Mrs. Bradley, don't you want to tell your side of the story? I'm meeting with your husband, or should I say ex-husband, tomorrow. I would think you'd want to say your piece as well."

Rachel caught the image of protestors in front of her church. "Get out. I'm not saying it again." She picked up the phone to call the police.

Julie started for the front door. "Fine, we're leaving." She placed a business card on the counter. "If you change your mind, give me a call. We're going to tell this story, Mrs. Bradley. With or without you. It's your choice."

Rachel slammed the door and cut off anything else the young woman was saying. She didn't want to hear it. She turned toward Shelly. "How could you let them in this house?"

"Mom, I asked you. You said, sure. I thought you heard me."

"You could have told me it was newscasters."

"What is going on? Why are they protesting at our church?"

Rachel started crying. "Oh, Honey. I didn't think anyone would notice. We're such a small church. We're not on anyone's radar. How did they find out and more importantly, why do they care?"

"You   mean   about   Dad?"

Rachel nodded her head. "Yes, about your father. About us. About our church. About our faith. Who gave them permission to drag our private lives into the living rooms of the whole community? This is hard enough."

"Mom, what did she mean when she called Dad your ex-husband?"

This was not how she wanted her girls to find out. There was nothing she could do now. All three of her girls would know before the week was out. She had to do damage control. "Honey, I filed for divorce."

Shelly's face went white. "You what? But why?"

"Why do you think? Have you seen your father around here lately? I would think the answer to that question is obvious."

Shannon bounded down the stairs, entering the kitchen in a whirlwind. "Who was at the door?"

Rachel and Shelly looked at each other. Even though they sometimes didn't see eye to eye, they still understood one another better than the others. Rachel responded. "It was News Five. They wanted to ask me questions about your father and our church."

Shannon was stunned. "You mean, this is going to be on the news? But, why?"

Rachel shook her head. "I guess they consider this news. Especially since the whole nation is in a spiritual tug of war on this subject. When a Bible believing, fundamental pastor announces he is gay and leaves his post, it becomes news."

Shannon turned to the television, which was recapping the protestors at the church. "Why are they protesting?"

"They seem to think your father was fired and that is discrimination."

"But, he quit."

"You know that and I know that. Unfortunately, the gossips who drew attention to this didn't clarify that he'd quit. Besides, he never told the church why he was quitting. He only told the four of us. How News Five found out is beyond me."

Shelly joined the conversation. "Mom, you know we've all told someone. You've talked with Jessi and Mark, I've talked with Emily. Shannon's at least told her counselor and who knows how many people Sam's told. She's probably bragged about it to anyone who would listen."

"I suppose. It was naïve of me to think we could keep this in the family. I guess we're going to have deal with it. I need to call your father. I'm gonna go upstairs." Rachel took a look at her dried out sandwich and threw it away.

"Mom? I'll make dinner, okay?"

"Thanks Shelly. I appreciate it."

Rachel tentatively dialed the phone. She had let her last encounter with Ryan shake her up. She didn't need to complicate her emotions. She had just made the decision to put the exclamation point on the end of their relationship then he shows up on the scene showing regret. She couldn't take that. She didn't want it. Not now. It was too late.

She breathed a sigh of relief when she got his voicemail. "Ryan, it's Rachel. Please give me a call. I really hope you didn't start this three-ring circus. I just don't need this right now." She ended the call then looked out her bedroom window, across the street toward Dillon's house. She could use a shoulder to lean on about now. She picked up her phone and pressed number two on speed dial.

"Hi there."

"Hi yourself."

"Is that you peeking out your bedroom window?"

"I sure hope so. I couldn't imagine who it might be otherwise."

"I saw the news van pull in. Any thing I should know about?"

"Yeah. About that. Things might get crazy around here for a while. Shelly is making dinner. Mind if I come over for a little while? I could use an ear and a shoulder."

"My ear and shoulder are yours. I'll be waiting."

Rachel smelled garlic and felt her stomach protest. Nerves were not good on her appetite. She descended the stairs as Shelly placed the pasta bowl on the table.

"Hey, you're just in time. Angel hair pasta with garlic cream sauce and a tossed salad. Best I could do on short notice and a near bare cupboard."

"It smells wonderful. I'll get your sister."

All three sat around the table, mostly pushing their food around on their plates. All three tiptoeing around the events of the evening.

Shannon ventured into the shark-infested waters. "Did you get a hold of Dad?"

"No, I left a message for him. He's probably working."

Shannon nodded her head and allowed silence to reside over the dinner table.

Rachel took a few bites, thankful for her daughter's attempt at bringing normalcy to their lives. Shelly excused herself then Shannon followed suit, leaving Rachel in the company of a wood salad bowl and her over sized pasta bowl. She cleaned up the mess and refrigerated the leftovers before heading to Dillon's. She left a note in case either of the girls came looking for her, although she doubted that would happen.

He was waiting for her with a glass of wine.

Rachel sipped from the glass before softly kissing his lips. "Hmmm, you taste like wine."

Dillon closed his eyes. He did not want to consider what she tasted like. She wasn't his. Not yet. "Come on. Tell me about your night."

Rachel kicked off her slip ons and tucked her feet underneath her. She breathed deeply, the scent of the wine soothing her nerves. When did having a glass of wine with Dillon become normal? She didn't remember when she went from declining the soothing liquid to expecting it. So much had changed. October had turned windy and cold. Before she knew it, Thanksgiving would be knocking on their door. The holidays were going to be the worst. How would they all get through them? She lifted her face and remembered the question Dillon had asked then told him about it all.

He wrapped his arm around her and pulled her close. "Everything is going to work out, you know that, right?"

She sighed. "Sometimes I wonder. The holidays are almost here. I worry about the girls, especially Shannon. She's so insecure. Sometimes I feel like she's going to shatter into a million pieces and I'll never be able to put her together again. I have nightmares of her sitting on the wall then falling. I can hear the chanting in the background. 'Shannon Bradley sitting on the wall. Shannon Bradley had a great fall.' And I'm the one who couldn't put her together again. I startle awake, shaking. Some nights it takes me a while to get back to sleep."

"Tell you what. Next time you have that nightmare, call me and I'll talk till you fall back asleep, okay?" He tilted her face so he could see her eyes. "I'm here for you, Rachel."

"Thank you, Dillon. You have no idea how much that means to me."

"I have an idea. Maybe we can go away for Christmas. Maybe a change of scenery would help everyone get through the holidays without incident." He thought for a moment. "Do you guys like to ski?"

"Yeah, we do. I'm not very good at it, but as long as I have a bunny hill I'll be content."

"Well, I have some friends back in Colorado with a gorgeous cabin in the mountains. Why don't I give them a call and see if it's available over Christmas. I think it would be good for all of us."

"Oh Dillon. I'd love that. I won't say anything until you know for sure. I know Shelly will be ecstatic. I'm guessing Sam won't want to go. She'd probably only come down for Christmas day and then she'd want to be with her father. Shannon could go either way." Just the thought of getting away brought tears to her eyes.

"Hey, I was hoping to make you happy, not sad."

"I am happy. I just hadn't given any real thought to getting away. Just the idea of it makes me feel lighter."

"Well, would it make you feel better if I give them a call now?" He glanced at his watch. "It's only eight thirty there."

"Could you?"

He took his arm from around her and went into his office. Rachel could hear his voice but couldn't make out what he was saying. As he returned to the family room, the grin on his face said it all. "It's all ours. Five bedrooms. A floor to ceiling stone fireplace. A wall of glass, the only thing separating us from the grandest views nature has to offer. A gourmet kitchen where I will cook for you and your lovely daughters. Plenty of room for all of us, no matter who decides to go. Oh, and don't forget your swimsuit. There is a hot tub on the deck. I'll look into making flight arrangements once we know who is going. It'll be my Christmas present to your family."

"Oh Dillon. It sounds like heaven." She cuddled back up in his arms, relaxed and at peace. If only every moment of everyday could be like this. She noticed the wine helped too. Maybe she'd pick up a bottle for home. After an hour of making plans and drinking wine, Rachel unfolded herself from Dillon's arms and picked up the wine bottle. "Mind if I take the rest of this with me? I'm gonna sink into a hot bath and this just seems to fit."

"You're gonna kill me, you know that? Yes, take the wine." He leaned in and gently kissed her. It would be so easy to take advantage of her like this. With every sip of wine her inhibitions took flight. "Go, before I do something I'll be sorry for, we'll both be sorry for."

Flirting with her smile, she had no idea the wine turned her simple flirt into something sultry and provocative. She'd never played with alcohol before. She had no idea how easy it would be to be bad.

Dillon sent her out the door with her bottle and watched her turn toward him from the middle of the street. He motioned for her to keep going. It would have been so easy to take her to his bed. She was playing with fire and didn't know it. He wasn't sure he wanted to tell her.

155

Chapter Twenty Four

Mark entered the shelter, this time by invitation. It seemed Terry had decided to hear him out after all.

Marie was waiting for him in her office. "Well, hello there Pastor Mark. How are you today?"

"I'm doing pretty well. How about yourself?"

"About as good as expected. There's something to be said for that when you're almost seventy."

"Almost seventy? I wouldn't have put you a day over thirty."

She cast him a sideways smirk. "You keep flirting and I'm gonna have a talk with your wife."

He laughed and lifted his hands. "Fine. I'll behave, promise."

"It seems Terry has had a change of heart. It's funny how that happens. The closer to death they become, the more willing they are to listen. Not everyone accepts Christ before they die, mind you. But some do. We have to try, right?"

Mark nodded his head. The moment for laughter had passed.

She motioned for him to sit then sat beside him. "Let's pray before you go up. He's in a bad way. Stubborn, that one. I wasn't altogether sure he'd ever agree to see you."

Mark bowed his head and let Marie take the lead. She'd been working with AIDS patients for years and although he'd known her but a short time, he knew and recognized the spirit of love radiating from her. That kind of love only came from one place, Christ. He listened to her voice. She'd been talking to her Savior for many years and was comfortable in his presence. He could always tell.

"Father, you already know why we're calling on your name. Your word says only the Holy Spirit can draw a man unto himself. We are but tools, vessels to be used at your discretion. I pray for Terry. I pray that you would ready his heart to accept and embrace you. I pray for Mark, for the wisdom and sensitivity required to reach this man who has been hurt so terribly. I pray for a connection, a relationship to be formed between these two men. Father, I pray that Terry sees Jesus in Mark. I pray he recognizes the great love you have for him and that he does not have to spend eternity alone and in pain. Father, reveal yourself to him in the precious name of Jesus. Amen."

Mark felt Marie squeeze his hand then opened his eyes and nodded his head.

She stood up. "His room is upstairs to the right, third door on the left. He's expecting you. He's but a shell of his former self, so don't be too surprised." She started to walk toward her desk then turned. "I'll be praying for the both of you."

The stairs were wide and curved upward toward a sitting area on the landing. Mark noticed the over stuffed chairs and shelves of reading material. What an inviting place. He'd have been distracted himself had he not remembered why his palms were a sweaty mess. He wiped them on his jeans then turned to his right, counting doors as he walked the hallway. He reached the third door on his left and lightly knocked. He heard a weak man's voice coming from the other side and took that as permission to enter.

The man lying on the bed couldn't be the same vibrant protector Ryan had told him about. His skin was nearly translucent, simply a light covering for his bone structure. His face was hollow. His eyes only housed fear and pain. And there was a sadness about him, a lack of hope that can only come from a person close to death and fearful of eternity. Mark tried to hide his surprise, his discomfort. Remaining stoic was more difficult than he'd imagined. He watched as Terry searched him for signs of repulsion. *Lord, help me be you.* He extended his hand and introduced himself. "Hi, I'm Mark Jenson. A friend of Ryan's."

157

Terry didn't say anything. He watched this man who was clearly out of his comfort zone. Sure, he knew he was a pastor and he'd probably seen death hundreds of times, but Terry was betting he'd never been this close to a dying gay man with AIDS before. Most pastors just didn't go there.

Mark waited for him to say something, anything, but the man continued to study him with his eyes as if all the answers to the questions were found beneath the skin and eyes this close to death could see that deep. Mark felt in his spirit that he should remain still, remain quiet, so he took a seat near the bed and waited. Clearly this man was looking for something. Mark quietly prayed.

Ten minutes had passed. Terry was impressed. If he'd come to save his soul he wasn't in a hurry to do his Christian duty and leave. "So, you're a friend of Ryan's?"

Mark nodded. "Yes, I am."

Terry knew if he asked him why Mark had come, he'd start preaching so he avoided that. He wanted someone to talk to, someone to remind him he was alive. Even if a preacher wasn't his first choice, there sure weren't many people lining up at the door so he'd take what he could get. "Do you have a family?"

"I do. My wife Jessi and we have four children."

"Four huh? That's a bunch."

"Yeah, it is. They keep us on our toes."

"How old?"

"Well, our oldest, Ethan, would have been seventeen this year but he died in a car accident when he was five. Our daughter is twelve and the twins, both boys, are six."

"Man, sorry about your oldest. That's harsh."

Mark nodded. *Was this the open door he was supposed to walk through?*

Terry continued to dominate the conversation. Mark continued to let him. It didn't take long before Terry's eyelids starting blinking in slow motion so Mark stood to leave. He quietly walked toward the closed door.

"Will you come back?"

"Do you want me to?"

"Yeah, I do. You're not what I expected."

"Would tomorrow at the same time be okay?"

Terry attempted a laugh. "It's not like I'm going anywhere."

"All right then, I'll see you tomorrow."

Mark sat down in Marie's office and took the cup of coffee she offered. He was disappointed. He'd not shared the love of Christ like they'd prayed for and time was growing short. One look at the man and it was obvious he wouldn't be around too much longer. He shook his head.

The man sitting on Marie's settee may be a pastor, he may have experienced a lot of heartache, but he sure had a lot to learn. "Don't be too hard on yourself. Did he reject you?"

"No, not really. We just didn't talk about anything of importance. I mean, we talked about the differences in Wisconsin and Illinois. The states he'd traveled through. We discussed my family. What he did for a living. Everything but the really important stuff."

"I see." Marie poured her tea and stirred in some sugar. Many had told her that she shouldn't use the white stuff but old habits were hard to put to rest. Besides, she was seventy. What harm could it do now? She sipped the hot fluid and closed her eyes. How could someone be so smart yet so dumb? She set the fine porcelain cup on its saucer and sat down in the chair opposite Mark. "Did God share everything with you the day you got   saved?"

"Excuse me?"

"Did you know everything there is to know about God, or at least the really important stuff the day you met him?"

"Well, of course not."

"Exactly. He didn't tell you everything the first day he met you, even though he knew you were dying and on the road to hell. He gave you a little at a time. He gave you the chance to get to know him before he sprung the hard stuff on you. He gave you an opportunity to build a relationship. That is what you must do with Terry if you want to earn his trust and his ear. He may listen to you if he knows you are concerned with all of him, not just his mortal soul. He doesn't know yet how unimportant this body is. To him, it's everything. It represents all the hurts and lost possibilities. It causes him pain and heartache. Yet, with every tear he holds on because his body is all he has to hold on to. He has no hope. This is it, in his eyes, the end of the road. You must show him you care about him, all of him, then maybe he'll trust you to lead his soul."

Mark thought about what she said as he drove toward home. He knew this, he knew how important relationships were, but because time was short he had wanted to rush into witnessing to him. What if he died before he had the chance to try to present him with the truth? He would have to trust God to know what he was doing. What was the alternative?

Chapter Twenty Five

Rachel groaned when the alarm clock went off. Her throat felt like it was on fire. She sipped from the water glass sitting on the nightstand. *Ugh. I feel terrible.* She called Dillon to let him know he was going to have to handle classes today without her. She loved her job, loved working with the kids, but she knew the signs and ten to one she had strep. She'd be seeing her doctor today.

She made an appointment for early afternoon, turned off her phone then cuddled back up in her comforter. Sleep was what she needed. Everything else would have to wait.

Ryan arranged to watch the broadcast with Rachel and the girls. He even asked Sam to come home for the occasion. He remembered his afternoon with Julie well. He had spent three hours with the newswoman, going over his story, clarifying his story, and correcting her as she recapped his story. By the time they finished he was satisfied she would do him justice. She didn't seem the type of person who would purposefully sabotage anyone. Nor did she seem a spiteful person. He looked at his watch. It was supposed to be on the six o'clock news. He always thought it rather catchy they called themselves News Five at Six. Just a little over eight hours to go. He shouldn't have taken off work. He would have had plenty of time to get to the house before the news started. Then again there were no guarantees. It was better to be safe than sorry. *Lord, this is it. This is the door you opened. Thank you for this opportunity.*

Rachel left the pharmacy with her prescription in hand. *Eww. Antibiotics that smell like rotten eggs are just wrong.* She swallowed the nasty smelling pill then set her water bottle in its holder. As she headed back home for bed, she remembered Ryan was coming over to watch the news. She really didn't want to watch the lady reporter who had invaded her home, but apparently this was big news and was going to solve all their problems. All she really wanted to do was sleep. She glanced at her watch. At least he said he'd bring pizza. That gave her enough time to take a nap before the news started. She drove into the garage and headed straight for bed. She resisted the urge to down her nighttime cold medicine, at least until the news was over. She pulled the comforter up around her chin and closed her eyes.

"Mom, hey, it's time to get up. Dad's here."

Rachel opened her eyes to her youngest daughter's hopeful stare then shut them again. *Already?* "Okay, I'll be right down." *At least it's only a half an hour.*

She pulled her sweats over her pajama pants, pulled her hair into a ponytail and stumbled down the stairs and onto her favorite chair. She put her feet on the ottoman. This is where she'd stay. She wasn't waiting on anyone. They could take care of themselves. The smell of pizza enticed her but swallowing would be an issue so she ignored it. Shelly brought her a large bottle of cold water. She croaked out her thanks and took a long swallow. The cold felt good on her throat.

The introduction music from the news program caught everyone's attention so they all filed into the living room with their pizza and soda. Rachel was surprised, it actually felt like old times. It wasn't too long ago she would have done anything to see all of them spread around the living room. She wasn't sure that was the case anymore.

The newscasters were straightening papers on their desk, smiling and chatting while the music played. The anchorman looked into the camera just as the music was fading. "Good evening. I'm Jared Mitchell with News Five at Six." Everyone listened attentively as he and his co-anchor highlighted a few world news stories. "Now for your local news. Julie Prescott is standing by with our human interest story. Julie?"

"Thank you, Jared. I'm here in this blue-collar town where life idles by, neighbors know one another and there is a church on every street corner, well, maybe not every corner but close. It's on such a corner that we find Hope Center, a small community church where up until recently this man, Pastor Ryan Bradley, was the pastor. Everything changed the day Mr. Bradley decided he could no longer go on living a lie. It was here he traded in a primarily homophobic life for a life of truth and courage."

Ryan watched in horror as the camera slowly panned the church and protesters rang out their demands, wanting his position restored. The scene changed as he recognized his eldest daughter, Sam, being interviewed.

"My dad can't help who he is. It would be a travesty if he weren't allowed to continue preaching because someone so long ago twisted scripture. It isn't fair really. And it's not how my God operates. My God loves everyone and wants everyone just as they are. God is love."

Sam was beaming. He cast his daughter a questioning look as she took a small bite of her pizza. She just shrugged.

He turned back to the television and didn't recognize the man on the screen until she introduced him. "Oh no."

Julie was interviewing Terry, who was emaciated beyond recognition. "This is Terry Schmidt, Ryan's partner since their adolescent years. Terry is dying of AIDS. What should have been a long, healthy relationship for both men ended in travesty for Terry when Ryan found religion. Because modern day Christianity dictates homosexuality a sin, Ryan felt compelled to leave his soul mate in exchange for a life of bitterness and regret. Terry, despondent and depressed, regrettably lived a life in and out of relationships, trying to find someone that would make him forget his one true love. This is the price hate crimes breed."

Julie turned toward the camera. "I believe Ryan Bradley says it best." The camera panned to him. "I was so young. He was there for me through the hard times. I came to depend on him, at first our relationship was like that of two brothers, a protector if you will. Then our bond developed into much more than that. I'm so sorry for what I have done."

The next scene was Julie, once again, in front of the church. "We tried to interview Mrs. Bradley but she denied us an interview. We have since learned that Mrs. Bradley has indeed filed for divorce and has also left the church of her upbringing since the firing of her husband. The elders of Hope Center have also denied us an interview. It truly is a sad day in America when a man is discriminated against for something he has no control over. We can only hope for a better tomorrow. Back to you, Jared."

Ryan was speechless. He turned to Rachel who had tears streaming down her face. "That is not what I said. She, she twisted it. She mixed it up. We talked for hours. I thought she would tell the truth."

Rachel watched her family through her tears. Shelly was holding onto Shannon and both girls were crying. This was supposed to make everything better, not worse. Neither Sam nor Shannon knew about the divorce until now. What a way to find out. Sam was looking smug, like she had a secret. "Sam? What is going on?"

"What do you mean?"

Rachel didn't have the energy for games. Her throat was on fire and she could barley talk above a whisper. "Sam, I'm not in the mood."

"Fine. I know Julie. I know her from church. I told her about you and Dad. She's a good friend of mine and she just wanted to help Dad. She understands, really she does. She knows what it's like to be denied love because of religious beliefs."

The look on his daughter's face made him want to slap her. "Your friend twisted every word I said. Your friend is a liar."

"Dad, she only wanted to help you. She didn't want you feeling pressured and bullied by the religious establishment any longer. She knows the pressure you're under to conform. They want to change you, to hold you down. We both knew you needed help staying true to yourself." Sam started for the kitchen then stopped. "Look, we can read between the lines. You're beginning to feel guilty, like you made the wrong decision, but you didn't. You'll find happiness again. And Mom will be happy with Dillon. This is all for the best. The traditional church has gone too far with its message of hate. I hate to eat and run but I have to get back." Sam placed her plate on the counter and let herself out through the garage door.

Ryan turned to Rachel. "Rach, please, let me explain."

"Ryan, not now. I am so embarrassed I'm not sure I can show my face in this town again."

Shannon screamed out. "You, you're embarrassed? What about me? My whole family is on the six o'clock news, my dad is gay, my mom has filed for divorce and already in another relationship and the church I grew up in is being picketed. You think you're life is ruined?" She ran, sobbing, up the stairs.

Shelly just held her knees and rocked, quietly crying. "I guess that's it then. I can stop imagining you will get back together. It's over, right?" She wiped her eyes and followed after her sister.

Rachel stood up. "You know how to let yourself out." She followed her daughters upstairs and left Ryan standing in the living room.

Ryan looked around the room and raised his fist to God. "You, you did this. I thought you loved me. I thought you were going to fix this." He dropped to his knees and sobbed. It was over. There was no hope.

Chapter Twenty Six

Rachel removed the lid from the roaster oven and basted the stuffed turkey. The whole house smelled like Thanksgiving. The sweet potato soufflé was baking in the oven. The cranberry salad was made. Vegetables were in the steamer. The rolls were rising and would go in last. Dillon was bringing the mashed potatoes, green bean casserole and two pies, pumpkin and pecan. Rachel and Shelly made an apple pie as well as a blueberry pie.

The table was set for six with her fall tablecloth and matching napkins. Rachel loved using her harvest serving dishes. She prayed dinner went well. During dessert, she and Dillon were going to tell the kids about going to Colorado for Christmas. Hopefully that went well. She had already talked with Ryan and they decided that Shelly and Shannon should both go to Colorado. He had no idea how long Terry would hold on. Besides that, he would be working long hours in the pre-Christmas rush and wouldn't be around much. Mark and Jessi invited him to spend Christmas day with them. Rachel had to admit, she felt a little jealous. Given the circumstances, she understood. At least she would be with the people she loved. It wouldn't be right for Ryan to be alone on Christmas. The girls would celebrate with him the week before.

She pulled out the sweet potatoes just as the doorbell rang. "Shannon, can you get that?"

"Yeah. Sure. Why not?"

Rachel gave her daughter a warning look and turned back to the oven. The rolls were next. They looked perfect.

Dillon and Jacob walked in with full hands. "Good thing we live so close. It's freezing out there. If we'd had to go any farther, the potatoes would have gotten cold."

"Just put the food on the table. There are some hot pads ready."

"Dillon, would you help me put the turkey on the platter?"

"Sure thing." He took a deep breath. "Smells delicious."

She used the turkey drippings to make the gravy, pulled the rolls out then sat down to dinner. The two combined families were seated around the table. Even Sam came home for the occasion. They bowed their heads and Rachel prayed a simple prayer of thanksgiving.

Dinner was a success. The food was fantastic. Everyone got along. Rachel was hoping that was a good sign, that the girls would be excited for the trip. The group voted to put off dessert until after the dishes were done. Shelly and Jacob went downstairs to play pool while Shannon and Sam retreated to their upstairs bedrooms, leaving Rachel and Dillon to do the dishes. "No wonder they wanted to wait for dessert. What ever happened to the cook resting while everyone else did dishes?" Truth be told, she didn't mind cleaning up. Especially since Dillon was working by her side. "Are you nervous?"

Dillon leaned against the countertop and pondered her question. "No, not really." He took the dishtowel from her hands and pulled her toward him. "This is about us. This is about you getting a break from everything going on. If the kids are supportive, well, it'll be a bonus. If not, then they'll have to deal with it. I am looking forward to having you to myself for a whole week." He bent down and gently kissed her lips. "And I'm not going to let them spoil our fun."

She laid her head against his shoulder. "You have no idea how good that sounds."

"Now that ,my love, is where you are wrong. I know exactly how good it sounds."

Rachel eyed the pies sitting on the counter. "Well, it's time to see who is supportive and who isn't." She put the apple pie in the oven on warm while she sliced the pumpkin, pecan and blueberry pies. "I have never liked pumpkin pie. Isn't that weird?"

"That means there'll be more for me."

She picked up her phone and texted her girls. "Sometimes modern conveniences are a blessing. Much easier than yelling for them."

They heard Shelly and Jacob's feet pounding the stairs from the basement. "I think those two will be supportive."

She nodded in agreement. "I think you're right. It's Shannon who concerns me the most."

He squeezed her hand. "Time will tell."

Jacob and Shelly raced for the counter. It was good to hear laughter in the house. "That was close. I'm not sure who won."

Shelly held her side. "Clearly I did."

Jacob was quick to defend his efforts. "Yeah, I don't think so. I beat you by a mile."

Shelly grabbed a piece of blueberry pie. "You don't exaggerate much do you?" She turned toward Rachel. "Mom, can we take our pie downstairs? We're in the middle of a game of pool and I'm winning. I don't want to lose my touch."

"Well, actually, we want to talk to you kids about something. So, let's sit at the table."

Shelly cocked her head and questioned her mom with her eyes. Rachel just smiled and slightly shook her head no.

Shelly acknowledged the look that passed between them and sat down at the table. Shannon entered the kitchen and chose a piece of pumpkin and Sam texted Rachel back telling her she was on a diet. "I'll be right back. Seems my oldest is going to be difficult."

Dillon called after her. "Do you want apple with ice cream?"

"Yeah, that'd be great."

It wasn't long before Rachel returned to the dining room with Sam in tow. Rachel sat down next to Dillon. He began. "We have a surprise for you."

Shannon gasped and about choked on her pie.

Rachel stepped in. "Calm down and listen Shannon. I think you're going to like this." She nodded to Dillon to continue.

"We're all going to Colorado for Christmas. We have a beautiful cabin in the mountains. Unlimited skiing. Gorgeous scenery." He looked at each of the kids. "Merry Christmas."

Shelly squealed. "Really? We're really going to the mountains for Christmas?"

Jacob piped in. "Oh, you better get your game on. I'm so beating you down the mountain."

Shelly ran for the basement door. "In your dreams!"

Jacob followed, laughing and telling her all about Colorado.

Rachel yelled after them. "So, you approve?"

"Uh, yeah, Mom. I can't wait to tell Emily."

Sam was next. "I'm sorry to be such a downer, but I already made plans for Christmas. I hope you don't mind. I'm going with a friend to Jamaica." *with a male or female friend?*

Sam seems very secretive

Having already figured this would happen, Rachel forced a smile. "You know I'll miss having you with us for Christmas, but I understand. You're growing up and have a life of your own. Just be safe, okay?"

"I will. We're meeting some other friends there. Just hanging out away from all the drama, ya know. I'll be fine." She kissed her mother's cheek. "I'm sure you'll have fun. You be safe too." She started to walk away then turned back to her mother. "I've decided to go back tonight. I hope you don't mind. I know I'll miss the monopoly tournament but I have to work in the morning. You know, black Friday and all. Everyone is required to work at some point in the day. Gotta love retail."

Rachel watched Sam as she walked up the stairs. "When did she grow up?" She felt a protective hand cover hers and remembered Shannon was still sitting at the table with a half eaten piece of pie. "Well, what do you think Shannon?"

"I think I'll stay here with Dad. If you don't mind that is. I mean, I am a grown up too, right?"

"Your dad and I already talked about it and we decided it would be best if you go with us to Colorado."

"What? I'm almost twenty years old. Why do you get to decide for me?"

169

"I think you know why. Until your therapist decides you are no longer a threat to yourself, you are under your father's and my care. Unless you'd like to spend the holidays in a facility?"

"Well, why can't I stay with Dad? I'd be in his care."

"He figured he'd be working a lot due to the shopping season. He doesn't want you alone in his tiny little apartment. And we think the change of scenery would do you good."

"Mom, I don't want to go."

Rachel sighed. "I'll talk to your dad. But, I'm not promising anything."

Shannon took the hope that was offered and returned to her room.

Dillon poured Rachel a glass of wine. "Maybe it wouldn't be such a bad thing if she stayed here."

Rachel rested her head in her hands then looked at Dillon before responding. "Does it make me a horrible mother to agree with you?"

"No. It makes you human. You can only take so much."

"What if I offer to let Ryan stay in the guest room here? That way Shannon will at least be home. I work all day, too, so it's not like she has to be babysat all day. I just don't want her hurting herself out of depression while we're gone." She took a large swallow of her wine. "Whether she admits it or not, she likes having us all around. It gives her a sense of security."

"Do you think you should talk to her counselor about it?"

"That's a good idea. We'll wait to make a decision until then. But, Colorado is around the corner. I can't wait to go." Rachel felt the warm tingling sensation she experienced when she drank wine, which was more and more often. She liked how it muted the voices pounding in her head, demanding her attention. She leaned back, content in her relaxed state and closed her eyes. She opened them when she felt Dillon's gaze upon her. "Yes?"

He reached over and ran his fingertips along her cheek. "You are so beautiful."

She tilted her cheek into the palm of his hand, the warmth adding to the rush from the wine. "Shall we move into the living room, by the fire?"

He took her hand and helped her to her feet then followed her to the couch with the wine in hand. "I love a warm fire on these cool evenings. This is what home is all about." He snuggled in close and held her hand. She laid her head on his shoulder, enjoying the moment.

"Mom?"

Rachel adjusted slightly trying to see Sam who was standing behind her. "You leaving?"

"Uh, yeah. I'm ready to go. You look comfy." Sam leaned over the back of the couch and kissed her mom's cheek. The advantages of having an open living space meant you could spy on your mom and her boyfriend for a moment from behind before making your presence known. *Looks as if things are progressing quickly with these two. Maybe Dad will be free to live his life as it was intended.*

Rachel started to get up and Sam stopped her. "Mom, you don't have to get up. It's all good. I'm leaving now anyway. Just stay where you are."

"Okay, I love you. Drive safe."

"I will. I'll make sure to come home the weekend before you leave for Colorado. We'll talk about plans later, k?"

"Sounds good."

Rachel listened to Sam's car start then settled back in, enjoying the close proximity to Dillon. She breathed deeply, memorizing his scent. "You smell good."

He chuckled. "So do you. You smell like apple pie, turkey and stuffing and I could just eat you up." He playfully nuzzled her as he tickled her sides. She laughed and pushed his hands away. She turned her head at the same moment he turned to look at her. Their faces were a mere inch apart and suddenly the mood was serious. She leaned toward him, kissing him before she had time to think. This time the kiss was much more than innocent affection. It was a kiss that promised more than either of them were ready for and more than Rachel was free to give.

Shelly and Jacob chose that moment to enter with the monopoly board. "Ahem. Kids in the room."

Rachel whispered. "Perfect timing, wouldn't you say?"

Dillon knew he was wearing the truth all over his face. "Definitely."

Chapter Twenty Seven

Val was restless. She could feel a pull in her spirit to get on her knees. Rachel had been on her mind more and more and she felt an urgency in her to pray on Thanksgiving. She couldn't put her finger on it, but she knew the Holy Spirit was leading her so she had to obey. She finished putting the leftovers in the refrigerator while Herbert was talking to Ryan in the living room. They had invited him when they had inadvertently found out he was spending Thanksgiving alone.

She hadn't made a feast like years previous, but she did manage to bake a stuffed turkey and make a pumpkin pie. The rest came out of boxes. There was only so much she could do. There were no complaints as far as she could tell. Both men were nursing the cups of coffee they'd had with their pie. She kissed Herbert and let him know she was going to her room for a while. Of course, he would understand she needed a nap but she didn't want to alarm Ryan so she let him think it. She did need a nap and maybe when she received a release, she would indulge and lay down for a while. She didn't like to mislead her husband.

Once in her room, she pulled a couple of pillows onto the carpet and knelt down by her bed. Her heart literally hurt in her chest. The constant flow of tears brought about relief. "Lord, what is happening? Show me." Val prayed through her tears, through the pain. Her girl was in trouble, that much she knew. "Lord, protect her. Keep your angels all around her. Don't let the enemy have his way with her, Lord. Reveal truth to her. Open her eyes. Give her understanding. Oh Father, I know how much you love her. She's playing with fire right now. She's venturing in waters too deep and too dangerous. Only you can protect her, Lord. Only you can lead her to safety."

Val prayed until she could pray no more. Exhaustion won and she crawled into her bed. She knew the situation wasn't resolved, but she also knew her Lord was bigger than anything the enemy could throw. There was no question who would win. The question was, how much damage would be done before the war was over?   She closed her eyes and dreamt of angels and demons in full warfare. The prize was a family on the brink of destruction. Who would win? Who would claim this family as the prize? Val tossed and turned, inhibited yet somehow free by all the armor she wore in her dream. She was fighting alongside the angels. She was growing weary. An angel of death lunged at her as she opened her eyes. She purposefully slowed her breathing.

Val felt one lonely tear escape as it turned cool upon her pillow. She whispered toward heaven. "Lord, who? Me or Rachel?"

Chapter Twenty Eight

Rachel removed the last Christmas box from the storage space in the basement. Shelly, Shannon and Jacob were taking them upstairs as she dug them out. She wiped a spider web off her jeans. She and Dillon had decided that both families would decorate her house for the holidays. It made sense as they would be celebrating the week before Christmas with Sam and it worked out that Ryan was going to stay at the house with Shannon. Besides, Rachel hated the idea of not decorating. Even knowing she was going to be gone for the actual day, she still wanted to spend the better part of December enjoying her decorations.

She followed Jacob as he carried the last box for her. "What time did your dad say he'd be here?"

"Should be any minute now. He had a few errands to run. If you want to know what I think, I'm guessing he went Christmas shopping." Jacob tripped on the stair and almost fell. "Oh, he said he'd bring lunch so don't make anything."

"I was just going to order pizza, so that works." Rachel laid the wreath on the table. "Have you cut down a Christmas tree before?"

"No, my mom never really went all out for the holidays. She was always too busy. We still celebrated, I mean, she got me gifts and all, but we didn't do the tree thing or the lights. She always said it was a pagan celebration anyway."

Rachel made a mental note to ask Dillon about that later. "Just put that box on the stack over in the corner. We'll go through them later."

Rachel moved to the stove to make a thermos of hot chocolate while Jacob went in search of Shelly. Manhattan

Steamroller was playing in the background and she was humming along to the melody of God Rest Ye Merry Gentlemen when cold hands pressed against the back of her neck. She shrieked. "Dillon, you almost made me drop the thermos."

"Are you sure you want to go out in the woods in this cold?"

"Dillon, are you getting cold feet?"

"Getting? No. I already have cold feet. You want to feel those, too?"

"Oh sure, you can ski all day in the snow but you can't go cut down a Christmas tree?"

"Okay, okay. You got me. I give up. Can we eat first?"

"Well, that depends on what you brought for lunch." Rachel raised her eyebrows trying to decipher the smells coming from the brown paper bags sitting on her counter.

Dillon began pulling cartons of Chinese food out of the bags. "Does this answer your question?"

"It does. And by all means, we can eat first." She leaned in and allowed her lips to linger on his. "Thank you."

"You're welcome. If I knew that would be my reward I'd bring Chinese home every night. You want me to call the kids?"

She kissed him again. "Why don't we wait a minute? Those cartons keep the food hot, don't they?"

Dillon pulled himself away. The bolder she got the harder it was to control himself. He had to put some distance between the two of them. "I'm getting the kids. We'll run out of daylight if we don't get moving. You want to get that tree, don't you?"

Rachel pretended to pout. "Fine. I'll get out the plates."

Dillon sighed a breath of relief. It wasn't that he didn't desire her physically, he did, more than he had a right to. He was still unsure of her intentions and whether or not she would actually go through with the divorce. One moment he was sure she was his, then he'd catch her with this far away look in her eyes, like she was longing for something, or someone in the past. He called for Jacob and Shelly.

The three teens loaded up their plates and talked all at once. Even Shannon seemed to be enjoying herself. Rachel took a bite of her eggroll. "I love these things." She opened another little box. "Cashew Chicken. My favorite."

Dillon marveled at how she was so easy to please. "You have a lot of favorites, don't you?"

"I do. Especially when it comes to Chinese food."

Coats, hats, mittens, gloves, boots and wool socks were flying around the room. "I'm sure we have enough to outfit an army. There's bound to be something here that will work for everyone."

Once everyone was dressed like they were going to the North Pole, they ran for Dillon's truck. Rachel and Dillon put the saw and the other supplies in the back, gave each other a quick kiss and headed for the Christmas tree farm.

Rachel couldn't stop laughing. The whole trip was one Christmas carol after another and there wasn't a one in the bunch who could sing. "I sure hope none of you want to sing professionally. This is terrible. Wonderful but terrible." They sang even louder.

After a full afternoon of snowball fights, snow angels and hot cocoa, Rachel found the perfect tree. "This is the one."

Dillon came up from behind her and locked his arms around her. "How do you know?"

"I just know. That's how this works."

He looked at the tree from his position behind her, trying to see it through her eyes. "It is pretty. It's big. Will it fit in your living room?"

"It'll fit. We'll need to take off a little from the bottom, but that's okay. We'll make it work."

Jacob volunteered to do the cutting while Dillon held the tree with a gloved hand. It didn't take long and they were dragging the tree back to the truck.

Shelly walked along side her mother. "Are you doing okay?"

Rachel nodded. "Yeah, I'm good." She smiled at her daughter. "Really good. How about you?"

Shelly nodded as well. "Yeah, me too. I thought I might not be, but I am. This is fun."

Rachel looked at Shelly. "How is your sister doing?"

"I'm surprised. She's actually having fun. I haven't heard one negative thing from her all day."

"I suppose her improved attitude might have something to do with staying here with her dad while we're on vacation. That was one of the requirements her counselor added to the conditions. Having a good attitude is a decision. We don't always feel like being positive, but we can choose to be so anyway."

"Well, whatever the reason is, I like it. I hope she stays this way. I mean, she's always been somewhat moody, but lately I can't stand to be around her." Shelly looked apprehensive. "Mom, is it mean of me to be glad she's not going with us?"

What could Rachel say? She felt the same way herself but she couldn't admit that to her youngest daughter. It wouldn't be fair. "I think we all need a break. It'll be good for everyone. Besides, now we won't have to worry about Romeo."

Shelly ran to catch up with Jacob who was pulling the tree. Rachel watched the two of them chat as they walked and wondered what they talked about. Dillon was walking along side Shannon and she wondered about their conversation even more. She was content to walk and watch her family. She thought about how easy it was to include Dillon and Jacob in that category and sighed. So much had changed in the last six months.

Once home, they put the tree in its stand in the corner of the living room. It would be ready to decorate after a night of warming up. Rachel had put on a crock-pot of corn chowder before they left. That with some sandwiches made for an easy, warm your bones kind of late supper. Dillon and Jacob left for home with promises to be over early the next day to help decorate.

Dillon hung out at the door while Jacob bounded through the snow. "You were right. This was fun."

"It was, wasn't it? It's one of my favorite Christmas traditions. I love to sit here in the evening with all the house lights off and just stare at the glowing tree. A fire going and a hot cup of tea just round out the experience. This year, I'm going to sip on a glass of wine and think of you. Oh, a new tradition. I like the sound of that."

She kissed this man she was beginning to depend on, this man who was working his way into her heart. She pulled his face closer to hers and felt the beginning stubble on his cheeks. The square cut of his jaw, the gently falling splay of hair across his forehead, the vivid green that consumed her when she allowed herself to be lost in his gaze, were all reasons to be attracted to him. Yet, the reason she was falling in love with him had nothing to do with those physical traits and had everything to do with who he was as a person and how much he loved her. For the first time in years she felt loved, wanted and desired. Why did she still feel guilty? Did she not deserve to be cherished?

"What were you thinking just then? You got that look, like you were uncertain."

She closed her eyes and shook her head. "Nothing. I just can't imagine a more perfect moment. I don't want it to end."

Dillon knew there was more to it than that. He'd gotten to know her, her looks; her facial expressions were all beginning to make sense to him. All the time they spent together, at home, at work, at play had given him the opportunity to scrutinize her and learn everything he could about her. He knew when she was sad, when she was playful and when she was contemplating. He knew her anger, although those displays were rare. And best of all, he knew her heart. "We'll have a million more moments like this. I promise."

Rachel considered his words. Could he really promise something like that? Did he have the authority? "I hope so."

She bid him goodbye then went to her room where she waited for his light to come on. When he pulled the curtain back and waved, she waved back then climbed into bed. She closed her eyes and dreamed of other Christmases, Christmases when the girls were younger. When Ryan was the one cutting the tree and dragging it to their van flitted through her mind in bite size portions that threatened to disrupt the joy she currently clung to. She turned over and briefly opened her eyes then closed them again. Perhaps she wasn't fully asleep. Maybe she willfully brought those memories to mind. Maybe she was comparing.

She forced her mind to shut down and closed her eyes. This time she fell into a dreamless, restful sleep and didn't wake until the sun was streaming through the crack in her curtains.

Rachel rubbed her eyes. It was Sunday morning. Instead of getting ready for church like she had always done in the past, she spent a leisurely half hour in bed before turning on the shower. She could hardly believe it was after nine. When did she become such a sluggard?

She dried her hair and applied moisturizer and lip gloss. She gave herself a once over in the mirror and decided she didn't look bad for her age. She was growing old gracefully.

The cinnamon rolls were the kind you bought in a tube at the grocery store. Rachel found she liked some of these convenience foods she'd tried since going back to work. These were almost as good as homemade. Maybe even better. She put the pan in the oven and started the coffee and tea water. She glanced at her watch then started a fire. By the time the cinnamon rolls were done, the girls were up and ready to decorate and Dillon and Jacob were knocking on the door. Rachel looked around at the decorations spilling from boxes.

The only box that remained was the box with Ryan's ornaments. She needed to give those to him. The only time during the day she'd felt morose was when she'd had to separate out his ornaments. She marked the box and tucked it into the hall closet.

The room was magnificent. The girls had insisted on colored twinkling lights since they were little. Maybe someday she'd have the all white ones she wanted. Then she pictured grandchildren and smiled to herself. Maybe not.

Shelly and Jacob were drinking hot chocolate and eating the cookies she'd managed to make. Shannon was fidgeting with the manger scene. Dillon was sitting in the recliner with his mouth slightly ajar and a soft snore emitting from his parted lips. The tree was aglow. The angel kept watch. Even the outdoor lights were on and lit up. It had been a full day.

Rachel smiled and whispered. "It's beginning to look a lot like Christmas."

Chapter Twenty Nine

Terry knew Mark would walk through that door any minute. He was ready for him. They had spent many afternoons skirting around the real issue, and that was the attitude Christians had toward homosexuals. *When will they understand we just want the same rights as them?* He was armed and ready to finally have it out. He wanted answers. He wanted to know how God could make him who he was then condemn him in the same breath. He had read many accounts of how the Bible had become the twisted distorted book it was. The hatred poured out on homosexuals was man's doing. Not God's. It derived from homophobes who were so self-righteous, so sanctimonious, they had nothing better to do than look down their noses at those who were different than them.

Mark felt Terry's animosity when he walked through the door. The man's body may be failing but his attitude was full strength. "So, what's got you in a bad mood today?"

Terry felt his anger rise to answer. "You. You and every other self-serving, hate filled Christian I've ever been unfortunate enough to meet. That's what."

"Oh, is that all?" Mark sat down. "Now tell me something I don't know."

Terry couldn't believe this guy. "All right, fine. I'll tell you. For thousands of years Christians have used the Bible to justify their hatred. They have murdered in the name of Christianity. They used the Bible to justify slavery and dominate women. Some have even used it as a weapon against the Jews for killing Jesus. Now these same groups of people are using the Bible to justify their hatred toward homosexuals."

Mark cocked his head. "I agree with you."

Terry stopped speaking, stunned. "What do you mean you agree with me, you're a Christian, why aren't you defending your people?"

"Because, you're right. There have been so many atrocities committed in the name of Christianity it's unfathomable. And yes, some people hate homosexuals in the name of Christianity. I do not deny that. I do want to make one point though. Those people are not God. Not everything done in the name of Christianity accurately represents God. And God hates no one. He loves everyone and made a way to himself through his only son, Jesus Christ."

Terry didn't like this kind of argument. It wasn't an argument. It wasn't what he expected to hear. He moved to point two. "Okay" He stuttered. "Christians are hypocritical. They pick and choose which parts of the Old Testament they want to follow. I mean, they preach on what an abomination homosexuality is, but they certainly don't stone their children when they disobey. And I sure see a lot of Christians eating bacon."

Mark pursed his lips and nodded his head. "Terry, do you think there is a difference between murder and jay walking? Is one a more serious offence than the other?"

"Well, of course."

"Are both of these offenses against the law?"

"Yes."

"Do you think it would be fair of a police officer to give a murderer a warning like he might with a jay walker or perhaps the jay walker should spend the rest of his life in prison because he broke the law?"

Terry saw where this was headed and saw the futility of his argument. He became frustrated. "What about David and Jonathan?"

"What about them?"

"Uh, they were lovers. The Bible clearly states they loved each other."

"You're right again. They did love one another. So, a male cannot love another male without it being sexual? A man cannot love his son without him thinking or acting in a sexual manner? The Hebrew word used in 1 Samuel chapter eighteen for "love" is ahab which is commonly used for a love between a man and wife, a parent and a child and between friends. There would be a whole lot of story twisting going on if you came to the conclusion through that word that David and Jonathan were lovers."

Terry felt as if he were grasping at straws. He'd never been in a discussion with someone who was educated on the arguments for homosexuality in the Bible. Most people he had come across had a blind faith and didn't know why they believed what they did. "Why do you guys pick on homosexuals? Why don't you go after murderers and liars? I don't see you hating thieves."

"First off, we don't hate homosexuals. Second, I have yet to meet a liar who is trying to make lying legal or a thief trying to legalize their theft. You are the ones trying to justify your behavior. My question for you is, why do you feel you need the Bible's approval for your actions? If you don't agree with it, why not just say, the Bible is against homosexuality but I don't care because I don't agree with the Bible? I would think that would be the more honest approach."

Mark continued. "Terry, you keep talking about hate, about how Christians hate homosexuals. You consider the words in the Bible as words that promote hatred and hate crimes. I ask you this, if you were running into a building and I knew for a fact that building was about to blow up would it be love if I let you go because that is what you wanted to do, or would it be love if I tried to stop you? Even if you fought me tooth and nail, because you were bound and determined to get into that building, and you hated me for stopping you, would it be love if I let you go? Or do you think when the building exploded in every direction, blowing out windows and flames shooting through the roof, would you realize then that the reason I cautioned you, the reason that I warned you was because I loved you? I share Christ with you, not because I hate you. I warn you of your sin, not because I want to see you suffer, but because I love you."

Mark took a sip from his water bottle. "All the time I hear people say God loves everyone. And I agree, he does. But, to see the benefits of his love, we must first repent. We must turn from our sin. It's not enough that God loves us. We are told over and over again in scripture to repent. John the Baptist tells us in Matthew Chapter 3, *'repent for the kingdom of heaven is at hand.'* 2 Peter 3:9 says *'The Lord is not slow in keeping his promise, as some understand slowness. He is patient with you, not wanting anyone to perish, but everyone to come to repentance.* Matthew 11:20 tells us *'Then Jesus began to denounce the cities in which most of his miracles had been performed, because they did not repent.'* Are you seeing a pattern here? We're called to repent, to turn from our wicked ways. All of us. Sinner and saint. Homosexual and heterosexual. Adulterer, liar and thief. We are all called to repentance." Terry was angry. He didn't expect his arguments to be countered with intelligent replies. He wasn't ready for this. "Look, I don't believe in your Bible. I don't believe in your God. Just leave. I don't want to hear any more of your nonsense."

Mark stood up to go. "Terry, God loves you. Jesus died for you. He created you in his image. A body, a spirit and a soul. Your body is dying. We cannot deny that. It will return to dust. Your soul on the other hand will live forever. It's up to you where that will be, heaven or hell." Marked turned and walked out the door.

Chapter Thirty

The plane taxied down the runway then lifted off. Rachel could hardly believe they were on their way. It ended up being just the four of them. Ryan had agreed to stay at the house with Shannon and Sam was already in Jamaica. Rachel was surprised when she didn't receive a request for money. Maybe Sam really was growing up.

They had had a nice Christmas celebration the weekend before, just her and the girls. Rachel had been proud of the shopping she'd done. Each of the girls received clothes, books, a cd or two and a necklace with their birthstone. It was something she'd never been able to do before. Now that she was making her own money, she felt she could spend it as she saw fit. And she wanted to treat the girls. This Christmas was hard on them all. She did all she could do to make it up to them.

They would exchange small gifts with Dillon and Jacob in Colorado on Christmas. She and Shelly planned on taking a mom daughter day to shop. She hoped she found the perfect gift for Dillon to show him how much she cared for him. The trip was Dillon's gift to everyone. Rachel felt her shoulders lighten as soon as she sat in her seat. She was glad it wasn't a long flight.

She took Dillon's hand and closed her eyes. She needed this vacation.

Dillon watched Rachel relax. This is what he'd hoped for. He felt the diamond ring in the pocket of his jacket then ordered a bottle of champagne from the stewardess. He hoped the kids didn't mind sitting in coach. There were only two seats available in first class and while he normally didn't spend the extra money on such luxuries, he'd wanted to treat Rachel to a first rate vacation. Most likely the two teens were listening to music and planning their ski vacation. He was thankful they got along so well. He handed the glass to Rachel then toasted. "To us."

She gladly accepted the bubbly liquid and touched her glass to his. "To us." She sipped the sweet fluid and leaned back against the roomy seat. "So this is how the other half travels." She leaned toward Dillon and whispered. "I've never traveled first class before." She hiccupped. "And I've never had champagne before." She hiccupped again.

"You don't say?" He refilled her glass.

Two hours later as they exited the plane, Rachel was feeling quite happy. She raved about everything. She'd never ridden in a limousine. When Dillon popped the cork of another bottle of champagne, she happily tilted her glass. "I love this stuff." Another hiccup.

Dillon was laughing as well. The teens found their parent's behavior a tad bit amusing as well as a bit embarrassing. Shelly had never seen her mother drink so much, in fact, before Dillon, she'd never seen her drink, let alone seen her tipsy.

Jacob shrugged it off. "It's harmless. They're not driving. Besides, a good friend of Dad's provided this car, as well as the champagne. We wouldn't want to offend him. It was a gift. A special occasion is what Dad told me."

Shelly questioned him. "A special occasion? What does he mean?"

"I don't know. Dad didn't tell me. I could wager a guess though, if you want me to."

Shelly shook her head. "No, I'd rather you not. Let's just enjoy ourselves." She watched her mom and was glad to see her refusing any more champagne. She must have realized what she was doing. She leaned back against the soft leather and inserted her ear buds. Two hours later, Jacob nudged her awake. She was surrounded by mountains. The view was amazing.

Her mom smiled at her. "It's beautiful."

"Wow. Why have we not come here before? Shannon and Sam are going to be so mad they missed this."

The four of them exited the car as the driver removed their luggage. He helped them inside the cabin then left.

Rachel turned in a circle. "You call this a cabin? Where I come from this is a mansion." She set out to explore. The house was exquisite. She wouldn't mind getting lost and never coming up for air.

Dillon watched every expression. She was as excited as a child on Christmas morning. The wall facing the mountain range was all glass. She just stood there, staring. She turned, looking for him.

"Come here." She held out her hand, imploring him to come take it. "I could stand here and look at that all day. It's simply breathtaking." She turned to him. "Thank you."

Dillon couldn't imagine anything he wouldn't do to make her happy. He kissed her hand. "You're welcome. Want to see your room?" He took her hand and led her upstairs. She had the same magnificent view from her bedroom. "I may never come out."

He picked her up and carried her back into the hallway. "Not if I have anything to do with it you won't." He set her down then took her by the hand. "Come on. I want to show you the rest of the house." Together they explored the house. They passed Jacob and Shelly as they traveled. The two teenagers had started with the basement level and the walk out patio and worked their way up.

Jacob questioned his dad. "Does it matter who sleeps where?"

"I put Rachel in the master. See if Shelly wants the other end of the hall."

"Dad, she wants one of the downstairs rooms. Is that all right?"

"Yeah, that should be fine. Are you taking the other one down there?"

"It might be better so we don't interrupt. We'll probably be staying up late, playing pool and swimming. We could get loud. We are teenagers on vacation ya know."

Dillon took his son aside. "You will respect her, won't you?"

"Dad. Sheesh. We don't think of each other like that. We're practically brother and sister. That is what you have in mind, right?"

Jacob continually surprised him. "You don't mind, do you?"

"No, I think it's great. She's an awesome lady. It's about time you found someone to spend your life with."

Dillon hugged his son. "Thanks. That means a lot." He pulled away.

He heard Rachel calling for him and took off to find her. She was standing before the decorated Christmas tree in the large great room. "Dillon, look. It's the most beautiful tree I've ever seen."

He snuggled up behind her. "I'm interested in a different view at the moment."

She turned into his arms. "I should think about supper. The kids are probably starving."

"It's already been taken care of. The refrigerator is stocked and we have dinner reservations at eight. We're eating with the Williams family. They own this place and are good friends of mine." He looked at his watch. "That gives us a couple of hours. Do you want to lie down for a little while? It's already been a long day."

"That sounds heavenly. Would you let Jacob and Shelly know when we'll be leaving? I'll be down in an hour and a half." She kissed his lips then retreated to her bedroom.

Rachel stood by the window, staring as the sun set behind the mountains. The reds, yellows and oranges were a brilliant backdrop for the incoming clouds. She peeked in the master bath and seeing the enormous soaking tub, she opted for a bath instead of a nap. She delighted in the choice of bath salts and oils available. She found the towels and washcloths and as she searched, she found a wine cooler with a selection of wines as well as wine glasses.

She groaned. "I may never get out."

After forty-five minutes of soaking, she forced herself to dress for dinner.

Dillon heard the water running and chuckled. She found the master bath. It was an amazing bathroom. Columns surrounded the deep, oversized soaking tub. A huge walk in master shower with multiple showerheads, all aimed to massage an aching body. A dressing table, sinks, bidet, steam room, wine cooler and all done up in rich marble with low lighting. There was everything anyone could possibly need to disappear for a few days. He sure hoped Rachel didn't lock herself in there. He'd have to break the door down because he wasn't spending this vacation alone.

He relaxed in his own room, which was well appointed. Although not as nice as the master, he had some gorgeous amenities of his own. Rich cherry wood furniture with carpet so thick, so deep, his feet were nearly buried. The heated floors in his bathroom and the walk in shower, similar to the one in the master, beckoned him. First, he tucked the diamond ring in the inside pocket of his suitcase. He didn't want to be walking around with that thing in his pocket the whole vacation. If everything worked out, he'd be engaged on the flight home. He never thought he'd fall in love again. Boy was he wrong.

They were eating with his friends, the ones who owned the cabin, or mansion as Rachel put it. Dillon put on his jacket and tie and hoped Jacob remembered his. Dining with the Williams was not a casual affair. He emerged from his room confident in his appearance then proceeded to find Jacob and Shelly. Both of the kids were dressed to the nines. When Rachel announced she was ready, he literally had to remind himself to breath. She was spectacular. Her black velvet dress stopped just above the floor and while the front scoop was very respectable, the back hung in gentle folds that exposed most of her back. She was stunning. He spun her around to see her in all her glory. She wore pearl drop earrings and a pearl necklace, both were her mothers and her hair was pinned up casually and showcased her long, elegant neck. Dillon covered her shoulders with her wrap then led her to the waiting car.

Rachel felt like Cinderella. She leaned over to whisper in Dillon's ear. "Pinch me. I need to make sure I'm not dreaming."

Dillon laughed out loud. "You're not dreaming. Although I admit you do look like something out of a dream, my dreams to be more specific." He still stared at her. She had no idea how beautiful she was. He took her gloved hand in his own and attempted to calm her insecurities. She'd been worked over. Her womanhood had been thrown in the fire and scorched. Somewhere in the process she lost her confidence. Who wouldn't? To be replaced by someone of the same sex as your partner would throw anyone into a tailspin. "You're beautiful. And you are going to be exquisite at the dinner party. Who in their right mind wouldn't love you?"

Her eyes thanked him. She needed to hear that. Her normal relationships consisted of other mothers, ladies in her church and other pastors' wives. She didn't rub elbows with millionaires. When Dillon told her she'd need to bring some formalwear, she thought about backing out of the trip. She's not sure what she had expected but it certainly wasn't hob knobbing. Dillon assured her it was for only one night. The rest of their time was their own. And she could wear jeans and sweaters to her heart's content.

They were dining at the top of the mountain in a glass restaurant attached to an elite ski lodge that Dillon's friends owned. The very same ones she'd be dining with. She prayed she wouldn't do or say anything stupid.

She allowed Dillon to guide her by her elbow after she made sure Shelly and Jacob were close behind. She made a point to kiss her daughter's cheek. "You look lovely."

Shelly made goo-goo eyes at her. "Ooh la la. So you do."

"Really? I don't look silly, like I'm out of place?"

"No, Mom. You really are beautiful."

The view from the restaurant was splendid. Of course, that came as no surprise. They were dining on top of a mountain. It didn't take long before Dillon was introducing her to the Williams. It was a brief meeting. They had been good friends with his late wife and while he still considered them friends as well, they ran in very different circles. They were also entertaining guests from overseas. In all, Rachel thought there were fifty to sixty dining with them. A jazz band was playing softly in one corner while each course was served.

After dining on such delicacies as caviar and quail and ending with a black truffle soufflé for dessert, Rachel logically would have chosen her bed as her next resting spot. Dillon had something else in mind. He pulled her close on the dance floor and gently swayed to the smooth saxophone and bass. She ended up having a wonderful time.

The surprise came on the ride home when Dillon announced they could have the house for another week. Originally, someone else had been scheduled to stay over the New Year. But, they had to cancel at the last moment giving Dillon and Rachel a wonderful place to celebrate New Year's Eve.

Shelly and Jacob had been invited to a youth shut in at the lodge. The Williams' teens were hosting a party of their own. Dillon assured Rachel the kids would be fine and they'd have a great time. It also gave him the opportunity to propose in the quiet of the cabin with no interruptions.

"Shelly, are you sure you want to go? You don't know them too well."

"Mom, I had a blast and you should see the schedule for the shut in. We'll be skiing all day. There'll be a fire on the deck at night. They have a huge theatre room to watch movies in. Yeah, I want to go. Can I?"

"I suppose. Dillon and Jacob know them well. We can trust their judgment."

Dillon felt his insides stir. He could hardly wait until New Year's Eve.

Chapter Thirty One

Mark had been visiting Terry regularly over the course of the past month. He'd established somewhat of a relationship with him, at least as much as Terry would allow. His distrust for pastors, really all Christians, kept him from truly sharing his heart.

He tried to be quiet as he sat down in the chair near the bed. The chair had developed a creak over time and Mark winced when it announced his arrival. Terry stirred.

Mark waited for Terry to wake up and get comfortable. The activities so many took for granted took him great effort to accomplish. The pain was excruciating, even with the pain patches.

"So, I didn't scare you away? I thought after our last visit you'd never be back."

"You won't get rid of me that easily." Mark thought about their conversation the day before yesterday and how it had gotten heated. It hadn't been his intent to upset Terry, but he had to hear the truth.

Terry watched him with a level of respect he begrudgingly handed out. He didn't want to like this man of the cloth. He wanted to hate him for all he stood for and for all the hurt people like him dished out. But he found he couldn't hate him. He had been through his share of troubles, too, and for some reason, he actually acted as if he cared. Terry half grinned, half smirked. "Then I guess I'll have to try harder today."

Mark took the bait. "Give it your best shot."

"Oh, a challenge. I like that."

Mark acknowledged Terry's wit. He was smart. His mind was still strong even though his body was failing. "Should we pick up where we left off?"

"Okay." He wasn't comfortable talking about the Bible. He only knew the verses that were planted in him by those who were fighting for the rights of homosexuals. And he had to admit, after his last conversation with Mark, even he thought some of their explanations were a stretch. "So, you were telling me that God created us in his image, body, soul and spirit. And if I remember right, our body will return to the dust from where it came but our soul will live eternally. I get that, if you believe in that sort of thing. But, the job of our spirit makes no sense."

"Think of your spirit as the power source behind your body and your soul. It can be good or evil, clean or unclean, holy or unholy. In other words, you get to choose who your power source comes from, God or Satan."

Terry looked at him like he'd grown a tail.

"Not making sense?"

Terry shook his head.

Mark opened his Bible. "Okay. Jesus puts it like this in the book of John chapter three verses five and six. 'Jesus answered, "Very truly I tell you, no one can enter the kingdom of God unless they are born of water and the Spirit. Flesh gives birth to flesh, but the Spirit gives birth to spirit.' In other words, a person must be born physically. We must come from our mother's womb and be born into this world. If we wish to spend eternity with God, then we must also be born of the Spirit. Meaning, we must replace the evil spirit within us, the one that is self-serving and replace it with the Spirit of God. That is how we come to have the Holy Spirit within us. He will not enter us without permission. He will not take away our free will. It is our choice."

"So, you are telling me we're possessed and it's our choice who possesses us? God or Satan? That, my friend, is epic."

"Well, that is one way to look at it. We certainly don't have the power within us to do anything. We get our power from a source, be it good or evil."

193

Terry thought about this information for a moment. "So what happens if we don't replace the evil spirit within us with God's Spirit?"

"Revelation twenty thirteen through fifteen says 'The sea gave up the dead that were in it, and death and Hades gave up the dead that were in them, and each person was judged according to what they had done. Then death and Hades were thrown into the lake of fire. The lake of fire is the second death. Anyone whose name was not found written in the book of life was thrown into the lake of fire."

Terry looked horrified. "That's harsh."

"I suppose it is. But, God cannot be in the presence of evil. He made a way for us to spend eternity with him. We get to choose. We are the ones to decide. We can accept him for who he is, for all that he has done or we can continue to deny him. Our eternity lies in our own hands." Mark watched Terry digest this information. He was more inquisitive this time. He seemed more interested in the Word and what it actually said. "Terry, I wouldn't be a friend to you if I didn't tell you that you must choose before you die. Doing nothing is also a choice. It means you deny what Christ did for you on the cross. It means you will spend eternity separated from God."

He wished he had more energy. He wished he had more time. The little time he had left was slipping away. The time he spent coherent was even less. He had to make a decision. Mark made a good argument he would admit that. He needed to think. But first, he had to rest. He needed to be fully aware before he could make that kind of decision. He closed his eyes.

Mark rose and walked down the hall. Every day Terry put off making a decision was another day closer to death. He prayed he wouldn't wait until it was too late.

The phone rang from somewhere in his dream. It was Jessi who shook him awake. "Hon, the phone is for you." She fell back into bed.

He put on his glasses and peered at the alarm clock. "Who calls at three in the morning two days before Christmas?" He pulled his robe on. "This must not be good news."

It was Marie from the shelter. Terry had died in his sleep. She thought he'd want to know. He'd arranged to go see her the next morning. He debated back and forth on when to call Ryan. He opted to wait and call him in the morning. There wasn't anything anyone could do now. He returned to bed.

Jessi was waiting for him. "Bad news?"

He sat on his side of the bed and sighed. "Yeah, Terry died in his sleep."

She sat up and touched his arm. "You know you did everything you could."

"I know. I just pray there was some way of knowing. He had the information. What did he do with it?"

"We may never know. You were obedient. That is all the Lord expects from you. You did your part. Remember, we plant and he reaps the harvest. Only the Lord can lead the lost to salvation." She pulled him over beside her. "Did you call Ryan?"

"No. I'll call him in the morning."

She lay back against her pillow. Mark followed suit. "We've seen it all, haven't we?"

"I suspect there is a great deal we'll never see. And be glad we didn't." Jessi shook her head. "There's too much hurt in this world. I'm so glad I have Jesus. I couldn't do this without him."

He turned toward her. "Me too. How do people keep going when they have no hope? What's the point?"

"I don't get it either." She cuddled into his shoulder. "I'm so glad God gave me you." She kissed his cheek.

Mark reached over and turned off the light.

The next morning Mark met Ryan at the shelter and packed up the few possessions Terry owned. Marie met them in the foyer. "Can you come in my office for a minute?"

Marie mainly addressed Mark. "Terry has no living relatives. His mother passed away a couple of years ago. He has a small life insurance policy to cover his funeral. He wants to be cremated. Also, he wanted you to have a small service here at the shelter. Are you okay with that?"

Mark would take any opportunity given him to preach the gospel. If the service was held in the shelter, then most of the residents would probably be in attendance. "Yeah, I can work that out."

Marie nodded. "Good. Will the Saturday after Christmas work for you?"

Mark checked his calendar. "Yeah, I can arrange it."

It was almost Christmas and neither Mark nor Ryan were in the mood for lengthy conversations, so they remained standing. Marie opened her desk drawer and removed an envelope addressed to Mark. "This is for you."

He took the envelope from her. By the light in her eyes, he correctly guessed she already knew the content. "We'll talk more after Christmas."

She waved goodbye then went about caring for the other residents in her care. Mourning took place in private. Her residents needed to see love in action at all times. Every waking moment was a testament to Christ. She always had to be ready to answer for the hope that resided in her.

Mark and Ryan went for coffee and Mark read the letter out loud. It was short, sweet and to the point.

Mark,

You'll be glad to know I did it. I answered the call within me. And just like you said I would, I feel better than I ever have. I have spent every waking hour poring over the gospel of John, not that I had many of those, mind you. It would seem to me there are so many like me, so many men and women hurting and leading a life that leads straight to hell. Be my voice. Tell my story. Give them reason to hope like you gave me. Perhaps God will give me a voice from the grave through you.

Your faithfulness and dedication, even when I didn't deserve it, have shown me what it's like to be sold out for Christ.

Thank you for your friendship. Thank you for not giving up on me.

Please tell Ryan I'm sorry. I had no right to disrupt his life and I understand why he sent you in his stead. If he hadn't, I don't think I'd be where I am. One of my dying prayers is for his family to be restored to him.

As I read in the book of John, I read the story of Nicodemus and the word was opened to me. Those verses you shared with me about being born of both the water the spirit came alive within me. I now know with a confidence that I have everlasting life in Christ.

See you on the other side,
Terry

Mark and Ryan openly wept over their coffee. Knowing that Terry would spend eternity in heaven, that even now he had no more sickness, no more pain, gave them hope that God was still in control. In the midst of all their mistakes, God could make things right.

Chapter Thirty Two

Val hummed to herself as she pulled the baked mashed potato dish out of the oven. Aunt Merry had invited them to share Christmas dinner. She was thankful. She didn't have the energy to make a big meal for just the two of them. With all the kids coming in for the anniversary party in March, they felt like they couldn't take the time or the money to travel the distance twice in such a short amount of time. She understood. Times were hard and her kids were feeling the pinch.

She had mailed a box of cookies to each of her kids and instead of shopping for each grandchild, she sent them each some money. That would have to do for this year. Of course they understood. With her being sick, they didn't expect anything. She was thankful she was able to surprise them.

She put the small stockings she stuffed for Jessi's kids in the bag, along with the peanut butter cake she'd made then went in search of Herbert. She found him lying in bed, fully clothed and snoring. She nudged his leg. "We're gonna be late."

He sat straight up. "Yep, just resting my eyes."

"I suppose you were snoring on purpose too?"

"Yep. Meant to do that."

"Humph. I need you to carry the potatoes to the car."

"Okay. I'm comin'."

"Now be careful driving. I don't want our back seat covered in potatoes."

"You got it."

"Herbert. Are you listening to me?"

"You know I am."

"Are you going to drive carefully?"

"Don't I always?"

"Oh dear. Then I'll hold the potatoes."

"Good idea."

Despite the crazy man behind the wheel, they arrived at Mark and Jessi's in one piece. Even the potatoes made it to the table with no apparent damage. That was a blessing.

Jessi gave Val a hug. "How are you feeling?"

"I about had a heart attack on our way, but that didn't have one thing to do with the cancer." She gave her husband a dirty look. "No thanks to you."

"Woman, I've been driving this way for fifty years. If I ain't killed you yet, I probably ain't going to."

She tilted her chin into the air, signaling she was finished having that particular conversation.

Herbert went in search of the guys who were huddled around the television watching football.

Jessi bit her lip to keep from laughing. "Your baked mashed potatoes look amazing. I think Aunt Merry is getting everything ready in the kitchen. I'm gonna go check on her. Do you want to go in and have a cup of tea?"

"That'd be just the thing to settle my nerves. I got so tense holding on to that handle in the car, I may need a muscle relaxer. I guess tea will have to do."

Aunt Merry had already heated the water and to Val's surprise, Shannon was arranging a vegetable tray. "Well, if it's not one of my very favorite people in the world." She gave Shannon a big hug. "Hi sweetie. I didn't know you were going to be here."

"It was just me and Dad at home so Mark and Jessi invited us over for dinner. Neither one of us wanted frozen pizza or take out."

"Well, I don't blame you there. Not on Christmas, anyway."

Val looked to Jessi and Merry for an explanation. Both shook their heads slightly so she took the conversation in another direction. "Was Santa good to you?"

Shannon grinned. "He sure was. I got the cutest new bunny slippers, a new sweater and this." She lifted the necklace up so Val could see it. "It's my birthstone."

Val stepped closer to Shannon and squinted her eyes. "It's beautiful. Garnet for my January baby." She turned her attention to Merry. "Well, how can I be of help?"

Merry handed her a cup of tea. "You can sit down at the table and drink your tea. As soon as I'm done glazing this ham, we'll have fifteen minutes or so to sit and chat. Then, we can take all the food to the table."

Merry put the ham back in the oven and joined the other ladies at the table. It felt good to sit down. They had a full house. Sheila, Mark's sister and her family were there. Even Patty, Jessi's mom, flew in to spend the holiday with her grandchildren. The twins had her in a mean game of Sorry. Olivia was reading. The men were watching football and by the time the ladies finished their tea, dinner would be ready.

Merry listened to all the sounds emanating from the friends and family gathered in the house. This is what Christmas is supposed to be like. Her heart was so full it was near bursting. These people, she loved every one of them. She smiled, content with the world, then stood and took out the ham. "Time to eat."

Chapter Thirty Three

Christmas passed in slow motion in the mountains. They had spent a casual day of opening gifts, playing games, sitting in the hot tub and eating grilled steaks and shrimp. The trip was the emphasis so gifts were kept to a minimum. Rachel and Shelly had spent some time shopping in the village and had found some unique gifts for both Dillon and Jacob. The day was labeled a success. The rest of the week passed quickly.

With all the skiing, Rachel was ready to spend New Year's Eve sitting by the fire, relaxing. The kids had left early and wouldn't be back till noon or after the next day. Rachel was a bit nervous spending the night in a house all by herself with Dillon. They spent the afternoon lounging, watching old movies. They had just finished Breakfast at Tiffany's when Dillon insisted she go and run a bath. She was all too happy to oblige. A bath sounded wonderful.

Rachel lingered in the bath. By the time she got out, the sun had set. She dried off with one of the luxurious towels provided. Her skin felt soft and hydrated. "I'm gonna miss this."

She padded into the bedroom and resting on the bed was a set of beautifully wrapped boxes. Puzzled, she opened the first one. Inside was a magnificent emerald green dress. She slipped it over her head and it felt like silk as it slid over her body. The dress was a bit shorter than she normally wore and the neckline plunged a little deeper, but why not? She wasn't the pastor's wife anymore. She was thankful she took the time to shave her legs because coming out of that dress her legs would definitely be in the spotlight. The next box housed a pair of stilettos. She hoped she wouldn't have too far to walk in these or she'd break her neck. The third box, which was the smallest of the three held a pair of emerald earrings. She gasped then put the teardrops in her ears. She looked at herself in the mirror. *Apparently, we're going out. I guess I'd better put on some make up.*

Rachel was ready for a party. She had to admit, she looked good. Really good. She descended the stairs to candlelight and soft music playing. And something smelled delicious. The table was set for two. Dillon stood, looking debonair in his tuxedo, leaning against the bar with two glasses in his hand.

He offered one to Rachel. "You look amazing."

She noticed his polished wing tip shoes, his pressed pants and his well-tailored jacket. "I could say the same for you." She accepted the drink he offered then tipped her glass. "Champagne. My favorite. You do know how to spoil me. Thank you. The gifts are lovely. The earrings are perfect. You've done so much, how can I thank you?"

He kissed her lips and murmured, "I'm sure I'll think of something." He led her to the table and pulled out her chair. "First, dinner." She sat down then he removed the dome lids over the plates.

"When did you have time for all this?"

"My darling, I had it catered, of course."

They dined on oysters, lobster and scallops, steamed asparagus and the largest, sweetest strawberries Rachel had ever had.

Her stilettos brought her eye-to-eye with Dillon as they danced the evening away, just the two of them. Her glass was rarely empty and she found herself free from any thoughts or doubts that plagued her. They kissed, they laughed, and when he brought out the Godiva Chocolates, she thought she'd died and gone to heaven. Never in her entire life had she been treated this way, like she was the most important person in the world.

Dillon watched the clock hands carefully. It was nearing midnight. He was nervous. Would she say yes? "Should we do our own private count down or should we look on with Times Square? They delay the broadcast so we're in the same time zone."

Rachel finished her champagne and kissed him. "Let's countdown ourselves."

Their faces mere inches a part, they counted backwards in unison until the clock chimed midnight. Dillon kissed her again, this time more possessively. He dropped to one knee and pulled out a beautiful blue velvet box. "Rachel, will you make me the happiest man alive? Will you marry me?" He opened the box revealing a platinum two-carat round cut diamond engagement ring then looked at her with hopeful eyes.

Rachel felt her mouth drop. She stared at the ring then diverted her eyes to Dillon's who was still waiting for her response. Did she love him? Did she want to spend the rest of her life with him? She pushed those thoughts to the back of her mind. The champagne confused every sane thought she might have had and combined with the expensive food, the romantic setting, the absolutely gorgeous ring, and the handsome man on his knee Rachel nearly yelled, "Yes! Yes, I'll marry you."

He stood up and put the ring on her finger. The two of them watched the ring as it dazzled in the firelight. He brought her to him. "I never thought I'd love like this again. You're mine now. No one else's."

"I like the sound of that."

His eyes locked with hers. He took her hand and together they climbed the stairs.

Chapter Thirty Four

Dillon watched her as she slept. Her head rested on his shoulder and her hair was fanned out on the pillow under his arm. Her lips curved in a gentle smile and her eyelids fluttered slightly. She was dreaming. He'd like to think he was the object of those smiles. Perhaps he was. She had said yes. She stirred, then mumbled. There were so many things he didn't know about her. Apparently one of those things was she talked in her sleep. He listened to see if he could make sense of anything she was saying. She seemed to be stirring awake. She cuddled into him then he clearly heard her say, "Ryan." He tensed. Surely she didn't think she was in bed with her soon to be ex-husband?

He cut her some slack. She'd been married to the same jerk for twenty-three years. She'd never been with another man. It was only natural she'd be confused.

She blinked her eyelids a few times then opened them. She seemed confused for a moment then adjusted her head so she could see him. It was when she smiled fully he knew she was awake and aware that it was his arms that were holding her.

He kissed her. "You stay right here. I'll be right back."

She yawned. "Am I allowed to go to the bathroom?"

"Fine. Then get back into bed."

"I won't argue with that."

Rachel stood in front of the mirror and stared at herself. For the first time in twenty-two years she allowed a man to touch her out of wedlock. She thought perhaps she might have grown horns over night; somewhat like when Pinocchio's nose grew when he lied. Nope, she still looked the same. In the back of her mind she heard a still small voice, pulling at her. She refused to listen. She hadn't been back to church since she went and sat with Val and saw all the women whispering behind her back. She'd been ready to trust God then, to give everything over to him. But it hurt. It hurt knowing that somehow she was being blamed or at the very least pitied. And it hurt knowing that God would let her down. She had done her best over the years to be the submissive wife, the good mother, and the good pastor's wife. This was the payback she got? Maybe being good just wasn't what it was cracked up to be.

She looked at the rock on her finger and smirked. She held it up to the light and watched it dance. No one would pity her now. So she and Dillon jumped the gun a little bit. At least she knew he desired her. Was that so wrong? She had to admit the champagne had made it easier. It sure helped her ignore that voice in her head. She brushed her teeth and ran her fingers through her hair.

She returned to bed just before Dillon walked in the door bearing a tray with breakfast. "Oh, something smells good. You need help?"

"Nope, I got this. You stay where you are."

Dillon slid the tray onto the bed. Rachel's stomach growled. "I guess I'm hungry."

"Let's see what we can do about that. I have scrambled eggs, bacon, fresh strawberries, croissants, coffee and orange juice." He mounded her plate with food then served himself. "I'm famished."

They lingered over breakfast and enjoyed the quiet. She liked being with him. It was a comfortable place to be, as long as the voices didn't start up. She felt justified. Besides, as soon as the divorce was final they'd be married.

Dillon kissed her hand. "Any regrets?"

She shook her head. "Not a one. You?"

"Oh, no. None. I just wanted to be sure you're okay with everything."

"I am. So stop worrying. I'm a big girl. I know what I'm doing."

He set the tray aside and pulled her down beside him. "Do you know how much I love you?"

She giggled. "I'm guessing I'm about to find out?"

He laughed. "I'm going to love being married to you."

Two hours later Shelly and Jacob burst through the front doors, both jabbering away. "Mom, you just won't believe how much fun we had. We went skiing and snowboarding. My favorite was tubing. Oh my gosh, it's a blast. Then when we got back to the house we went snowmobiling on their property, at night. It was so beautiful. You would have loved it. And Mom, their house is so beautiful. If you think this one is awesome, you should see that one. It's huge. They even have an indoor pool." Shelly yawned. "We didn't go to bed. I'm exhausted."

Dillon laughed. "I wondered when you were gonna come up for air."

Rachel kissed her daughter. "Why don't you guys go take a nap? Unless you want to eat first?"

Jacob rubbed his stomach. "No, I couldn't eat another bite. I'm stuffed. We had a huge breakfast."

Shelly nodded in agreement. "Good idea, Mom. I'll be up in a little while."

Rachel addressed her comments to their retreating backs. "I think we're going to take a walk, so if you don't see us you'll know where we are."

She slipped her boots and jacket on then took Dillon's hand. "The property is beautiful. So many trees. I love how the sunshine filters through them."

"I've always loved coming here. The longer we were able to stay, the better. There's something to be said for breathing clean mountain air."

Rachel watched Dillon's warm breath escape with each word he spoke. She looked at the brilliant blue sky. "Why is the sky blue?"

He grinned. "Is this a rhetorical question?"

"No, I just wondered why it always looks blue."

"I can answer that. It's due to Rayleigh Scattering."

"Huh?"

"To put it simply, the sunlight scatters off the molecules in the atmosphere. The shorter the wavelength, basically the blues and greens, the better this process works. Reds and yellows have longer wavelengths. Those wavelengths are better seen closer to the sun, which is the reason for the yellowish sun, and the beautiful sunsets."

"Well, my answer would have simply been that God created it that way. I had no idea he went through all that to accomplish it."

He stopped walking. "Do you not believe in evolution?"

She paused. "Well, no. I believe God created the universe. Don't you?"

"I've never really given much thought to God."

"How can you look at the world and not think about God?"

"I guess I wasn't raised that way. Religion wasn't part of our lives. My mom and Dad were science professors and God was never part of our home life. Of course, it doesn't bother me at all that you believe in God. I can respect that. To each his own, right?"

Rachel heard the voice again, warning her. She changed the subject. "Should we tell the kids or wait to see if they notice the ring?"

"Let's give them until we go to bed tonight. I don't want them wondering why we're going into the same room."

Rachel froze. That would mean Shelly would know they were sleeping together. Was she okay with that? She could justify sharing his bed when no one knew, but she'd taught Shelly that a physical relationship was strictly for a husband and wife. What kind of mother would she be if she openly went against what she supposedly believed in? "Can you just sneak into my room after we know they've gone to bed?"

Dillon shook his head. "Sure, we can do that." He paused. "You're not embarrassed, are you?"

"No, it's not that. She'll know we're engaged. It's just, I've always taught her sex before marriage is wrong. I'm just not ready to deal with that yet."

"Okay, we'll take it slow. I'm good with that."

"Thank you."

Dillon and Rachel needn't have wondered if the kids would notice. Shelly woke up from her nap hungry and offered to help Rachel make pasta. The ring had completely slipped her mind until Shelly lifted her hand and stared at the rock on her mother's ring finger. She looked her mother in the eye. "You got engaged?"

Rachel smiled. "Yes, isn't it exciting?"

Shelly wasn't smiling back. "Mom, you're still married."

"It's only a formality, Shelly. I've filed for divorce. It will be final in March. That's only three months away. I can be engaged. Isn't it okay that someone actually loves me?" She put the pasta in the boiling water. "Can't you just be happy for me?"

Shelly's stomach lurched. "Yeah, Mom. Sure."

"And Shelly, don't say anything to your sisters or Dad. I want to be the one to tell them."

Dinner was quiet. Dillon figured the kids were still tired, and with Jacob he was correct. Rachel knew the real reason for her daughter's attitude. She thought of all the girls, Shelly would've been the one happy for her. She guessed wrong.

They all gathered in the great room and watched The Holiday before both kids made their excuses and headed to bed for the night. He pulled her close. "Dinner was wonderful, thank you."

"You're welcome."

"Feel like sitting in the hot tub?"

"Now you're talking. Let me go get changed."

Chapter Thirty Five

Rachel walked through her front door and immediately felt the stress she left behind. Even with a rock on her finger.

Dillon carried her suitcase up while she followed behind with her bathroom bag and carry on. He set the bag down and turned and kissed her. She tensed up. It was one thing to be physical in neutral territory, or perhaps even his place, but she didn't think she'd be able to here in the room she shared with Ryan. It just wasn't right.

He questioned her with his eyes.

She brushed it off. He'd think she still had feelings for Ryan. "I'm fine. Just tired."

"Why don't I come over later? We could tell Shannon the good news together." He paused. "Or do you want to tell her by yourself?"

They heard a noise in the hallway then a voice. "What good news?"

The door hadn't been fully shut. Rachel closed her eyes. She'd been dreading this moment. She had no idea how Shannon would react. Well, she had a pretty good idea but hated the thought. Shelly had gotten over her attitude when she'd caught up on her rest. The next morning she'd approached Rachel with an apology and a hug. Sam would be thrilled that she was getting on with her life. It was Shannon that made Rachel question her decision. And at the same time, she knew it wasn't Shannon's life, it was hers. Shannon would grow up and have a life of her own. She would make her own mistakes and celebrate her own victories. Why should Rachel live to please her almost twenty year old daughter?

Rachel fully opened the door and plastered on the brightest smile she could muster. "Hi, Honey. I missed you. Did you have fun with your dad?" She embraced her daughter.

"If you can call going to a funeral for some gay guy fun, then yeah, I guess I had fun."

"Terry died?"

"Yeah, he had AIDS, remember?"

"You don't have to be like that, Shannon. I asked a simple question. It didn't warrant the attitude."

Shannon, embarrassed by her mother's reprimand in front of Dillon, retreated to her room. "When you feel like sharing your good news, you know where I am."

Rachel rested her head on the door jam then looked at Dillon. "Sometimes I wonder if beating my head against this thing would help."

"I'm afraid I cannot allow you to do that. You'd be hurting my future wife and I just won't stand for it." He wrapped his arms around her. "Come here, let me hold you for a minute." He whispered in her ear. "I'm going to miss you tonight."

She had to admit after so many years of marriage, she didn't like sleeping alone. "I'm going to miss you, too."

"We can rectify this you know. Just let me know when you're ready. We don't answer to your kids."

"I know, and I will, promise. Just not yet."

Rachel saw Dillon to the door. "I'll try and come over later."

He looked her in the eye. "I love you, Rachel."

She watched him walk across the street then went in search of Shannon. She knocked on the door. "Hey, it's me, Mom. Can I come in?" Rachel heard movement on the other side of the door.

"I'll be down in a minute."

What is she hiding from me now? "Okay, I'll be at the table. You want a cup of tea?"

"Um, no. Thanks."

Rachel descended the stairs and put on tea water. Somehow the cold was different in Wisconsin than it was in

Colorado. She started a fire then poured her tea. Shannon sat down at the table right after she did.

"I see you're wearing long sleeves again. Is there something I should know about?"

"Mom, can we not make this about me? Besides, it is winter. I'm cold. You're supposed to have good news, remember?" Shannon smiled to lighten up her tone.

"Yes, well, I think it's good news and I'm hoping you will as well. Dillon has asked me to marry him and I said yes." She held out her hand for Shannon to see the ring.

Shannon felt her eyes fill with tears. "How could you? How could you do such a thing?"

"I'm sorry you feel that way, but this is my life, Shannon."

"Your life? What about my life? What about Shelly and Sam? What about Dad?" Don't they have a life, too? Have you even considered how this will affect all of our lives?"

"I have to make the best decision I can. I'm responsible for me. No one else. You're almost twenty. You will live your life as you see fit. I'll do the same with mine." Rachel stood up. "And you will treat Dillon with respect or you will no longer live under my roof, do you understand me?"

Shannon was having difficulty breathing. "I can't believe how selfish you've become. I bet you slept with him, didn't you?"

Rachel's hand reached out and slapped Shannon across the face. "Don't you dare talk to me that way."

Shannon smirked. "That's what I thought. You make me sick."

Rachel was seeing red. "Get out of my house. Go live with your saint of a father."

"Don't worry. I'm leaving. I wouldn't stay here if you paid me."

Shannon ran upstairs for a few things then slammed the door on her way out.

Rachel sobbed into her hands. *What happened to my perfect life?* She wiped her nose then picked up her now cold tea and dumped it in the sink. She found a wine glass and poured herself a glass of wine instead. She needed it to calm her nerves and think. What was she going to do about Shannon? She couldn't leave her out in the cold. She had to call Ryan.

The doorbell rang as she picked up her phone. She opened the door, knowing it would be Ryan. Shannon probably called him while she was upstairs. "Hey. Come on in."

"Thanks. Shannon asked me to come get her. She said you two got into some kind of a fight."

"Yeah, I pretty much kicked her out."

He nodded. "Yeah, that's what she said. Want to tell me what happened?"

She motioned for the dining table. "Sit down. You might as well hear it, too."

Ryan noticed her glass of wine and hid his surprise. The girls had told him she was drinking, but he didn't want to believe them. He sat down and said nothing.

"Do you want something to drink?"

"No, I'm good. What's going on?"

"Dillon asked me to marry him. I said yes. Shannon didn't like it so much. Which, had she stopped there, I could have handled that. But, the way she's been talking to me lately, I just won't stand for it."

Ryan looked at the rock on her left hand and swallowed hard. *Lord, do you see that? How can I compete with that?* "You're right. You shouldn't have to deal with her being disrespectful. A week or two at my house and she'll be ready to apologize. I have a small television set with a couple of local channels and that is it for entertainment. She'll get a lumpy pull out couch for a bed and a two-burner apartment stove to cook on. There just isn't much else. Of course, my Bible is always on the table so maybe a few days of reading that will remind her of how she was raised."

"Well, thanks." Rachel remembered her manners. "Shannon told me about Terry. I'm sorry."

"Yeah. Death makes us come face to face with our own immortality. I'm thankful I got things straightened out with God. Every day I find myself on my knees, grateful for his mercy. I could have died in my rebellion. Instead, he was patient with me and welcomed me home like the prodigal son I was."

Rachel could hear the voice in her head, imploring her to return to her first love. She took a large drink of her wine then remembered who she was drinking with. She felt her face turn red then justified her actions. *Jesus himself turned the water into wine. I can have a glass if I want to.*

Ryan noticed her discomfort and changed topics. It was obvious the Holy Spirit was dealing with her in his own way. "Have you told Sam yet?"

"No, I haven't had a chance. I don't expect she'll take it hard though. You know how much she wants both of us to be happy and be who we really are."

"Yeah, about that. I've wanted to talk to you for a while now. I thought that reporter was going to do a good job and tell the truth without twisting every word I said. I learned my lesson there."

"Ryan, look, you don't have to explain anything to me. I understand. I can't say I wasn't hurt, but I've gotten over it. I'm happy now." She reached over and placed her hand over his. "Just be happy for me, okay?"

He stood up. He couldn't stand to see another man's ring on his wife's finger. True, she filed for divorce, but it wasn't a done deal yet. He had to leave before he messed things up even more. "I truly do want you to be happy. I'll always want that for you."

She stood up and kissed his cheek. She lingered a few seconds more than she should have. Why couldn't she just let go? He'd been gone since June. It was January. Seven months had passed. "I want you to be happy as well. Goodbye, Ryan."

She closed the door behind him and finished off her wine.

Ryan opened the door of his car and climbed in. The heat wasn't working the best. You'd think a guy working at a car dealership would at least have a car with heat. "Looks like you're living with me."

"Suits me just fine."

"Okay. I hope you're not expecting much."

Ryan drove across town and into the parking lot of his building.

"Where are we?"

"This ,my daughter, is your new home."

Shannon turned up her nose. "You have to be kidding me?"

"Nope, I kid you not. This is where I live. Come on, let me show you home."

He opened the door for her then went to the wall heater unit and turned up the heat.

"It's freezing in here."

"It'll get warm soon. Not super warm, but at least better than it is now."

Shannon turned in a circle then saw the only door in the place. "What's in there?"

"That would be the bathroom."

"This is it? Where do you sleep?"

He pointed to the couch.

Shannon saw a bug run across the floor and she screamed. Ryan quickly killed it with his shoe. "It won't hurt you. It's hard to be bug free in apartments. Besides, they're looking for a warm place to sleep too."

"Oh, this is gross. I can't stay here."

"You haven't given yourself much of a choice, have you?"

She thought back to her conversation with her mom and swallowed. "I guess not."

Ryan turned to the small kitchen area of the studio apartment and smiled to himself. So much for a week or two, this girl wouldn't last more than two days. He had to face facts. His girls were spoiled. They had no idea what living hard was like. He could make it easy on her and take her out or at least order in, but if she really wanted to see how the other half lived, she could have it in all its glory. He opened the freezer. "We

215

have Salisbury steak, pepperoni pizza or meatloaf. Take your pick."

Shannon looked confused.

He held up the three Banquet dinner choices for her to choose from and waited for her response.

"You actually eat that stuff?"

"It's really not bad. You'll get used to it."

"I've decided I'm not all that hungry."

"Well, maybe you should watch how I make it so you know for tomorrow. I'll be working all day and well, this is pretty much all we have to eat." He smacked another bug on the little counter. He watched her turn green and almost laughed out loud.

Dillon watched the drama happening across the street. He hoped Rachel was okay. He picked up his phone. "Hey beautiful. Want some company?"

"I was just putting on my jacket to take Romeo for a walk. Want to go?"

"Yeah, I could go for some fresh air."

He met her outside and together they walked around the block as Romeo smelled and marked his territory.

Rachel was learning to be forward. "Want some company tonight?" She looked to see his reaction. "It was a tough evening."

"I'd love some company. Have you eaten yet?"

"No, I didn't have the energy to deal with it."

"No worries. I have that much covered. I was about to put on a chicken stir-fry. You interested?"

"Sounds great. Want me to bring anything?"

"No, I think I have everything we need." He kissed her at her front door then went to start dinner.

Rachel let Romeo in the house and checked her messages. Shelly texted and wanted to know if she could spend the night at Emily's. They had so much to catch up on. Rachel texted her back and said, sure. Ryan had left a voicemail about his and Shannon's evening so far. Rachel found herself laughing. She could just imagine Shannon turning on the water and hearing the pipes creaking in the walls. She'd freak. Add having to drink water from a rusty faucet, and she was surprised Shannon wasn't crawling back home. Ryan wasn't going to get her any special groceries until tomorrow after work. She'd have to suffer through a full day without her normal luxuries, like bottled water.

She attached her phone to the wall charger and left for Dillon's. She didn't plan on staying overnight so she didn't think twice about leaving it at home.

Rachel was laughing so hard it hurt. She'd never been drunk before. Yeah, she'd gotten tipsy on wine and champagne, but tonight, Dillon made her a sour apple martini. Then another and another until she'd lost count. The voice in her head was quiet. The girls were gone. She didn't think it would hurt any and besides, now she knew what the fuss was all about. All through college she'd had opportunity after opportunity to drink and she'd always said no. She had been so serious, such a stick in the mud. What could it hurt? She wasn't driving. She was at her fiancé's house so she wasn't in danger. She could think of no reason whatsoever to not drink her troubles away. And downing those martinis didn't take an arm-twisting. They were better than Kool-Aid.

She didn't remember taking her clothes off little by little as she lost at darts. She didn't remember going in the hot tub with no clothes on. She didn't remember throwing up and she didn't remember ending up in Dillon's bed. She remembered

217

nothing. Nor did she hear her phone ringing from across the street as she slept until early afternoon the next day.

Chapter Thirty Six

Where is she? Ryan ended his call. He had to be at work at seven and when he'd left, Shannon had been soundly sleeping on the pull out couch. He had been trying to call her since ten to see if she wanted to get something to eat for lunch. He was feeling guilty about making things harder for her than they had to be and wanted to make it up to her.

At first when she didn't answer her phone, he thought she might have braved the shower, so he waited and tried again. But, at eleven when he didn't hear from her, he began to worry. The nagging in his spirit could only be the prompting of the Holy Spirit so he left work, much to the chagrin of his boss, and went home to check on her. What he found made his blood curdle. One look at her and he dialed for an ambulance.

Shannon was hanging on. He had to reach Rachel. He had tried again and again, but no answer. Shelly wasn't answering her phone either. He couldn't leave the hospital. If the doctors or Shannon needed him, he had to be there. He kept praying she would get to her phone or realize the battery was dead.

Rachel groaned and winced. Her head was killing her. Just opening her eyes caused pain to shoot through her temple. What happened last night? She looked around the room. She didn't recognize where she was and she started to panic until she saw Dillon walk in the room, a smile on his face.

"Oh, good, you're awake. I thought you were going to sleep the day away."

"I'm not sure there's anything good about it. What time is it?"

"It's coming up on one thirty. I take it you've never been drunk before?"

"No. And I never want to do it again." Just the thought of drinking made her run for the bathroom. She hated getting sick. She wiped her mouth and found some mouth rinse then went back to Dillon's bed and collapsed. "What am I wearing?"

"Well, since you threw your clothes all over the house last night, I put you in one of my t-shirts to sleep in."

"I did what?"

"Oh yeah. You're what we like to call a fun drunk. You get happy. Loud. And you do things I'm guessing you wouldn't normally do. Like losing all your clothes playing darts."

Rachel was horrified. "No!"

Dillon shook his head. "Yes. And that's not all. You just had to go outside at two in the morning, in your birthday suit I might add, to get in the hot tub."

"I did not."

"Oh, yes you did. I had a heck of a time keeping you quiet. It's a good thing it's so cold outside. Everyone's windows are shut up tight. Even then I think we attracted some attention."

She covered her mouth and ran for the bathroom, again. She yelled out from her perch by the toilet. "Did anyone see me? Did they know it was me?"

"No, I'm pretty sure your secret is safe. Of course, I saw you and believe me, it was quite the show."

She touched her hand to her forehead. "Do you have any aspirin?"

"It's right here on the tray." He handed her a glass of water and the pills.

She downed the pills. "Has anyone tried to call me?"

"Not that I've heard. But then again, I don't remember seeing your phone. You didn't bring your purse over last night, I do know that much."

She frowned. "I'm so embarrassed."

He sat down next to her. "Don't be. Everyone needs to completely let go once in a while. And you have a lot of years to make up for."

"If this is what letting go is like, I'm not sure I'll be "letting go" again anytime soon." Rachel looked at him with terror in her eyes. "Tell me Jacob wasn't here."

"Relax. He wasn't here. He spent the night with a buddy from school."

"Thank you, thank you, thank you. I wouldn't have been able to show my face around here ever again." She looked at the Bronco's t-shirt she wore to bed. "Did you happen to find all my clothing? I probably should get dressed and go see about my phone. At the very least Shelly has tried to call about coming home."

Dillon pointed to her neatly folded clothing on the dresser. "I gathered it up and folded it. I don't wash women's clothing. I tried that once with my wife and was strictly ordered to never touch her clothes again. After shrinking her two hundred dollar sweater, I learned my lesson."

Shelly reached for her clothes. "This is great, thanks." She waited to see if he was going to leave.

"What? You're not turning all modest on me now are you?"

Rachel was appalled. "I don't remember being anything but modest."

"All right, fine. But as soon as we're married, this will stop." He bent to kiss her head. "You are beautiful. Even when you're hung over."

After the door closed she pulled off the t-shirt and got dressed. With the pain shooting through her skull, it was slow going. She emerged a few minutes later and waved off all offers of food. All she wanted was to take a hot shower, put on some fresh clothes and fall into her own bed. She promised to call him later then left for home.

Rachel opened the garage door with the code then let herself into the kitchen. She heard her phone beeping, indicating she had a message.

Four missed calls. Three from Ryan and one from Shelly. She was certain Ryan had more stories to tell on Shannon and Shelly probably wanted to be picked up but first, she had to take a shower. She smelled like a brewery. It was a necessity.

Rachel walked in her shower and stood underneath the hot water. She closed her eyes and let the water beat against her shoulders. It felt so good.

She went for comfort. She had no plans to go anywhere, although at some point she'd need to go to the grocery store, so she pulled on some sweat pants. She knew she should call Ryan back and make arrangements for Shelly, but the bed was pulling her hard. *I'll just lie down for a few minutes. They can wait a little longer.*

She felt someone shaking her and saying her name. She was having a hard time distinguishing between her dreams and reality. Finally it sunk in, someone was trying to wake her. "Mom, come on. Wake up."

Rachel cringed. "What?

"Mom, listen to me. You've got to wake up. Shannon is in the hospital. She tried to commit suicide this morning and they're not sure she's going to make it. We've got to get to the hospital. Dad has been trying to call you all day. Where have you been?"

Rachel was instantly alert. "Oh dear God." She pulled on her socks and tennis shoes. "Come on. Let's go."

She grabbed her purse and phone and was pulling out of the garage within minutes. Rachel was having a hard time seeing to drive through her tears. *What have I done?*

She and Shelly ran into the emergency room. Ryan was pacing. "Oh thank God. I've been praying you'd get my messages."

The first thing she noticed was his clothes, which were covered in blood. Probably Shannon's. The thought caused her eyes to well with tears. "I'm sorry. I plugged it into the charger and forgot to turn it back on. How is she?" Rachel winced at the deception.

Ryan shook his head. "It's touch and go. They got the bleeding to stop but by the time I got to her she had already lost

222

a lot of blood. She's in surgery now to repair the damage in her arm." He started crying. "This is all my fault. I shouldn't have been so hard on her."

Rachel held her husband. "It's not your fault. It's mine. I'm the one who fought with her. I could have been more understanding and less selfish." She released Ryan then sat down in a waiting room chair. "Tell me what happened."

"When we got back to my apartment, if you could call it that, she was clearly appalled. I thought I was teaching her a lesson, in being grateful for what you have and respectful and not taking what you were giving her for granted. I really thought she was taking it in good form. I mean, she clearly didn't like my place, but she didn't freak out."
I made a bed on the floor and she slept on the pull out couch. I woke up at six and was headed to work by six forty five." He looked as if he were going to throw up. "I tried to call her, to tell her I'd pick her up and we'd go to lunch, but she didn't answer. I started getting a bad feeling." His look said she knew the "feeling" he was talking about. "I drove home as fast as I could and I found her, bleeding, passed out, lying on the bed. I called for an ambulance then tried calling you and Shelly. Sam is on her way."

Rachel's guilt rose with the bile that was threatening to send her to the bathroom. She'd been passed out drunk when her daughter was bleeding to death. "Was it an accident? Did she just cut too deep this time?"

"We won't know until we can talk with her. She had cuts going across her arm from the wrist to the elbow on her left hand. It looks like she passed out before she could do the same kind of damage to her right arm. If she had managed to get to her right arm, we probably wouldn't have got to her in time." Ryan started crying all over again. "Rachel, what if this had happened when I was rebelling? What if I had dismissed the voice of the Holy Spirit like I'd done so many times before? Our little girl would have bled to death; she wouldn't have made it because of my selfishness."

Rachel knew exactly what he was talking about. If saving Shannon had been up to her obeying God's voice, her daughter

223

would be dead. The thought about destroyed her. Some mother she was. She held Ryan and cried with him. He had no idea her tears were tears of repentance while his were gratefulness.

Shelly watched her mother and father. She hadn't seen them get along this well since before her father left. She wondered if her sister's attempted suicide would somehow change things. She hadn't stopped praying. Even when her mom showed her the ring, even when she apologized for her attitude, she hadn't stopped praying that God would provide a miracle. Should she tell them this was her fault? She was praying for a miracle at any cost. She never would have sacrificed her sister. Never. She kept her tears quiet. Every heated drop reminded her of her sins, of her selfishness.

Ryan and Rachel sat for several hours, waiting for news on Shannon's condition. Mainly, they commiserated in their own silence. Occasionally one of them would remember something particularly endearing that she had done as a child.

Rachel watched as one by one, friends joined them. Val was the first one there. She quietly sat down next to Rachel. Rachel could tell she was praying. A short while later, Herbert joined her. Mark, with a change of clothes for Ryan, Jessi, Aunt Merry and Olivia were next. Church members started filing in, including the ladies who had whispered behind her back. Today she saw them for who they really were, ladies who messed up, just like she did. She felt her heart swell in love for them when they hugged her. Word got out and soon the waiting room was full of prayer. Watching them pray, watching them with bowed heads praying for her daughter was more than Rachel could take. She dropped to her knees in the waiting room and cried out to God. This was family. These were the people she needed to be surrounding herself with. She felt hands on her back as the people who truly loved her prayed with her. *Oh God. I'm so sorry.*

She didn't know what tomorrow would bring, if she'd ever share her life with anyone, but she knew Dillon wasn't the man for her. His lack of faith should have been her first clue. She took the ring off her finger and put it in her purse.

She chose to ignore God's gentle reminders and followed her flesh. She was so afraid of being alone she allowed her fear to control her and she cast aside the One who would truly never leave her. She felt her soon to be ex-husband kneel beside her. She knew she still loved him. In fact, he's the only one she had ever loved. Maybe someday she would find true love again.

Even if Ryan weren't gay, he would never forgive her for what she'd done. She doubted she'd ever be able to forgive herself. She rocked on her knees somewhat calmed by his presence, yet just being near him also reminded her of her indiscretions.

Rachel wiped her nose with the tissue Val handed her as the surgeon walked into the waiting room. She looked for Ryan. "Shannon has made it through surgery. She's had several blood transfusions and quite a few stitches in her arm to repair the damage. We won't know if she will be able to use her arm until after some healing takes place. There will be permanent damage." She looked to Rachel. "If your husband hadn't found her when he did, there could have been even more damage, possibly even death. Normally a suicide attempt cutting across the wrist is the least likely to cause death. But, because of how many cuts she made, and the depth, well, let's just say she's one lucky girl."

Ryan looked directly at the surgeon. "She's blessed."

"Well, whatever you want to call it is fine with me. I just know that things could have been a lot worse." She continued. "She will be in here for a few days so we can watch her. I have called her counselor and she is on her way. Since this is her second attempt, at least that we know of, you should discuss treatment options." She let that thought sink in. "I'll have a nurse take you back shortly to see her. Her counselor will tell you how you should act toward her. She needs support right now more than anything else."

Samantha arrived looking tan and refreshed, although worry creased her forehead. "How is she?"

They filled her in, then sat back down and waited some more.

Shannon's counselor had come, just as the surgeon said she would. Together they discussed what to say to her, to tell her they loved her and they're glad she's alive. She admitted these things were common sense, but Ryan and Rachel would be surprised at how many people cast blame in situations like this. They looked at one another. They'd been playing that game since they'd gotten there.

Finally, Ryan and Rachel were led to their daughter. Each of them wiped away the tears outside the door and put on a smile for her sake, as well as their own.

She wasn't awake for long. They only had a couple of moments to tell her how much they loved her. She was still attached to multiple tubes and medical contraptions. Medicine was still being pumped into her body. Her arm was bandaged and her face was so pale it was nearly white. Rachel bent down and kissed her cheek. "I love you. I'll be here when you need me."

"That goes for both of us. We're not going anywhere."

Rachel held open the door. "Your sisters are going to come in. They want to see you."

Shannon opened her eyes and whispered. "I'm sorry."

Rachel didn't know what to say so she just smiled. They were all sorry. They had all done and said things that should never have been done or said. The questions was, could they heal and could they go on from here?

Ryan and Rachel thanked everyone for coming. Most everyone left after they went to her room. Knowing she was out of immediate danger they sent Sam home with Shelly then prepared to camp out for the evening at the hospital. They wanted to be there when she woke up.

After everyone was gone, Rachel stepped outside to call Dillon. She owed him that much. She saw several missed calls from him. He answered on the second ring. "There you are. I was about to send out the cavalry. I wasn't sure you survived after the night you had."

"Oh, I survived. Actually, I can't talk long. I'm at the hospital. Shannon tried to kill herself. She just came out of surgery."

"Oh, hon. I'll be there as soon as I can get there. You shouldn't have to go through something like this alone. Why didn't you call me right away?"

"I'm not alone. Ryan is here, too. I'll give you a call if I need you, okay?" She ended the call and went back into the waiting room.

Ryan was looking pretty tired. "Feel like getting some coffee?"

"Yeah, that sounds good. I'll let the nurse know we're going to the cafeteria."

"Good idea. Maybe a little food will give me some energy."

"You know, you can go home and get some rest. I'll call you if anything changes."

He pushed the button for the elevator. "No, I'll stay here with you. This is where we both belong. After we know she's doing well, we can both go home and get some sleep."

Shannon continued to remain stable. Ryan and Rachel ended up sleeping propped up against one another on one of the love seats in the waiting area. It wasn't the most comfortable way of sleeping but with Ryan's arm around her and her head on his shoulder, she fell into a comfortable resting position.

Ryan felt her breathing slow down against his shirt. He felt the warmth of her body next to his. He never thought he'd hold her like this again. He was horrified that his daughter had been at the brink of death, but if God used this to restore his family, he'd take it. He leaned his head back against the wall and closed his eyes.

Chapter Thirty Seven

Rachel knocked on Dillon's door. She had come home to change and shower but knew she had to do this. He opened the door. "Hi there." He stepped aside so she could enter. He wrapped her in his arms and attempted to kiss her. He felt her tense. "What's wrong? I mean, besides the obvious?"

She handed him the ring. "Dillon, I can't marry you."

"Why, what happened? Is it Ryan?"

"No, it's not Ryan."

"Is it something I've done? I said I would come be with you. I hope you're not upset with me for that."

"No, that's not it either. It's not anything you've done or haven't done. It is about who you are. You are a wonderful man and a great father. You are kind, and giving, smart and funny. You are so many good things and someday you will find the woman who is perfect for you. But that person is not me.

"The one difference we have, the one thing I cannot accept, is you are an unbeliever. The person I marry has to be as strong a believer, or stronger, than I am. And I believe with my whole being that God became flesh and was born as Jesus. I also believe he created the universe, even the blue sky. He died for me and he rose again and someday I will spend eternity with him in heaven. He is my very reason for being. I'm sorry but that is the one thing I cannot compromise. I tried to deceive myself into thinking I could, that I could be someone I'm not. It took my daughter being on the threshold of death for me to realize what a fool I've been."

Dillon sat down. His world had changed overnight. He thought he'd found the woman he could be with forever. Why couldn't he change? He looked at her expectantly. "What if I became a Christian? What would I have to do?"

Now she smiled. "I would never allow you to become a Christian for me. Believing in Christ is something you must do for yourself. When the yearning to know him becomes so strong, so strong that remaining apart from him is just not an option that is when you accept Christ." She kissed his cheek. "Please, I ask two things of you. First, will you forgive me? It was wrong of me to enter into a relationship with you. Instead of trusting God to be everything I needed, I allowed myself to depend on you. It wasn't fair to you." He tried to contradict her, but she wouldn't let him. "Second, I ask that you truly seek Christ. Would you ask him to reveal himself to you? Because when that happens, you won't be able to turn him down."

He felt the tears but refused to wipe them away. He nodded and committed to finding out if there really was a God. Maybe it would take his mind off losing her. She walked out of his house and out of his life. At home she erased his number from her phone and deleted him from her facebook account. Next, she poured two bottles of wine down the drain and threw the wine glasses away. She'd never allow anything to come between her and her God again.

She found her Bible tucked in her nightstand and took it with her back to the hospital. She couldn't undo what she'd done, but she could start over from here. She knew it wouldn't be easy. She'd dug a pretty deep hole. But, she'd do her best to follow God's will for her life, no matter what happened in her future.

Rachel sat down next to Ryan. She insisted that as soon as she got back, and she promised him it wouldn't be long, that he should go home and get some rest. Besides, she would be able to spend most of the day in Shannon's room. It would be much easier than the waiting room. She could read her Bible and pray. She had a lot of catching up to do.

Together they walked to their daughter's room. She had been moved to the top floor of the hospital, which was the psychiatric ward. Ryan didn't want to go back to his apartment. He didn't have the energy to clean his apartment and wash all the bedding before he got some rest. "Rachel, would it be okay with you if I crashed in the guest room?"

She thought of the mess he would be facing at his apartment. "Yes, of course. Why don't you take your bedding to the house and wash it while you're there."

He sighed. "Thank you. I'm so exhausted. Between sleeping on the hard floor the night before and in the loveseat here last night, I'm about to drop. I appreciate it."

Ryan went by the apartment and got a change of clothes and his bedding before going to the house. He started the washer then climbed the stairs and asked Shelly to switch the laundry for him. The guest room had a shower, for which he was thankful. Afterward he set his alarm and collapsed.

Shannon hated being confined. Her counselor had been to see her and her mom was basically camped out in her room. She just wished she could leave. She tried to tell them she hadn't tried to kill herself. She just started cutting and found she couldn't stop. They didn't believe her. They told her the end result was the same. She'd almost died."

She glared at her mother. How could she just sit there, like nothing was wrong and read her Bible? She asked to speak with her doctor, alone.

Rachel stood and stretched. She could use a sandwich. She'd lost track of time. She left the room so Shannon could have some privacy and spent a half hour in the cafeteria. When she got back to the third floor, her things were sitting at the nurses' station. The nurse smiled apologetically. "I'm sorry, but it looks as if Shannon has requested no visitors."

Rachel raised her eyebrows. "What do you mean, she's requested no visitors?"

"Sometimes our patients do that. The reasons vary as greatly as the patients. As you know, when someone tries to take their life, there are other issues involved. It is in the best interest of our patients to attempt to follow their wishes while they are here." She handed Rachel her Bible and jacket and escorted her to the door.

Rachel drove home, dumbfounded. Shannon really kicked her out? She shook her head. *Surely she isn't still mad about our fight the other night?* Although Shannon did know how to hold a grudge, Rachel would never have suspected her to hold onto her anger through all this. Then again, what did she know? She was only the mom.

She decided she had better get some groceries. First, she drove through and got a latte. She needed caffeine. She bought the ingredients for a meatloaf and mashed potatoes. She looked at the wine rack then dismissed the thought. She couldn't possibly have a problem with alcohol in that short of a time, could she?

Rachel could hear Ryan snoring when she walked in the house. *Some things never change.* She found his bedding in the washer and switched it over then began making the meatloaf. She was still trying to figure Shannon out when Ryan came downstairs a couple of hours later. "Hey, I thought you were staying at the hospital."

She set her tea cup down. "That was the plan. Until your daughter kicked me out."

Ryan's jaw dropped. "You're kidding me?"

"I wouldn't kid you about something like that. She actually asked for me to be removed from the room. I went to get a sandwich and when I returned, my things were at the nurses' station. I was escorted from the floor."

"Are we all banned, or just you?"

"The nurse told me she'd requested no visitors, but I too was wondering if it was just me. As much as I hate to admit it, I believe that could be the case."

Ryan sighed. "I wonder if I should go back up and find out what's going on?"

"It might not hurt. Do you want to eat first? I made a meatloaf and mashed potatoes and gravy."

"I was hoping you'd ask me. It smells fantastic and I'm starving."

Rachel set the table and called Sam and Shelly to eat. It almost felt like old times. Shannon was the only missing family member.

Much to Rachel's surprise and delight, Samantha actually ate a plate of food. Romeo didn't get a single bite from the table. Maybe after seeing the self-imposed torture her sister went through Sam realized it wasn't healthy to starve herself. One could always hope. Dinner was a success.

Ryan helped clean up then went to the hospital to see if he was on the "no visitor's list." Rachel handed him his clean bedding as he walked out the door. "Hey, thanks. This helps a lot."

"You're welcome. Let me know what happens, okay?"

"You bet. If I'm allowed in, I'll talk to her and find out what's going on."

She closed the door and wandered around the room for a while before plugging in her laptop. She had a message from Dillon.

Hey Rachel,

I'm sorry things happened the way they did. I hope we can still be friends and work together without things becoming too complicated. I thought this would be an easier, less painful way for me to contact you. I still think the world of you.

All my love,
Dillon

Rachel shut off the computer then picked up her Bible. She said goodnight to her daughters and closed her bedroom door. She ran a bath and lit some candles. Next to the tub were a wine glass and a half empty bottle of wine. She felt the pull to drink it then refused and dumped the contents down the bathroom sink. She threw the glass in the trash and climbed in the tub with her Bible. She only needed Jesus. He would sustain her and give her the courage to face her lonely days. He would be her strength. She was sound asleep by eight o'clock.

Chapter Thirty Eight

Rachel helped carry Shannon's suitcases from the car. She had agreed with her counselor to get inpatient help. Shannon looked like a different person. Rachel hoped that was the case. She could hardly believe it was March. She was still working with Dillon at the college and while she was tempted at times, she kept their relationship strictly platonic. He on the other hand tried everything to get her to see the error of her ways. Spring break had just begun so she had a full week to strengthen up.

She wanted to take the girls shopping for new dresses. Herbert and Val's fiftieth wedding anniversary would take place on Saturday and she felt they all needed something new after such a long winter. She spent most of her time these past few months reconnecting with the girls, mending those relationships that had been terribly jeopardized in the name of self preservation.

Her and Shannon's relationship was at the top of the list. She had made the hour and a half drive every Saturday to Milwaukee to visit her daughter. At first, Shannon refused to see her. After a couple of weeks, when Shannon realized her mother would visit regardless, and after two weeks of counseling sessions, she agreed to spend some time with her. They even had the opportunity to participate in some mother daughter counseling sessions, which was good for both of them.

Shannon realized that her mother's choices, while she may not agree with them, were hers to make. Rachel had to admit Shannon was an adult and she had to give her the space that she needed. In order for Shannon to feel like the adult she was, she needed to get involved in life, go back to school and get a job. She had to do something that would qualify her as an adult in her parents' eyes and thus be worthy of being treated like an adult instead of the dependent daughter she currently was.

Ryan set the last suitcase at the bottom of the stairs. In January when everything had happened, when Rachel broke off her engagement to Dillon, he thought things would fall into place with them, that they'd get back together but Rachel had kept her distance. Any attempt at talking to her beyond a casual 'how are you doing?' was promptly squashed. She wanted nothing to do with him. She was even going through with the divorce. He was crushed. "So, I'll see you at the party then?"

Rachel nodded. "Wouldn't miss it for the world."

He kissed Shannon's cheek. "I'm really proud of you."

She smiled. "Thanks, Dad."

Rachel waited patiently for Samantha to arrive. She was also on spring break and had agreed to come home to go shopping and attend the party. The only problem was, so far she was a no show. Both Shelly and Shannon were becoming impatient. Rachel was, too, for that matter. She'd tried to call her several times but Sam wasn't answering. Rachel decided to leave. When she called back, she could tell Sam where to meet them.

The girls spent a full day enjoying the spring like weather. The ongoing bet in the family was regarding when their last snowfall would be. It was always later than anyone projected. Though once March arrived, you could count on a least a few nice days as teasers. Sam finally called in the early evening, apologizing. Apparently she'd forgotten that she'd made other plans. She realized she should have called sooner but time got away from her. She did promise she'd be there on Saturday though.

Val's family had done a wonderful job decorating the hall. Rachel remembered dreaming about the years she and Ryan would spend growing old together. She was happy for Herbert and Val, she truly was, but part of her was sad. Her divorce would be final the following week after a short court appearance. She knew Ryan didn't understand why she wouldn't hear him out, but if he knew what she'd done, he wouldn't attempt reconciliation. She was saving him the trouble.

Rachel looked around for Sam. She hoped she made it. Sam had been distant since January when she'd come down for her sister's hospital stay. Rachel knew something was up, but had no clue what.

Finally she saw Sam come in on the arm of a good-looking young man. Rachel looked at her daughter. There was something different about her. She looked healthier. Rachel remembered the meatloaf dinner that Sam actually ate. Rachel shook her head. With Sam, you just never knew what was going to happen next.

Samantha waved to her mother then walked toward her. "Mom, this is Craig. Craig, my mom, Rachel."

Rachel welcomed Craig and gave her daughter a hug. "You look gorgeous." Sam was wearing a yellow dress that hung in folds and ended just above her knees. Against her tan skin, she looked fresh and springy. "I love that dress on you. It's just adorable. I guess you didn't need my help shopping after all."

Sam looked a little sheepish. "Is Dad here yet?"

"I don't know. I haven't seen him."

"We're going to socialize for a bit. I'll see if I can find him. I want to introduce him to Craig."

Rachel pointed to a nearby table. "We're sitting there if you want to join us."

Sam acknowledged her mom with a wave then set off to find her dad. Her skirt swooshed as she walked. It reminded Rachel of a baby doll dress from her growing up years. No waistline, just a straight drop. She had to admit, the dress was wonderful for dancing.

Ryan got off work a little late so he arrived just as the party was getting underway. He had stopped off at home to change into something a little more celebratory and a little less "car salesman." Not that he minded having shirts with logos. At least the customers knew he was a salesman.

He spotted her from across the room. She stood alone, like she had been waiting for him all her life. Indeed she had, but he'd have to prove that to her. Something was holding her back. He wanted to tell her the truth about his and Terry's relationship. Once she understood maybe then she'd give him a chance.

He started walking toward her, willing her to look at him as he did. Halfway there, he was spun around by his oldest daughter. "Dad! There you are. I want you to meet Craig. Craig, this is my dad, Ryan."

He put his hand in the younger man's outstretched hand. "Good to meet you Craig." He raised his eyebrows at Sam.

"We're going to get some food. Do you want to sit with us?"

Ryan looked to where he last saw Rachel and she was gone. He looked around the room before he answered Sam. "Maybe. I'll find you if I do." He wasn't going to be deterred. She was going to hear him out.

Ryan found her sitting at a table with Jessi and Mark. "Mind if I join you?"

Mark stood up. "Not at all. In fact, now that you're here, I'm going to get a plate. The ladies wanted to wait until the line shortened up. I say no way. I'm hungry."

Ryan noticed Sam and Craig nearing the table. "I guess they beat us to it."

"I see that. Who is that with her?"

"Well, since this is the first I heard about him, all I can tell you is, his name is Craig. Other than that, I have no idea."

Sam walked by with a full plate, teasing her dad. "See, you should have come with us. I don't think they have anything left."

236

Ryan yelled after her. "They better not have run out. I'm starving."

Her laughter drifted off, as did the smell of her food.

Mark studied his friend. "Anything happening with you and Rachel yet?"

Ryan shook his head. "Nothing. Absolutely nothing. She's nice. She is thoughtful. But, she won't give me the time of day."

"And the court day for the divorce is next week, right?"

"Yeah. I think I need to kidnap her and make her listen to me."

Mark took a plate from the stack. "Do you think you could get the girls to help?"

"Good idea. Maybe come up with some sort of plan to get her alone. Something secluded where she can't get away from me."

"If it was warmer, I'd say go out on my boat. But, that's a little hard to do in March."

Ryan thought for a minute. "What if I kidnapped her in her own house? Made her dinner as a surprise? Had Jessi take her shopping, get her out of the house so I could get everything ready? Do you think she'd be game?"

"Yeah, she'd get involved. I'm not sure I've ever seen Jessi pray so hard. Well, maybe, but she's been praying just as hard for you two as she has for anything else. She just knows God is going to work it out. Do you want to work it out for tomorrow night? Jessi is planning to tackle some wallpaper project at the house. She could ask Rachel to help?"

"You mean it? That would be perfect. I'll make sure the girls are out of the house too." Ryan thought about it a minute. "Have her home by seven, sound good?"

"Okay. I'll fill Jessi in and she'll do her thing."

They filled their plates then went back to their table. The line had shortened considerably so Jessi and Rachel went next and were back within a couple of minutes. The four of them talked like they used to do. Ryan noticed how right it felt. He wanted more times like this.

Val kept a close eye on Ryan and Rachel. Everyone, and she meant everyone, was praying for them. That girl was keeping her distance. She had an invisible board between them that she refused to put down. She wished she knew what it was, but Rachel wasn't talking. Yes, she'd been coming to church and yes, she had recommitted herself to her faith, but when it came to Ryan, she wasn't giving in.

Herbert put his arm around his wife. "They're going to be all right."

She scowled at him. "And how do you know that?"

He looked down at the feisty woman who'd been his better half for fifty years. "Do you really think you're the only one who hears from the Big Guy?"

"So Herbert Harold Sutton, are you telling me there is nothing wrong with your hearing?"

Herbert looked around. "Did I say that?"

"That is what I heard."

"Woman, you hear what you want to hear."

"Husband, you don't hear when you don't want to. I know you turn down that hearing aid when it's convenient for you. Listening to God and not listening to your wife has to be some sort of sin. If you had been listening to me, you would've known they were gonna be all right cause I told you they were gonna be all right. Men."

"How am I supposed to know when you've got something useful to say and when you don't? We need a sign. If it's useful, make the sign and I'll know to turn up the old hearing aid."

Val hit her husband's arm and wandered off to hold her great grandson. Maybe then she'd have a serious conversation. Course, they would have to name that baby Herbert. Poor kid. She held him and cooed. "Some day you'll make some woman very happy. Just like your grandpa made me."

Rachel said her goodbyes. It had been years since she'd visited with Val's children. They had all married and moved and had kids who were now having kids of their own. She couldn't believe Val was having great grandchildren. She had seen her loving on the little guy. She wondered which of her girls would be the first to give her a grandchild? She doubted Sam would settle down anytime soon and Shannon wasn't even dating. Shelly would probably be first and she still had to finish high school. She would be waiting a long time.

Ryan gave her a hug and told her he'd see her tomorrow at church. She wished he'd stop trying. It wouldn't do any good.

Mark and Jessi were leaving too. Jessi had asked Rachel if she would come over the next day after church to help her with some wallpapering. Jessi would provide lunch if Rachel brought some old clothes and helped out. What were friends for, right?

Sam promised to give Shelly and Shannon a ride home so they could stay a little longer. Val's kids had hired a jazz band to play and they were enjoying both the music and each other's company. Shelly was still on spring break, so why not? Rachel drove home alone.

Chapter Thirty Nine

Sunday morning arrived with more sunshine and spring temperatures. Rachel had to peek at her garden. She knew nothing would be breaking ground yet, but just looking gave her such pleasure. She was surprised to see a few daffodils pushing through the earth. The thought of the pretty yellow flowers put a smile on her face. It wouldn't be long now.

Ryan sat with her and the girls. Even though she'd forgiven the ladies for their gossiping, she still felt like she was on display sitting with her soon to be ex-husband. But, the girls wanted to sit with both of them so what could she say?

Worship was wonderful as usual. Mark was the guest speaker and he spoke on being Christ to everyone you meet, regardless of what they look like, smell like, sound like or act like. His sermon was very good. It reminded her of when her husband preached. She was always convicted from the insight he gave.

Rachel stopped by home after church to feed and let Romeo out. After changing, she went for her afternoon wallpapering job at Jessi's. She had to admit, she had a blast. Aunt Merry had made a pot of homemade tomato soup and grilled bacon and cheese sandwiches.

Rachel was so full she had to force herself to move from the dining chair to the room to wallpaper. By the time she was finished, she was covered in sticky glue.

Jessi didn't look much better. "You sure you don't want to clean up here? I probably have something in my closet that will fit you."

"No, that's okay. I'll head home to a nice hot shower then I'm going to relax and catch up on some reading."

"Okay, well, I appreciate the help. Thanks a lot."

"You're welcome. When it's time to redo mine, I know who the expert is."

"Anytime."

Rachel walked toward her van. She was surprised Mark and Jessi still lived in this old house. It wasn't in the best neighborhood, and she knew that Jessi's Dad had left her with a good inheritance when he passed away. Of course, they did work and minister in this neighborhood, so it made sense that they would choose to live here. She drove across town and pulled up in front of the house. The lights were on. *The girls must be home.* She let herself in through the garage.

She could smell lasagna baking as soon as she opened the door to the kitchen. Candles were on the table. A salad was made and garlic bread was in a basket. *What is going on?* The girls were nowhere to be found and even if they were, lasagna was not their standard fare to cook. It smelled delicious. She hadn't realized she was hungry until she smelled the cooking food.

Ryan stood in the living room next to the lit fireplace. "Hi."

"Ryan?"

"Yeah. It's me."

"What are you doing? What is all this?"

"Well, your favorite, at least it used to be. And, I've been trying to talk to you for weeks. I need to say some things and you need to let me. I thought we could have a nice dinner then talk for a little while."

"Ryan, I know what you're trying to do and trust me, it won't work."

"You haven't heard what I've come to say. How do you know?"

"Because. I just do."

"Well, regardless, I want you to hear me out. If, after I'm finished, you still want to go through with the divorce, I won't stop you. But first, you have to listen."

Rachel sighed. If this was the only way to get him to stop fighting her on the divorce, then she'd have to sit through his explanation. "Fine. But I want your word when you're done and I haven't changed my mind, you'll not fight me in court on Thursday."

"Done. You have my word." He looked at her outfit. "Do you want to change before dinner?"

For a moment Rachel considered staying just as she was. Maybe it would aid in convincing him she wanted to be left alone. She reconsidered when she pulled her glued shirtsleeve from her arm. "Yeah, I better go change. I'll be back in a few minutes."

Rachel quickly showered and put on a pair of jeans and a t-shirt then returned to have dinner and listen to her husband's story. She got it, she really did. But she didn't want to hear how he came to love men more than women. And more than that, if he confessed, then she'd have to. Not that God didn't know what she'd done, of course he did. But, for whatever reason, what Ryan thought of her still mattered. And she knew if he didn't hate her, he'd be sorely disappointed. And she'd rather have a friendship with him than nothing at all. But, a deal was a deal.

She put her napkin on her plate. "It was delicious. You always did make the best lasagna."

"Thanks. And it always was one of your favorites." He stood up and pointed to the living room. "Let's get comfortable, shall we?"

"Ryan, are you sure this is something you want to do? We don't have to do this."

"I have to." He led her to the couch and sat down beside her. "Please, just hear me out."

Rachel nodded in agreement.

"Remember when I told you that Terry protected me from bullying when I was a kid?"

"Yeah."

"Well, my dad worked second shift and after work he'd go to the bar and drink as much as he could before they closed. He would stumble home, have a few more glasses of whisky then usually pass out. On my eighth birthday, before he left for work my dad told me he had a special present for me. He'd hardly looked at me for the first eight years of my life, and now he was going to bring me something special? I was so excited. I waited up as long as I could but two in the morning is pretty late and I ended up falling asleep.

I remember hearing noises and wanting to wake up but for some reason I was stuck in my dream. When I did wake up it was with a slap across the face. I still didn't know if I was dreaming or if my father was indeed standing over my bed, drunk and yelling at me. He forced me onto my stomach then I felt such a terrible pain I screamed. He clamped his hand over my mouth to keep me from screaming again. I was so afraid. so helpless. I had no idea what to do and when I tried to scream and couldn't, I bit him. He beat me with his hands until I hurt too bad to move. He then turned me back onto my stomach and finished what he started. This time, he used duct tape to keep me from screaming. My mom was passed out in the other room. She couldn't have cared less. At least he wasn't doing it to her."

Rachel held her hand over her mouth. She couldn't imagine anyone hurting a child this way. She tried to wipe away the moisture from her cheeks but the tears wouldn't stop.

Ryan handed her the tissue box. "I grew smart pretty quick. It took me a while though. Some nights he'd leave me alone. Other nights he'd come to my room and use me for his own satisfaction. On those nights I'd try and pretend to be sleeping or sick. I figured if I could make myself throw up, he'd leave me alone. I tried everything. He found me wherever I hid. Of course there weren't too many places a kid could go to hide.

Not only did I fear him, but I was also deeply ashamed. I knew what was happening was wrong but somehow he made me believe it was my fault, that there was something wrong with me and that if anyone ever found out, they would take me away and put me in a kid's jail. I believed him. I knew it was wrong. And somehow I'd asked for it so what he was doing had to be my fault."

Ryan took a drink of his water. "This went on for about six months when I came up with the bright idea to crawl out my window and hide on the fire escape. Even in the dead of winter I'd hear him come home and when I figured out I was going to have the pleasure of his company I would quietly climb out and wait. I knew I could go back in when my mother stopped screaming. I would know I was safe. He'd forced himself on her instead.

One night it was so cold, I remember thinking I wouldn't make it. The wind was freezing the tears against my cheeks. I must have made some noise when I slipped because I heard this voice, this kid who lived below us inviting me into his apartment. He didn't ask any questions; he didn't have to. He understood. His mom had had boyfriends who were a little more interested in him than they were her so he knew what I was going through. He took to hiding me on those nights. My dad still caught me on some nights. If the plant where he worked closed early, he'd catch me off guard. He also figured out where I was going. But Terry's mom would threaten to call the police if he pushed it.

By the time I was twelve my dad quit trying to force himself on me and by the time I was thirteen, my friendship with Terry had turned into something tragically wrong. He was three years older than me. We had each other. That was it. He was there for me, he stood up for me, he protected me. I really thought I loved him and besides, that kind of physical relationship had been a part of who I was for five years from the man who was supposed to love me more than anyone else. My understanding of love became terribly skewed. I was young and impressionable. My father had to love me and if that is what guys did who loved each other, then why not with Terry?"

Hearing the horrors that her husband endured broke Rachel's heart. How could she not know this? How could he have kept it to himself all these years? "Ryan, why didn't you tell me?"

Ryan shook his head. "I know. It was dumb of me. I should have told you everything. But I was afraid. I was afraid you wouldn't love me like I loved you, that you wouldn't understand. I was introduced to Christ right after I turned eighteen. I had a hard time giving up my old life. I didn't know how to trust God implicitly. I was pulled between two worlds. On one hand, here was the God father figure who supposedly loved me enough that he died for me. I found that kind of love, while desirable, a little hard to believe. But I wanted to believe it, I really did. On the other hand, there was Terry. He truly had been there for me. He had taken a punch for me on more than one occasion and had sacrificed his own well being to make sure I was taken care of. I owed him. Not only that, but I truly cared for him. I understood that a homosexual relationship was wrong once I got into some Bible studies and my shame became more acute.

When I met and fell in love with you, I knew that God had chosen you to be my wife. I thought about coming clean. Then I saw your morals and how good you were and I couldn't take the chance on losing you. I look back now and see how I didn't trust God to work out the details. I should have been completely honest with you. There have been so many times I've thought about when, out of fear, Abraham tried to pass off Sarah as his sister. That is about as close as I can come to making sense of what I'd done.

I battled the feelings I had even while in seminary, all the way until my senior year when I met you. You changed everything for me. You made me see what true love was, what it could be. You gave me the chance to redefine myself and make my life into what God had intended for me. You brought hope into my world. God knew I needed someone who would love me. You were that someone. No wait, you are that someone."

Rachel shook her head trying to talk between the sobs. "But you left me Ryan. You left me for him."

"No, Rachel. I didn't leave you for him. I left because I was confused. When he showed up every painful memory that I'd failed to deal with resurfaced. I was that little boy again who was hiding in corners trying to find safety. My world was falling apart. I've never been good at dealing with problems head on. If at all possible, I'd rather avoid them. You know that about me. When Terry showed up, I didn't want to run into his arms, I just wanted to run. I've never loved anyone but you."

He leaned toward her and took her hands. "Rachel, I promise you this. Since the day I said I do, I have never, nor will I ever touch another man or woman. I promise you, I have never been unfaithful to you. I've never even been tempted. Not even with Terry."

Rachel gasped. She had justified her behavior based on what she thought Ryan and Terry were doing. Yes, he was guilty of leaving her. And yes, he was guilty of running instead of dealing with their issues, but she was the one guilty of adultery. *Oh dear Lord, what am I going to do?* She thought about Ryan's confession and knew she had to tell him. She'd known this day was coming for months. She, like Ryan, had tried to run. She was just as guilty as he was. She had failed just as much, if not more. "Ryan, you can't love me. I don't deserve your love."

"Listen to me, Rachel. It's not a matter of can or can't. I simply do. When God joined us together, I committed myself to you. Nothing will tear us apart, not if we don't let it."

"But you don't understand." Her words spurted out in bits between the sobs.

"Talk to me, Rachel."

"When I agreed to marry Dillon, I…" She tried to finish her sentence. She really did. "Ryan, I did horrible things. I was angry. I was so hurt. When Dillon held me, I forgot I was unlovable. I justified my behavior because he loved me and had asked me to be his wife. I pretended it was okay." She cried even harder. "Ryan, that's not all. The day you tried to reach me when Shannon went into the hospital, I was drunk. I was throwing up and unable to function. When I did get back to my phone, and I saw you called, I went to sleep instead of calling you back. My little girl could have died while I was nursing a hangover. Who does that, Ryan? Who?"

She put her head in her folded arms and cried like a baby. Every tear she'd been storing up poured out of her.

Ryan was silent for a brief moment while he prayed. "Rachel?" He lifted her chin. "When Christ died for us, he did it in spite of every sin he knew we'd commit. He took every sin on his shoulders and he still hung on the cross even though he knew we'd mess up. He loved us that much. That is how I love you. That is what Paul meant in Ephesians when he tells husbands to love their wives as Christ loved the church."

Ryan wiped the tears from her cheeks. "Deep down I knew that there would be consequences for my behavior. I'm not going to say I'm not hurt, because I am. But, I don't blame you for that. I blame myself. When I stood at the altar and said I do, that meant as Christians, God became the head of our house. I promised to love you and cherish you through everything. I failed miserably and one day I will stand before God and answer for what I've done. I did not lay my own flesh down as Christ did for us; instead I gave in to confusion and fear. I didn't allow God to lead me. I will always regret what I've done. Always. But know this, I love you and I don't want to live my life without you. I forgive you, Rachel, will you forgive me?"

Rachel clung to her husband. These were the arms she wanted wrapped around her. This was the man who was supposed to be beside her. No one else. How could she have ever thought otherwise? She didn't know what was supposed to happen next, but she knew she would crawl through mud for this man who was as much a part of her as her own living, beating heart. "Yes, Ryan, I forgive you."

Chapter Forty

Ryan held Rachel's hand as he stood outside the old apartment building. Not much had changed. The fire escape, which had become his personal refuge, still rested outside his bedroom wall. It's funny how over time things become just that, things. They cannot hurt you or hold your memories hostage if you don't let them. When a person allows healing to come, these things that once held you captive become powerless.

Ryan had not seen or spoken to his parents in more than twenty years. At eighteen he left home for college and never looked back. When Rachel and he married, he told her his parents had died. If he had told her the truth, he would have had to come face to face with his past. Now that he'd addressed all the other lies his life had been built on, he had this last one to conquer. He had to face and forgive his mother and father. No matter what the outcome.

Rachel watched her husband work up his courage to enter his parent's building. She prayed that they had changed, that they had come to know Christ. She squeezed his hand. "Are you ready?"

"You are with me. Christ is with me. My father no longer controls me through fear. I can do this." He gave her a squeeze in return. "Let's go."

Together they walked up the four flights to the apartment that still housed his parents. It hadn't taken long to confirm that they were both still alive and that they still lived in the same place. A single light bulb hung from each landing, barely casting enough light to see shadows tiptoeing through the dark. Ryan wondered how many children might be hiding in those shadows.

They stopped in front of the old apartment. Ryan knocked. A gruff voice behind the door called out. "Who's there?"

Ryan tried to swallow but found his throat was so dry he could barely eek out a sound. He took a quick drink from his water bottle. "It's Ryan."

The door pulled open, the chain clearly still linking the door to the frame. A woman with dark blue eye shadow and bleached hair peered through the opening. "Ryan, is that you?"

"Uh, yeah, it's me."

"I thought you were dead."

"Well, clearly I'm not dead. Can we come in?"

"We? Who is with you?"

"My wife, Rachel. May we come in?"

The door closed. They could hear the rattle of the chain. Finally, the door opened wide enough for the two of them to enter. Ryan stood still, staring at the familiar surroundings. "Well, come in then. Don't stand there all day and let the neighbors see everything we got. We don't like people in our business."

Rachel followed Ryan into the cramped apartment. The smell of booze, unwashed bodies and dirty living almost flattened her. She prayed for strength.

Some guy was wresting an alligator on the television. The man sitting in the chair only slightly resembled the father he used to know. He had always been a big man. When Ryan was young, this man had seemed a giant. Now he looked pathetic and sad. He was glued to the drama on the screen. Ryan cleared his throat.

"You want something, boy?"

"Um, yeah. I'd like to talk to you."

"Then talk. Don't just stand there."

Ryan looked at the television set then back to his father.

"You think I can't do two things at once, boy? I'm not so old I can't hear you and watch this program. So talk."

"I wanted to come to tell you I forgive you."

For the first time since they had arrived, the man stopped looking at the TV and looked toward Ryan. The expression on his face showed that he had no idea what Ryan was talking about. "What the devil for?"

Ryan stuttered. "For what you did to me as a boy."

Dawning crossed the older man's face. "You didn't get nothin' you didn't deserve."

Rachel's mouth dropped but she stayed silent. As much as she'd like to let the old man have it with everything in her, her husband had to be the one to deal with his past, not her. She waited.

Ryan figured nothing had changed. "I disagree with you on that. No one deserves what you did to me. You put me through hell."

"You've said your piece, now get out."

"Once you listen to what I've come to say, then I'll leave. You owe me that much."

"I don't owe you nothin'."

Ryan's mom interjected. "Just shut up and let the boy say what he come to say."

The room was silent. His father clamped his lips shut.

Ryan looked from his mother to his father and wondered about the shift in power. She never would have gotten away with defying him in years past. "Mom, Dad, for many years I've allowed what happened to me as a child to control me. Because of my fear of facing my past, I've hurt those that I love the most. You may not know this, but after I left home, I attended Bible College." He looked to Rachel who encouraged him with her smile. "I got married to this beautiful woman standing next to me. We have three lovely daughters. I almost lost them. I lived a lie. In over twenty years of marriage, not once did I speak out about who I was or where I came from. My past caught up with me and almost destroyed our marriage."

Ryan took another drink from his water bottle. "When I look back, what I really didn't do was trust Christ. At age eighteen I accepted him as my Lord and Savior but what I really did was accept him on my terms. I didn't trust him with the really big stuff, like working out the details of my past. I felt I needed to lock that away so I might be lovable. Even though I knew Jesus loved me, I didn't see him as being more powerful and in control of my life. And he wasn't because I didn't give him control. I kept part of me from him. Partly because I didn't trust him but also because I felt I was tainted and too messed up for anyone to love me. But that's not how Jesus works. He loves us no matter what we've done or been through. He can mend our scars and heal our wounds. And even when your past is as dark as the deepest hell, he can shine a light where there is only darkness."

Ryan looked at his parents. "I guess what I'm trying to say is, he loves you. He wants to free you from the guilt and the pain you've been harboring. You must truly be sorry for your sin and you must accept that he is Lord of your life. If you can do that, then you can spend eternity with Christ in heaven. I've made a choice to forgive you for what you've done. It was up to me. I decided. Even when we don't feel like forgiving, making the decision, saying the words, can bring healing. I forgive you. I love you both and I don't want you to spend eternity in hell."

His dad looked at him for the second time. "Are you done yet?"

"Yeah, I'm done."

"Now get out." His father picked up his glass of liquor and turned up the volume on the television.

His mom followed him into the hallway. "He has cancer. The booze has all but killed him. He won't stop drinking though. Say's he doesn't care."

Ryan could tell there was something else she wanted to say. "What is it, Mom?"

"It's about your dad. He ain't really your dad. See, that's why he treated you so bad over the years. He knew you wasn't his and he was so mean to you."

For the first time ever, Ryan understood. It didn't make what happened to him right, but at least there was some sort of explanation.

"See, his step daddy, well, he did the same thing and as they say, the apple don't fall too far from the tree."

"Who is my real father?"

"Oh, your real daddy was such a nice man. A real gentleman. He didn't know about you, though. I tried to keep it quiet. That didn't work out so well."

She started to go back in the apartment. Ryan stopped her. "What is his name?"

"It's Robert, Robert Wilson. He lived upstairs from us back then. I think he worked as a television repairman." She turned to go. "That's all I know. And Ryan, I sure am sorry."

Rachel let Ryan think about what just happened with his parents in silence as they walked toward the van. When he'd told her they were still alive, dealing with his family members became part of the healing for their relationship. She had to know he was serious about standing strong in the face of adversity, no matter where the attack came from. She was certain that the closer they got to accomplishing the will of the Father in their lives, the more regular the attacks would come. They had to be ready.

Mark and Jessi had recommended they make this trip about them, about communication and intimacy. They had been counseling with their friends for a couple of months now and they were going through the couples' class with Family Life Today. So much had already been accomplished. Ryan confronting his parents was a huge step for him and Rachel was proud of him. "How are you doing?"

Ryan was almost to the hotel before he spoke. He let the information about his father take root. He wasn't ready to face the idea that he might have a real father out there, one that might actually come to love him if given the chance. "I feel like a ton of bricks have been lifted off my shoulders. I had no idea it would feel so good to free myself of that burden. I can't help but wonder why I waited?"

She turned to him and took his free hand. "Who knows why we do the things we do? Self-preservation? Fear? Doubt? Pride? I think the list can go on and on. The important thing is, you faced them, you forgave them, and you told them about Jesus. I'm really proud of you."

"Even though it was hard, I really do feel so much better." He pulled into the hotel parking lot. "Do you want to rest before we go to dinner?"

Rachel raised her eyebrows. "We could get room service."

"I like how you think."

Ryan put his arm around his wife and led her to their room.

Epilogue

Rachel pulled the box off the top shelf and removed the girls' keepsakes. The items in the bottom were what she sought out. She read the poems Ryan had written her when they were dating. Next Rachel removed a daisy that had been pressed between two pieces of wax paper. Ryan had given her a whole bouquet and one by one she destroyed them by pulling the petals off. He loves me, he loves me not. By the time she got it right, she had one complete flower left and she preserved it for the days of remembering. Love could be so fragile, just like this flower. Yet, from experience, she knew true love could be resilient enough to withstand even the fiercest of attacks.

She could hardly believe one year had passed since her life had nearly fallen apart. In many ways the year flew, in others, it crawled. Regardless, the passing of time trudges on, second by second, minute by minute, not bending or bowing to anyone.

Dillon had taken a job in another city at a different college. He said being this close to her was too difficult for him. This would be the second time he'd had to start somewhere new to keep the painful memories from overtaking him. She was glad he found a place to start over. She still prayed for him and he continued to fight the war that was being waged for his soul. Rachel prayed he would give in and let God have control. Only then would he find true happiness.

Finally she found what she was looking for. She pulled the packets of the carefully packaged seeds from the box. When she had started cross-pollinating flowers, she would never have dreamed she'd mix two so very different roses and come up with such a beautiful flower. Wasn't that just like God? He can take our messed up, sinful, self serving lives and make something wonderful of them. She marveled at what a little water, fertilizer, sunlight and love could do.

Rachel heard the light tapping on the bedroom door. "Come in."

Ryan stood before her. "You find what you were looking for?"

She held up the packets. "Sure did."

"Good, cause its time."

Rachel nodded and followed her husband downstairs. The back yard was full of people. A simple but tasteful buffet table was ready and waiting for the ceremony to conclude. Rachel smoothed the skirt of her dress and followed Ryan to the front of the group. "Okay, everyone, she's here."

The group gathered around. Shelly, her youngest was radiant. When the vacant lot next door to them came on the market, she and Ryan used some of her inheritance money to purchase it and put in a pool. Shelly had taken advantage of every minute she had to enjoy the backyard paradise her mom had created.

Shannon, her middle daughter, was still healing and seeing a counselor regularly. She was working part time and attending the local college where Rachel still taught in the horticulture department.

Her eyes fell on Samantha next. She had graduated from college with a degree in business. Rachel had to wonder when she'd find time to pursue her business world ambitions. She looked at her daughter's rounded stomach. When Sam and Craig had come to them, to tell her and Ryan that they were expecting a baby and were going to get married, she found the measure of grace she was able to extend enormous. She knew how easy it was to fall. A strong grace brought a person through the other side to redemption. She could hardly believe her first grandbaby would be coming in the fall. Rachel could hardly wait.

Ryan was standing next to her. He had left the dealership and was working full time in ministry, although not as a pastor of a church. He, with Rachel's support, began "The Truth in Love" ministry, which was just getting off the ground. God had even used the chaos of that television coverage for good. Ryan had been invited to speak and encourage men and women around the country who were struggling with their sexuality.

Rachel looked around. Everything the enemy had tried to take, God had given back many times over. She closed her eyes and thanked him. It was time for the ceremony to begin.

When, to her amazement, she'd been notified that she'd received a national award for her cross-pollinating of Forever Loved, she'd had a great idea. What about combining the award presentation with a vow renewal ceremony? She had searched her green house, all her files, everything for the seeds she'd so lovingly preserved. Only this afternoon did she remember she had put them with the box of items she had wanted to keep forever.

After receiving her award for her work in cross-pollination, she set the plaque aside and renewed her wedding vows. Ryan handed her a single long stem rose. She carefully took the flower from him, avoiding the thorns. She brought the sweet smelling rose to her face and inhaled deeply. She felt the velvet petals against her lips then looked into her love's eyes. Together, they recommitted themselves to loving one another through all their days. In spite of everything they had gone through, all the good and the bad, and knowing there were no guarantees in life, they both pledged to the other they would always be forever loved.

Letter To The Reader

Dear Reader,

Thank you for reading Forever Loved, book three in The Women of Prayer Series.

As a Christian author, I choose to write stories that challenge us. Forever Loved is no exception. When I set out to write, I am always seeking the heart of the Father on a matter before I begin writing. I pray for his leading and direction. I try to write a story that does more than entertain. I believe as a writer I will answer to God for how I used my earthly talent to further his kingdom.

There are so many issues in today's world that go against the grain of the gospel of Jesus Christ. We are a world plagued by sin and the lustful ways of the flesh. 2 Timothy 3:1-5 describes our world this way. "But mark this: There will be terrible times in the last days. People will be lovers of themselves, lovers of money, boastful, proud, abusive, disobedient to their parents, ungrateful, unholy, without love, unforgiving, slanderous, without self-control, brutal, not lovers of the good, treacherous, rash, conceited, lovers of pleasure rather than lovers of God— having a form of godliness but denying its power. Have nothing to do with such people."

In such a rapidly declining society, it should not surprise me that sins like homosexuality are being embraced by not only a Godless world, but by many who call themselves Christians. Churches like the one Samantha attends near her college are being raised up. These modern day Christian churches are more concerned with pleasing the ears of people than they are concerned with offending our most Holy God.

If you are a follower of my work, you will know I do not shy away from touchy subjects. I write according to my convictions, which are guided by biblical truth. While Forever Loved is fiction, Ryan's personal story reveals the horrors that are happening behind closed doors across the world. With the family unit in decline, with more stepparents, boy friends, gay partnerships and non-blood related siblings living under the same roof, we are seeing more and more cases of sexual abuse in the lives of our children. Statistically one out of four females and one out of six males will be sexually abused in some manner before they are eighteen years old. Can we really expect there to be no repercussions to the deviant behavior that takes place in the lives of the ungodly?

Where is hope? It's in us. We are the ones who are to bring hope to a dying world. We are the ones who should bring truth to a world that has been lied to and deceived. It is our responsibility to be Christ to our world. I challenge you today to make a difference in the world around you. Love someone enough that you present them with the gospel of Jesus Christ.

If you have a prayer request, please feel to email me. My team and I would be honored to pray for you. If this story has touched you in any way, let me know. If you are interested in receiving a PDF of the Reader's Discussion in a printable Bible Study format for your group's use, please email me and request a copy at Darlene@darleneshortridge.com or through my facebook, twitter, google + or linkedin pages. I'd love to hear your thoughts on Forever Loved or any of my other books.

If you or someone you know is struggling with a homosexual lifestyle, there are people who want to help. Please click on the following links for more information.
http://www.restoredhopenetwork.com/

There is a tab called "Get Help" on the Restored Hope Network. This tab will take you to a map and provide information for local support.
http://truthministry.org/
http://graceinaction.us/

If sexual abuse of a child is currently taking place in your home, get help immediately. Do not allow this behavior to continue. Call the police.

If you are an adult and have been sexually abused as a child contact one of following centers for help.

http://rainn.org/get-info/effects-of-sexual-assault/adult-survivors-of-childhood-sexual-abuse

Or call -800-656-HOPE

http://www.ascasupport.org/

In His Love,
Darlene Shortridge

Reader's Discussion Guide

The following questions may be used as part of a book club, Bible study or group discussion.

1) In writing this book I realized that I might receive negative feedback from some circles. There may be those in the Christian community who feel uncomfortable discussing issues such as homosexuality and the abuse of children. There may be those in the homosexual community, or those who support the homosexual lifestyle, that feel I have somehow misrepresented them in their beliefs. How did reading this book make you feel? Were you uncomfortable? What did you learn? Do you feel better equipped to answer questions regarding your faith in relation to God's position on homosexuality?

2) Communication is key to having a successful relationship.

   a) In Forever Loved we see an obvious lack of communication between Ryan and Rachel. When did their communication problems begin? When did they finally get on track in regards to honest communication in their relationship? Make a list of some of the reasons we fail to communicate with our spouse? I'll start that list off for you with a couple of mine: Pride, embarrassment, fear of rejection…you continue the list. When you finish, discuss some of these hurdles to openly communicating with your spouse.

   b) Ryan's fear of confrontation greatly contributed to his reluctance to communicate while Rachel was straightforward in her communication style. Because these two were at opposite ends of the spectrum in regards to their style of communicating, can you see why Ryan might have been hesitant to openly talk with Rachel? If you examine your relationships, which type of communicator are you? What can you do to make communicating more approachable for those you are in relationship with?

c) Look up James 1:19, Proverbs 15:1, Psalm 141:3, Hebrews 4:12, Ephesians 4:29 and 2 Corinthians 6:11-13 (This one makes me smile...imagine being able to freely communicate with our spouse?) Read each verse then discuss how the instructions in each verse can help you communicate in a positive way.

3) As Christians we love to use the phrase "love the sinner, hate the sin." And I absolutely agree with this phrase in principal. Unfortunately, many in the world have come to believe Christians hate sinners and feel they are superior to non-Christians. How can we more effectively love the sinner while standing firm against sin? Part of the discrepancy lays in the very different definitions of the word, love. What are some common interpretations of the definition of love? How is love defined in Scripture? In Forever Loved Mark attempts to explain Godly love to Terry by sharing the story of trying to prevent a man from running into a burning building. Read Romans chapter 12. Does this chapter concur with Mark's story? What do you think verse 9 means?

4) In the beginning of Forever Loved you, the reader, would have felt an enormous amount of empathy for Rachel. I have never experienced anything near what she went through, but I tried to put myself in her place to the best of my ability as I wrote the story. The gamut of emotions she would have gone through makes my mind wobble. When you found out that the roles were actually reversed, that Ryan never did go back to his sinful relationship while Rachel participated in an adulterous relationship were you relieved? Did you find yourself exhaling, thanking God that it wasn't worse? That brings me to my next

question. Do you believe one sin can be worse than another? Do you believe living a homosexual life is worse than committing adultery? The debate really goes both ways. What, according to Matthew 12:32, is the only unforgivable sin? Whatever your position on which sin is worse and why, any and all sin will send a person to hell if they are not redeemed by the blood of Jesus Christ.

5) Take a look at this scenario: A friend is selling snow cones on a hot day. She has her cute little apron on and she chats with the customers as she adds their syrup choices to their cups of ice. One gentleman makes a joke and she throws her head back in laughter. She then counters with a joke she heard that is equally, if not more, humorous. They both laugh out loud. She sees this as being "friendly." He sees this as "flirting." I see woman innocently cracking the door open to sin on a regular basis. Rachel's seemingly innocent relationship with her next-door neighbor led her on a path to disobedience and willful sinning against God. Do you believe a married woman can be a friend to a man other than her husband? What about through Facebook or in chat rooms? Why or why not? How does Proverbs 4:23 and 1 Thessalonians 4:1-8 support your answer?

6) Do you have an accountability partner? Imagine if Ryan and Rachel had Mark and Jessi as their trusted accountability partners. Of course there wouldn't be a story and you wouldn't be answering these questions but that is beside the point. A trusted accountability partner is someone you know intimately. She is a close, trusted friend. For me, I have several. Some are mentioned in this book by name. One wrote the forward to this book. She knows my heart. She knows the calling God has placed on my life. She also has my explicit permission to call me on the carpet when I choose to do something that goes against God's heart. I gave her permission to do that because I know her heart. Because I know she wants God's will for my life as well as hers. She loves God and his ways and she loves me. I trust her to always speak truth into my life. Do you have someone like this in your life? If not, go find her. Don't ask

someone who likes to tickle your ears or make you feel good (not that making you feel good is a bad thing, you just want someone who has the guts to be truthful). It is an honor to be someone else's accountability partner. It means she respects you. Read James 5:16, 1 Thessalonians 5:11 and Proverbs 27:17. According to these verses, what are the attributes of an accountability partner?

7) Every person, dead or alive, has been or will be hurt at some point in his or her life. Some, like Ryan, have experienced pain that runs so deep that it leaves its imprint on that person's soul forever. How does a person ever heal from such atrocious wounds? Some go to counseling their entire lives trying to understand the evil that was thrust upon them. What are some ways we learn to cope with our "scars?" It wasn't that long ago that I was in a group discussion and laughingly revealed something painful about my past. I made a joke about it. It was then I realized joking was my way to cope, or deal with my pain. I belittled the memory and made it funny. How do you cope? Does God want us to simply "cope" or does he have a more permanent remedy in mind? Read I Peter 5:10, Psalm 34:17-20, Psalm 147:3, Matthew 11:28, Psalm 23:3, Psalm 30:11 and Isaiah 61:3. According to these scriptures, does God want us to cope or be healed? How does that make you feel? Write down your favorite of these verses and place them where you will see them every day, perhaps on your bathroom mirror. When the enemy reminds you of your past, remind yourself that you are God's beloved and he wants the very best for you.

8) As a parent, one of the hardest things we will ever face is turning our children back over to God. When they are little we worry about outlet covers and slippery floors. When they are older we pray they will get a good education and choose a Godly spouse. Rachel worries about all three of her daughters in different ways, yet she is mainly concerned for one reason. Will they be okay with God before they die? Will they get their faith straightened out? I think most of us would agree a mother's heart is always turned toward her children. How difficult is it for you

to relinquish your children into God's capable hands? Some reading this have children living openly in sin and rebelling against God. Some of our children are flirting with the world. They want to expand their wings and learn for themselves. How do we trust him with our most prized possessions? First off, realize that nothing we have is ours, not even our children. We are but stewards of everything God has entrusted us with, yes that includes our children. They were his long before they were ours. What are some ways we can assure ourselves that our children will spend eternity with us in heaven? Hopefully prayer came to mind. Pray and pray and pray some more. Read Isaiah 55:11. What does that verse assure us of? Read Proverbs 3:5-6. What do these verses instruct us to do?

If you, the reader, have never accepted Christ as your savior and you wish to do so, please pray this prayer.

Lord God,

I come before you, a sinner. I believe in you and I believe your word is true. I believe Jesus Christ is your son and that he died on a cross so that I might be forgiven my sins and spend eternity with you. Without you, I am nothing.
I believe in my heart, that you, Lord God, raised him from the dead. Please Jesus forgive me for every sin I have committed or dwelt upon in my heart. Please Lord Jesus forgive me and come into my heart as my personal Lord and Savior today.
I give you my life and I ask that you take full control from this moment on.
I pray this in the name of Jesus Christ.

Amen

Please enjoy this excerpt from

Forever Faithful

Book Four of the
Women of Prayer Series

Darlene Shortridge

Chapter 1

Jackie lifted the coffee cup to her lips as she studied the picture on the front page of the newspaper.

Greg loved to see his wife's reaction to pictures of herself paving the way for a more conservative tomorrow. He came up behind her and put his hands on her shoulders. "Do you know that woman? She is one hot tamale."

Jackie swatted her husband's hand.

He bent down and kissed her cheek. "You look gorgeous, even in black and white."

She felt a nervous flutter. Today could be the day she becomes the next United States senator from Wisconsin. She'd find out when all the votes were tallied. "Am I doing the right thing? Can our family handle the scrutiny?"

He sat down at the table and poured himself a glass of orange juice. "Well, let's see. Have you ever been accused of sexual harassment in the work place?"

Jackie raised her eyebrows. "Gee, I hope not. Since I've been home the last eighteen years I can't imagine which one of our children could accuse me of that. Although I think unfair working conditions could pop up from my past."

"Okay, we'll check that one off the list. Next. Have you ever had a torrid love affair with anyone other than your's truly?"

"Greg, really?"

"Hey, just checking. These people mean business. They will find a skeleton if there's one to be found. How about an abortion?"

She shook her head. "That's disgusting."

"Money laundering?"

She folded the newspaper and set it aside.

"I'll take that as a no. Okay, fraud, addiction, or a lesbian girl friend in college?"

"Greg, you are being ridiculous. You know darn well I got most of my college credits by taking online classes from our living room."

"All right, I suppose you got me on that one." He paused. "Does that mean fraud and addiction are possibilities?"

She threw the paper at him. "Just stop. There is nothing. Period. I'm squeaky clean. No skeletons, no past to dredge up, no surprise endings to knock me out of the race."

He pulled her up and wrapped his arms around her. "Then I guess you answered your own question. Our family is tougher than it looks. And what scrutiny? We have a wonderful relationship and even with our "bad moments" we are a team that can't be beat. Our kids are fantastic. And more important than all of that, is we both know God has brought us to this moment. He has proven again and again that this is the road we are supposed to be on. It's time Wisconsin had a conservative voice that won't compromise on truth." He lifted her chin. "You are my Esther. And you are here for such a time as this."

The rushing of feet brought them both to attention. Two sets to be precise. "Mom, Anna took my sweater. The one with the pretty pink flowers on it."

Jackie removed her husband's arms from around her waist. "Anna, do you have Abby's sweater?" Jackie's heart went out to her daughter. "You know it's not yours."

Anna's bottom lip stuck out. "It's pretty. I want it."

Jackie held her hand out. "Give me your sister's sweater." She took the delicate white sweater and handed it to Abby then turned back to Anna. "Where is your sweater? The pink one with the butterflies?"

"I don't want that one."

Jackie kissed her forehead. "That is the one you picked out. So, that is the one you'll wear."

Breakfast could be a war zone with five kids and two parents. Today was an important day for all of them and it all started with a good breakfast. She took the pop tarts out of

Trent's hand. "Not today, Buddy. Today you get a real breakfast."

The whining began. "But, Mom, I don't like real breakfast."

"You do today." She put the pastry in a baggie. "You can have this tomorrow." Jackie stood over the stove and stirred the eggs. She'd made the bacon earlier so that would only have to be reheated for a moment in the microwave. She took a head count. "Okay, we're missing Ashley and Abigail. Trent, run up and get your sisters."

"Awe, Mom, do I have to?"

Jackie turned and gave him the look that dared him to say one more word then addressed her husband. "Greg, you have the toast going?"

"Yep, and not a one burnt."

"Then what is that I smell?" She only heard whistling in response. "Anna, get the jelly out of the fridge. Abby, you get the milk and orange juice."

Trent bounded back into the kitchen. "Trent, get out the plates."

"Ugh. I don't like eggs."

"Where are those girls?" Jackie turned the eggs into a bowl and set them on the table.

She stood at the foot of the stairs and yelled up. "Ashley, Amelia, where are you? Breakfast is on the table."

"Coming." Her oldest daughter's voice echoed from the bathroom. Both girls appeared at the top of the stairs and Jackie couldn't help but laugh. "Where do you think you're going dressed up like that?"

Amelia seemed appalled. "Mom, it's your big day. We thought we should look nice for you."

"I know what you're doing. The idea of being on television has you all fired up. As soon as we're finished with breakfast, I want you to wash that make up off your face." The three of them sat down with the rest of the family at the table.

Jackie kicked Greg under the table, hoping to dissuade him from busting out laughing. It didn't work.

"Come on, you have to admit, it's funny."

She passed the bowl of eggs. "I have to admit no such thing." She looked toward her daughters. Both were allowed to wear a little make up, although she insisted neither one needed it. Ashley's make up wasn't too bad but Amelia's was over the top. The amount of cover up caked on her face made her look orange. Add the dark blue eye shadow and the bright lipstick and she could have been mistaken for a clown. She tried to muffle her laughter. "Okay, so you're right." Pretty soon, everyone was laughing.

Ashley spoke up. "Mom, we thought we'd need more makeup because of the cameras."

"Oh, Honey. For this you only need to look like yourselves. Okay?" She bit her lip. "Besides, we won't see a camera until late tonight, possibly even tomorrow if the votes are close."

Ashley agreed. "All right."

Jackie remembered being sixteen and unsure of herself. Ashley was no different. Amelia, who always wanted to do what her older sister did, had twice the amount of base as her sister and the orange line stopped right at her jawline. She could have peeled it off, or scraped it off with a knife.

Breakfast resumed with everyone talking about the day ahead. Jackie noticed Trent had no problem polishing off his eggs and bacon. She shook her head.

"Ashley, you're going to meet us at the Civic Center tonight, right?"

"Mom, yes, as soon as play practice is over I'll be there."

Jackie nodded her head. "Just making sure. I want everything to go smoothly."

Greg took his wife's hand. "Everything is going to be fine. And you're going to win this thing. You'll see."

"I guess we'll find out tonight." She pushed her plate back. "Why did I insist on making a big breakfast? I'm too nervous to eat."

Seeing a slice of bacon on her plate Greg snatched it up. "It kept you busy. At least eat a few bites of toast. It's going to be a long day."

Once the kitchen was clean and all the kids were at school, Greg and Jackie went to the elementary school where they voted. The television crews were in place waiting for their arrival. She'd always placed a high importance on voting but today's vote meant even more. This is what her family had worked so hard to achieve.

She stepped behind the curtain then reemerged a couple of minutes later to applause. She had supporters everywhere. This was her town. These people knew her and Greg. They'd built a life here. They provided jobs with their business and volunteered. If it wasn't for the people of this town, she would never have run. In a million years she never would have imagined running for a US Senate seat. Apparently there were some who thought she could win. The financial backing had been enormous. She insisted on running a clean race. No mudslinging. Her commercials were done with taste and focused on the issues.

The Civic Center was decorated in red, white, and blue. Streamers hung from the ceiling. Balloons covered the platform and were arranged in clusters all around the room. A big banner, with her family's picture plastered across it, hung all the way across the stage. There were caterers working, preparing for the party to ensue. Win or lose, it would be a grand affair. This seat meant a lot to the conservative people of Wisconsin. Living in a blue collar town, she was surprised she had received as much support as she did. With the local automobile plant, there were a lot of factory employees who were being pressured by the local union to vote for her opponent. She wasn't as sure as Greg was that she would win this thing. It was a hard call.

She looked at her watch. Four fifteen. Her kids should be here any minute. A friend had offered to pick them up and bring them to the party. Jackie turned toward the door as the twins busted through and ran toward her. She hugged them to her. "How was school?"

"Wonderful. I got an A on my spelling test." Jackie congratulated Anna then questioned Abby. "How about you, Abby? How did you do on your spelling test?"

Her daughter began to pout.

Jackie knelt down and gave her a hug. "It's okay. We'll work harder next week. You'll get it. Spelling is harder for some people. But I bet you did really good on your math homework, didn't you?"

Abby brightened considerably. "My teacher said I got them all right."

"See, everyone has different gifts and talents. Didn't I tell you that?"

Abby shook her head.

Jackie stood up and gave Jessi a hug. "Thanks for bringing them after school. It saved me a trip."

"I didn't mind a bit. They're great kids, just like their parents." Looking at these girls reminded Jessi of her own twin boys when they were younger. "Besides, I miss having young ones around. My kids are all growing up."

"You're not that much older than us. You could always have another."

Jessi laughed. "No way. I'm done." She took her keys out of her pocket. "Mark and I will be back in a little while." She hugged Jackie and whispered. "You're doing great. Remember, we're all praying."

"Sometimes that's all that keeps me going. That, and knowing that God has ordained this. It's his plan, not mine." Jackie waved goodbye and watched her friend and mentor head out the door.

She and Greg had been attending the community church where Mark pastored for years now. Jackie often volunteered at their private school where all of her kids attended. She was so thankful they added on a high school before Ashley's freshman year. The girls were busy coloring. Trent and Amelia had already found friends and were hanging out with them. Another hour and Ashley would be here to help with them. It was going to be a long night but everyone, including the twins, wanted to be part of the winning celebration. She prayed they weren't counting their chickens before they hatched.

The hall started filling up. Important donors, other politicians, friends, and family were all on hand to lend their

271

support. Jessi's oldest daughter, Olivia, offered to keep an eye on the girls for Jackie. She was grateful. There were so many people vying for her and Greg's attention, she wouldn't have been able to keep close watch over them.

She was going from table to table, talking with everyone when it dawned on her, Ashley wasn't there yet. She fished her phone out of her purse and was relieved to see a text from Ashley: *Katelyn really wants to come tonight. Ok if I pick her up?*

Jackie returned her text with a simple yes, then went back to walking around the room.

Three hours later the newscasters were calling it. Jackie Adams was the new US Senator. She waved to the crowd and waited for the announcement. Greg hugged her with all his might. She couldn't believe she won. "Where are the kids? They need to be here with us."

"They'll be here any second." He turned and looked through the crowd and saw their children coming toward them. "Here they are now."

Jackie tilted her head to the side. "I only count four. Where is Ashley?"

"I don't know." Greg pulled his cell phone out of his pocket. No messages.

"I don't remember seeing her at all. Do you?"

He scratched his head. "No, I haven't seen her either."

Jackie heard the applause and watched everyone rise to their feet. It was time to go on. They would have to deal with Ashley later. Although a niggling in her stomach told her something was wrong, she approached the platform with her family, or most of her family. She waved and waited as the final speaker talked about her service and her attributes. Her family stood with her just behind the back curtain, to the side of the big banner. The clapping was louder, the lights were brighter. It was time to walk on the stage, as they had practiced. Just before she approached the podium someone placed a piece of paper in her hand. It was a note.

She opened it and read these words: Accept the Senate seat tonight and you will never see your daughter again.

About the Author

Darlene Shortridge is the best selling author of five contemporary Christian novels.

She is an accomplished vocalist and a compassionate speaker. She lives in Oklahoma City with her husband and son. Being a northern gal, she is quite proud of her developing language skills, especially when some dear friends taught her how to properly use the phrase, "Bless Your Heart."

You can visit Darlene at her website - darleneshortridge.com

You can also connect with her on your favorite social media channels.